The Witching Well

Hex After 40 Book 1

Shelley Dorey

DEDICATION

To the women
Worn out or blind-sided,
Who rebuilt their lives
The Happiness and Joy
Does come back
With a richness and depth
That will surprise you!

CONTENTS

ONE

M y fingers tightened on the steering wheel as white-hot rage burned through me for the *umpteenth* time. For the last six months, hardly a day went by where I wasn't overwhelmed by emotions. First was confusion, then grief, then financial despair, until I finally came to rage.

I'm okay with the rage. Confusion, grief, and financial anxiety all have their place, for sure. But ultimately, they're draining, sucking the life and energy out of you. But rage? Oh boy...let me tell you... Rage is empowering. And after the shitstorm my life had gone through for the last six months, I'm fine with being empowered.

Sure, I'm still in my mid-forties. Okay, closer to *fifty* than forty, but I'm sticking with "mid" for now, okay? Give a girl a break. Having gone from comfortable middle-class suburban housewife to divorcee in just twenty-four weeks takes its toll. Being pissed off is better than being a goddamn doormat.

Lately, the rage just pops into my head out of nowhere. And could you blame me? After twenty-three years of what I'd always considered a strong marriage, he calmly told me it was over, that it was time for him to move on. Move on? He said it as casually as if he were talking about the end of a movie!

That vow, "Till death do us part" had been amended to "Till the kids leave the nest." If I'd been privy to that postscript of our vows, I'd have done a LOT of things differently.

But no, I hadn't been aware, and as a result I'm driving along a winding road in the Catskill Mountains, towing a trailer with the remnants of my marriage, to start my new life.

"It wasn't supposed to be this way!" I shouted out loud for probably the thousandth time. "I held up my damn end!" My fingers throbbed from the death grip on the wheel.

Movement at the edge of my vision yanked me to the present. A flash of tawny brown sprang from the forest onto the blacktop. An animal the size of a medium dog but with feline eyes and a pointy tuft at the tip of one of its ears. My foot slammed the brakes, and time slowed like molasses.

"Noooooooo!" My truck skidded forward, inch by inch. Crouched low on its spotted haunches, the animal's head turned, and shining eyes peered at me. A bobcat! The slow blink of its eyes showed a flash of amber as it paused, waiting.

Shit! The truck kept barreling at it despite my foot locked on the brake pedal. My jaw clenched tight, and my arms braced for the sickening thud.

Suddenly the steering wheel wrenched free from my hands, spinning hard to the left.

"It's okay, Shannon. Trust me."

The words blared in my head as the front of the truck lurched toward a giant pine at the edge of the woods.

My head jerked back when the truck ground to a stop. Barely breathing, I saw the rough bark just inches from the hood, while a low branch brushed the side mirror on the passenger's side.

A quick look back to the center of the road showed the flash of a short tail, and a flurry of the big cat's paws before it disappeared into the undergrowth of the forest on the opposite side.

Time warped again back to normal, finding me gasping for breath while my heart hammered fast. What the hell just happened? That voice...My mouth fell open as it replayed in my head. It was Aunt Maeve's voice. I knew the sound of her countryside accent as well as the voices of my children.

But she's been dead and buried for years!

I shook my head from side to side staring at the steering wheel. Shit, my hands weren't even on it when it had turned all on its own! If not for that, I would have crushed that bobcat. Thank God I hadn't. But not from anything I'd done! That's for sure.

Aunt Maeve? It wasn't possible that she'd done this—saved that cat. Holding my trembling hands in front of me, I knew I hadn't spun the steering wheel. Yet it had happened. Sitting here with the truck angled across the road was proof that *something* had intervened.

"I'm freaking losing my mind. None of that should have happened." I took a deep breath. But it did. I don't know how, but it did. And that was Aunt Maeve's voice just before the truck swerved. All I could do was sit there, staring at the massive trunk of the pine tree inches from my front bumper. I gave myself a shake.

The view in the rearview mirror was another sobering sight. The U-Haul trailer I was hauling had jackknifed, taking up both lanes of the road. Everything I owned—my entire life's possessions of forty-six years—was in there. I was blocking the road, and who knew when another vehicle would come along? I was a sitting duck if I didn't get a grip.

"Shit!" I slammed the dashboard enough times to make my hand sore. Taking a deep breath for calm...I mean, seriously, I went from pissed off to scared witless and back to pissed off in about three seconds. I checked the dirt shoulder bordering the blacktop before gingerly toeing the gas pedal.

There were lots of breakables in that trailer, and if I wasn't careful, I could end up flipping the thing or get it mired at the side of the road. Holding my breath, staring at the trailer behind me, I feathered the gas pedal, easing the pickup gently forward. Slowly but surely, I managed to straighten out the trailer that held all the things worth keeping from my former life.

All the things?

"Not even remotely true, Shannon." I shook my head as I resumed my focus on the road ahead. I had two kids who I adored, both of them in colleges on opposite sides of the country. They'd totally freak out if they knew what had just happened. Hell, *I* was barely holding it together.

My kids… I could still see the tears in Jessica's face as the Ass-hat and I Skyped the family meeting, breaking the news to them. Thomas, her brother, had been stoic, the only sign of his anger being clipped questions about the house and finances.

"Stop it, Shannon! You need to concentrate on the road in case any more wildlife adventures jump out to welcome you." I'd think about all this later, when I was settled with a Jack Daniels in hand.

The GPS chimed in, "In four miles, turn right onto Greenbank Road."

Greenbank Road. That was a blast from the past. It had been a long, long time since I'd been back to the Catskills. Sunlight flickered through the wall of trees on each side of me before I crested the hill. The vista before me, a rolling wave of trees with the beginnings of fall plumage in oranges and scarlets made my eyes well up. I'd forgotten how gorgeous this area was after years of living in a city.

But more than that, it brought to mind better times. Happier times of my teen years, spending summers there with my aunt. That same aunt whose voice rang in my head minutes before.

Why hadn't I made more of an effort to visit her when she'd been alive and lucid? I'd always intended to, but life always got in the way. Alex The Ass Hat's idea of a family vacation was an annual week in Florida escaping the snow, but I should have insisted on visiting Aunt Maeve, even if only for a few times, to change it up. The kids had enjoyed Disney and the Florida Keys in our time away from Pittsburgh. No Caribbean trips and certainly no European journeys, that was for sure. He wasn't just an Ass-hat; he was a *cheap* Ass-hat.

When the lawyer handling Aunt Maeve's estate contacted me, Maeve was already in the ground, so I'd even missed her funeral. My stomach fell as the road suddenly took a dip going into the valley, but it was my guilt rather than the change in elevation that caused the unease. I should have come back to see her when she was alive.

In a single phone call, I learned that my favorite relative was dead and gone, and that she left me the small resort where she'd lived. The lawyer, a local who was also her lifelong friend, had told me the property needed a lot of work since Maeve had spent her last years in a nursing home. Ever since, for the last five years, I paid the property taxes until I could reach a decision on what to do with it. Ass-hat had urged me to sell it despite Aunt Maeve's request that the property remain in the family.

Now, after Ass-hat's financial chicanery putting multiple mortgages on our home, and the cost of the divorce, not to mention the kids' education, I'd barely walked away with sixty grand. Maybe that sounds like a nice chunk of money, but when you think about it...for twenty years I raised the kids and ran the household while he built his accounting firm.

For twenty years of "just being a housewife"—laundry, cooking, Mom's Taxi, checking homework, doctors' appointments, teachers' meetings, being the disciplinarian while he got to be "Fun Dad"—all the work of holding a family together was *my* job, and I did it happily. We were a *family*. So what if I chose motherhood over a career in journalism?

And as soon as that job was finished—when the kids fledged off to college, I was downsized. Sixty thousand dollars...three thousand dollars a year. My jaw clenched so hard my teeth made a grinding sound. He'd hidden money somewhere! That's what he did for a living, for Chrissake! How many other women had been cheated by their ex-husbands by this man's financial shell games? Ass-hat had *plenty* of practice by the time it came to put me out to pasture.

Now, Aunt Maeve's resort was my lifeline. At the very least, a mortgage-free roof over my head.

I noticed a gas station and 7-Eleven store. There was still a quarter tank of gas, but something told me to fill up. The small town of Wesley wasn't much farther now, but who knew if I'd be able to get fuel there.

It felt good to step outside and stretch my legs after the long drive. I won't lie—seven hours behind the wheel without a break was a record for me. But, oh man, I stood beside the truck feeling every creak and crick in my body as I stretched and tried to loosen up.

Before I reached the gas pump, the door to the store opened and my eyes widened in surprise. A guy with the chiseled features common in *GQ* models, his tall muscular body ambling smoothly toward a white truck, looked over at me and nodded. A smile stole onto his lips while his blue eyes narrowed, deepening the laugh lines at the corners.

I could feel my cheeks flush warmer as I returned his look, and it had nothing to do with my personal tropical moments that had started a year or two ago. This wasn't *that* kind of hot flash. Before I could turn my attention to the gas nozzle, he paused and took a step closer, eyeing me like I was his next meal.

"You look familiar. Are you from around here?" His voice was friendly and smooth as dark chocolate.

I froze. Was that a pickup line? I'd been out of the dating game since forever and not sure of the protocol these days. Not that I wanted to go down that road anytime soon— especially after Ass-hat's antics. Maybe I never would trust a man again. And if this was some kind of thing, him hitting on me, I totally didn't need this, not now.

TWO

O r did I?

I mean, for more than two decades, when a man would look at me twice, even though it felt good for the ego, I just dismissed it. But now?

Being "looked at" by an attractive man was… well, refreshing, okay? All right, more than refreshing; it was a boost to the ego. It's always harder on the ego being the dumpee than it is to be the dumper. And to be completely honest here for a minute, Ass-hat throwing me under the bus was the first and only time in my life a guy broke it off with me. All the boyfriends I had before we met in college were guys I eventually called it quits on. I'm just saying that my divorce hit me in places that had never been hit before.

Yes, this guy at the gas pump was watching me carefully. His eyes flitted up and down, taking me in, and…and it was a teensy scary—I've always been put off by being checked out by a man—but this time it also *felt good*. When his gaze came back up to meet mine and he held it, there were more than just a few randy images popping into the back of my head.

So randy I had to catch my breath.

What the hell did he say again? Oh yeah, the hick-town version of "Come here often?" I think…?

Oh yeah, he asked if I was from around here. After just a

couple of seconds of our stare down, I remembered my manners and shook my head. I tried to smile even though I was totally stumped. Believe me, if I'd met *him* before, I would have remembered.

Nope. I'm from Pittsburgh, but I spent practically every summer here, growing up. My aunt, Maeve Burke, lived just outside of Wesley."

His fingers threaded through a mop of dark hair that many girls would envy—myself included. He took a step closer and his eyes lit up. "*Shannon Burke?* Oh my God. I can't believe it's you!"

He stepped over and took the nozzle from me, showing perfect teeth when he grinned. "You don't recognize me, do you?" All the while he proceeded to fill me up, (*Stop that, Shannon!*) he smiled at me, making my neck become the same shade of embarrassment that my cheeks showed.

"I'm sorry but—"

"Steve Murphy! You don't remember the time I raced you across the lake and *beat* you? Or the gang of us having bonfires practically every night at Petrie Point?" He shook his head and laughed. "I guess I wasn't as memorable as I'd hoped."

I took in the dark stubble on his chin before looking closely into his eyes. "Steve Murphy?" The only Steve I could recall had worn glasses and had been so rail thin that a puff of air could blow him over. He'd been a Velcro kid, a hanger-on always trying to be cool, hanging out with us, even though we were six years older than him. It had been his brother Liam who I'd been interested in.

The guy looking back at me had the bluest eyes, and the contours of his face could easily be described as a panty dropper. As for his physique, he must have spent a lot of time at the gym lifting weights, from the way his jeans hugged his muscular thighs.

He slid the nozzle back onto the pump and his smile faded. "I was kind of a wimpy dork back then, I guess." After a moment he brightened. "So you're back to finalize your aunt's estate? That'll make Devon Booker happy, if you decide to sell.

He's been talking about development in the area. With so many people working from home these days, there's been an influx of folks from Albany and even the Big Apple." He looked around for a second. "Might be a Renaissance in the ol' Catskills."

"Wait. What? I don't know what I'm going to do with my aunt's property. I'd thought I'd just live there, at least for a while." Holy shit! I hadn't even hit the town limits and I was getting the latest town gossip.

He glanced at my trailer. "You're planning on moving into your aunt's old home?"

"Yup."

"You haven't been up here in a while, am I right?"

"Well…" Again, a wave of guilt came over me. Not for years and years despite the fact that Aunt Maeve had been my lifeline during my younger years. From the time I was seven years old until I finished high school, my summers at her place had been an oasis for me.

Before I could continue, Steve grimaced. "I live just past your aunt's place on the lake."

"So?"

"So the house is in pretty bad shape, Shannon. I stop by every so often to make sure it hasn't been broken into and vandalized, but I gotta tell you, it needs a fair bit of work. You might want to check into a motel." He glanced back at the orange U-Haul trailer. "You can store your stuff in my garage if you need to."

Even though he meant well, his advice raised my hackles. I had it with being told what to do. I'd listened to the Ass-hat when he'd discouraged me from pursuing a career when the kids were old enough to attend school. I could still hear his assurance that he made more than enough money to raise a family and look after our retirement. Being there for the kids and keeping the house running smoothly was all he needed from me. And *that* turned out to be a pile of bullcrap!

"Thanks, but I'll be fine there. I'm a lot more resilient than I look." Another thought popped into my head, and I blurted,

"Besides which, Mary-Jane and Libby would be pissed if I stayed in a motel rather than at either of their houses."

He nodded. "I remember. You three were thick as thieves back in the day."

"Yeah, we sure were. We've kept in touch, you know—Facebook and emails."

"Yeah, sure." He looked away for a moment. "Well, I better let you get to it while it's still daylight." Turning to me once more, his gaze was friendly. "If you need any help settling in, I'm not far away. In fact, let me give you my number." He slid his cell phone from the pocket of his jean jacket and we exchanged numbers.

"Thanks, Steve. I'll call you if I need anything." As he walked away, lifting his hand in a wave, I yelled to him, "Maybe we can get together for coffee or a drink sometime next week, if you'd like." Not a date or anything like that but it didn't hurt to have friends. *Friends with benefits?* My neck flamed at the random thought that had popped up in my head. Where the hell had *that* come from?

"Make it dinner on my dime and you got a date, Shannon!" He stood with his hand on the top of his truck's open door. "Oh, and I like your truck!" he added, giving me a two-finger salute. Without waiting for an answer, he climbed in and started the engine.

Well, we did have matching colors; mine was a candy-apple red while his was more of a burgundy. I glanced over at my Toyota. That Tacoma was my own "midlife" whatever. Sure, it was five years old, but it was in great shape. My minivan days were back in Pittsburgh.

I watched him wheel his red Dodge out of the parking lot, and then he was gone. There was a flutter in my belly as I walked into the convenience store to pay for the gas. "I like your truck?" What was wrong with me? The last thing I needed was any entanglements with anyone, let alone with a guy six years my junior! Even if he was pretty damned ripped and handsome as hell.

As I drove the rest of the way to Wesley, I realized

something weirdly nice. I was pushing fifty, recently divorced, but had enough game that a good-looking guy—no, a *great-looking* guy, came over to chat me up. And all during our encounter, I hadn't thought about, or felt any of the burning rage that had been consuming me over the past month. If anything, that spark of attraction was a good sign.

Right?

When I spied the grocery store on the outskirts of the town, I wheeled the Toyota into the lot. With my back straight and a sense of purpose, I went inside to get supplies to last me a week. This was a new chapter, if not an entirely new edition, in Shannon Burke's life. Yeah, I had already decided to resume my maiden name! I was free to buy whatever food *I* wanted. And if I felt like buying a bottle of Jack Daniels to toast my Aunt Maeve and my freedom, I'd do that too!

***

The closer I got to Aunt Maeve's house, that second wind of confidence dwindled to a mere puff. What if it really was too far gone to fix up? My funds weren't endless, and I could be inheriting a money pit that would sink me.

A flash of yellow caught my attention, and my eyes opened wider, seeing three bright balloons tied to the old mailbox at the end of Aunt Maeve's drive. What the heck? When I wheeled the truck into the laneway, bordered by grass that was more like overgrown hay and arching willow trees, I did a double take.

Two vehicles, a blue SUV and a white van with a colorful logo on the side, were parked in front of the old two-story home. I parked my truck next to them, and my hands flew to my mouth while tears rimmed my eyes. OMG! A tall woman with flowing blonde hair waved to me before she was joined by a shorter woman with strawberry curls framing a wide grin.

I practically flew from the truck, racing over to hug them. "Mary-Jane! Libby! What the heck? I wasn't expecting you—"

"Shannon! You think we'd let you arrive here alone?" Libby grinned at me, but her eyes searched my face.

"You're late! We thought you'd be here hours ago!" Mary-Jane held a half-empty bottle of wine out in front of her. "We started without you." She stepped away and grabbed a plastic cup from the railing, pouring a generous splash into it.

She handed it to me, and the three of us raised the cups, clicking them together before Libby blurted, "To Maeve! Bless her for bringing Shannon back to Wesley and to us!"

Mary-Jane snickered. "Not sure how much of a blessing this house is, but I'll drink to new beginnings and old friends."

Tears flooded my eyes.

"Hey, Shan, what's wrong? Did we make a mistake coming?" MJ asked.

"NO!" I cried, waving my hand. "Not at all!" It's just that..." I started to sob.

"I had so-called friends. I had so-called 'gal pals.' We'd shop together at Christmas. We'd even vacation together! But, but, when Alex decided our marriage was through...none of 'em...." I raised a pointed finger like a stiletto. "Not one damn one of them even so much as stopped by!"

Mary-Jane's lips were a thin line. "Some friends!" She exchanged a look with Libby before her tone softened. "Well, we're here for you, Shannon."

Libby set her wine down and stepped over to the door, opening it up. "I hope you don't mind, but we got an extra set of keys from your aunt's lawyer. He wasn't going to give them to me, but when I told him we wanted to do some cleaning and get it ready for you, he bent his own rule."

"What? You cleaned and—"

Mary-Jane interrupted, "And we had the power restored along with the internet. Don't get me wrong, it's no Taj Mahal, but there are clean sheets on the bed and lots more booze in the fridge."

Libby led the way into the house. "Mary-Jane and I cleared it with our families for tonight. We'll stay here and help you get settled in." She looked over her shoulder at me with a blank look. "That is, if you want us to. After what you've been through and the long drive, we'd understand if—"

"You're staying! Are you kidding me? I'd love that! I can't believe you two went to so much trouble." I stopped and looked around at the entranceway and the hallway leading to the living room at the back of the house. Memories of happy times spent there with Aunt Maeve collided with pent-up anger and sadness. My shoulders wracked with sobs and the tears flowed freely. To say I was a mess was an understatement. It had taken the love of my two friends to uncork that cauldron of emotion.

Mary-Jane squeezed my shoulder and murmured to Libby, "Let's give her some time alone, going through the place. We'll get her stuff from the truck."

THREE

I could smell as well as see the results of my friends' efforts to make the house more welcoming and livable. The air held a hint of lemon while the old Formica countertops and appliances showed not a speck of dust. I sighed as I gazed around the room. Walls that were once cheerful with a sunflower pattern were now dingy with strips of wallpaper hanging loose. I ran my finger along the scarred and worn wooden table where I could almost see my Aunt Maeve sitting as she shelled peas or played endless games of solitaire on rainy afternoons.

Slowly I wandered through the archway to the living room that encompassed the whole back half of the house. The leather sofa showed more sags than when I'd sat there with her watching television, and the loveseat had stuffing peeking out from a couple of the cushions. I looked out the big picture window with a view of the lake. That hadn't changed at all except the dock was tipped up on its side from years of winter ice pressure. I could just make out a couple of the tiny cottages she used to rent out before the curve of the shoreline obscured the others.

Turning, the set of stairs leading to the bedrooms above called to me. I'd check out the dining room later; we hardly ever used it anyway. The steps creaked as I moved up them. The wool runner centered with a flower pattern had been faded even when I'd lived there. The tangy scent of mothballs infused the air on the second floor. Aunt Maeve had sworn by the effectiveness of camphor in deterring not only bugs but rodents. Even to this day, whenever I smelled camphor I'd think of her.

The front door banged shut, and I could hear my friends' voices as they brought my stuff in from the truck. Moving past my aunt's bedroom, I went into the smaller one next to it where I'd always slept—my room. My gaze ran over the wrought-iron headboard of the double bed. I remembered painting it a vibrant purple, although much of the black under that color now showed through.

The dresser and chair had been dusted, and the duvet and pillow were new, but that was the extent of any upkeep in the room. Like every other area of the house, the wallpaper was in tatters, and the floor coverings were ancient. Yeah, the house needed a ton of work to bring it up to a livable condition, but the bones of the house were still good.

Steeling myself, I left the room and went into Aunt Maeve's old bedroom. The brightly colored patchwork quilt on her bed was an arrow that shot through my heart. I remembered her working on it, using the big frame she'd set up in the living room to quilt it by hand. Heck! Some of those stitches were by my own hand when she'd tried to teach me the art of quilting.

Seeing a framed print on the floor, I wandered over to pick it up. My heart sank lower at the familiar scene. It had been her favorite picture, one that she'd taken herself of a wishing well set in a glade of trees. When I'd asked her about it, she'd given me an enigmatic smile and changed the subject. It had meant something to her, something private. I'd always thought that perhaps it was connected to an old love of hers. And considering that she'd never married, maybe her heart had been too broken to ever go down that path again.

The sounds of a song drifted up the stairwell. I listened hard, and then words came out of my mouth all on their own. I swiped a tear from my cheek as I sang:

> *"When it hasn't been your day, your week, your month, or even your year...*

I'll be there for you."

I went over to the top of the stairs and looked down at Libby and Mary-Jane. They smiled at me and hooked their pinky fingers together, beckoning for me to join them. OMG! How many times had we watched episodes of *Friends* together? We'd made a pact to always be close like the gang on that sitcom. They were our heroes.

My finger linked with theirs and we laughed, still singing that old song by The Rembrandts. Even Aunt Maeve had laughed at the antics in the show as she stitched, sitting in the corner of the room.

Libby was the first to break off from the song, with a shout of joy, "That's us, gals! We're here for each other when the rain starts to fall!"

I snorted. "Rain? How about a torrential downpour?"

Mary-Jane put the fingers of her free hand over my lips. "You'll get through this, Shannon." There was a determination in her gray eyes that dared me to disagree. "You're home. Things will turn around, and you'll be better than new. I promise."

I couldn't help myself. I started to blubber. "I *had* a home! With two kids! And nowww…"

They gathered around me in a group hug. Cradling my head, Libby said, "Hush, honey. You said every summer, every single summer when you arrived, that coming here was like coming home." She was right; I did say that. Spending those summers here at Aunt Maeve's house had been a home for me.

"Like my childhood home?" I replied in a small voice.

Mary-Jane chimed in, "Exactly!" She gave me an extra squeeze. "So let's have that homecoming party, then!"

With a sharp nod, Libby added, "Hear! Hear! I second that! Let's get something to eat and then drink copious amounts of alcohol! It's not often that I get away from my tribe to get shit-faced with my friends." She broke away, still swaying and dancing as she walked into the kitchen. She may be carrying a few extra pounds around her waist but in the jeans and sweatshirt, she was busting a move.

Mary-Jane's eyes lit up. "I brought dinner! Lasagna, Caesar salad, and salted caramel brownies. No diets tonight, ladies! But I disagree with Libby; more libation is definitely in order first." She put her arm over my shoulder and herded me into the kitchen.

I laughed trying to steady myself and not bump into the doorjamb as we stumbled through. "This is from the world-famous Cat's Whiskers restaurant? Wow! Not only do you get this place ready for me, but you have my favorites. I can't remember the last time I had salted caramel *anything*!" It used to be our favorite ice-cream when we'd hang around the village green so many years ago.

Libby held up the wine bottle in one hand and my Jack Daniels in the other. "Pick your poison, ladies."

I shot a look over to Mary-Jane. "Our favorite nurse is now about to poison us."

Libby blinked innocently. "I'm not at work!" She gestured with the bottles. "So what's it going to be?"

I pointed to the Jack Daniels and then blurted, "Guess who I ran into when I stopped for gas? Steve Murphy! What the hell happened to little Stevie Murphy?"

Libby glanced over at me as she fished ice cubes from a bag and tossed them into my cup. "He started living at the gym, pumping iron. Plus, the contact lenses didn't hurt. He blossomed like a rose—"

"Till he knocked up, and married, Amy Grassley. They had a kid before she discovered she was more into women than men. I guess they had *that* in common at least." Mary-Jane filled her cup with wine and wandered into the living room.

"Wait! What? I don't remember any Amy. How long were they married before she—"

"Four years. And now she's with Suzanne Smith. You wouldn't know Suzanne either. She moved here about ten years ago. Steve and Amy had a boy, Byron. He's a good kid." Libby handed me the cup of whiskey over ice and led the way out of the room.

"How about you, Libby? How are you holding up?" I held

her eyes as I took a seat in the recliner. Her husband was killed in a car wreck six years ago, and she's raised their three kids alone since. My trip up for the wake and funeral was the last time the three of us had been together.

It was also, and I'm ashamed to admit it, the last time I visited Aunt Maeve. She was in the nursing home by then, and barely recognized me. Alzheimer's is such a wicked, wicked disease.

Libby tucked her feet under her butt, sitting at the end of the sofa. After a moment, she answered, "It was really hard at first. I hardly left my bed, let alone the house, for about a year. If not for Mary-Jane and my parents, I'm not sure I would have gotten through it. But now, I'm doing okay. There are days, though, with my second son, Jack, that I want to tear my hair out. But the other two make up for him, thank goodness."

Mary-Jane shook her head. "He's a good kid, just your rebellious teenager. Jack practically lives at my house, which is totally okay with my Zoe. *That's* the one we all have to keep an eye on. We try to keep the pair busy at the restaurant, waiting tables and helping in the kitchen with me but they're devious. But then"—she made an evil grin—"so were we at that age, right?"

Libby finished her drink and then signaled for me to hand my cup over. "Speak for yourself, MJ. You were the wild one, going from boyfriend to boyfriend. I only had eyes for Hank, even back then. Now, Shannon, you could have had your pick of any of the guys we hung out with. I think they counted the days till you were back for the summer."

I snorted. "As if! There was no way I was ending up like my mother, saddled with a kid to raise on my own. I'd spent my childhood in low-rent dives, going from city to city. I was totally fine with being a virgin, believe me."

I took a deep breath remembering those many evenings around the campfire with the old gang. "In retrospect, I kind of wished I'd gotten next to Liam Murphy. He was *hot!* Instead, I saved myself for the Ass-hat. But I've got two good kids, so I guess I wouldn't change anything about all that."

"Liam Murphy! That's a blast from the past. He was a great kisser! But nothing to write home about beyond first base. He's a corporate lawyer in LA now." Mary-Jane's gaze flitted between both of us over the rim of her plastic mug.

"You made out with *Liam Murphy*?" A glance at Libby showed the same shock I felt mirrored in her eyes.

Mary-Jane rolled her eyes. "What? Yeah, sure. You were the ice queen, Shannon, and Libby couldn't see past Hank. So, yeah, he made a pass at me." She stood up, primping the mane of strawberry curls cascading over her shoulders, totally vamping it up. "I wasn't always fifty pounds overweight! I might not have been as pretty as you two, but I was damned cute!"

"You slut! And I mean that in a good way, Mary-Jane. I-I'm just jealous," I stammered, before another thought popped into my head. "What's with this Devon guy that Steve told me about? He said he might want to buy Aunt Maeve's summer cabin colony to develop it."

A loud bang from the kitchen made everyone jump.

Libby stepped into the kitchen to take a look. She stood at the entranceway with a puzzled look. "That's weird. Your suitcase fell over, Shannon. I set it next to the table but it tipped. What the..." Her voice trailed off as she went into the kitchen, looking around to see if she could determine the cause.

I walked to the front door to see if it had opened from a gust of wind. But it was closed tight, and the window in the kitchen was also shut. When I entered the kitchen, Libby was stepping around my suitcase with her foot, pressing the floor.

She shrugged her shoulders. "Beats me, floor seems fine."

"Meh," I said, "I probably just packed it top-heavy." With an "oof," I righted it and set it against the wall. It had to weigh sixty pounds; no wonder it made such a loud bang when it fell over.

Libby leaned against the entranceway, her arms folded. "Don't sell this place, Shannon. Especially to Devon Booker. He's one shady operator. Besides," she added, looking around the fixer-upper that was the kitchen, "I think this place has real promise for you."

I spun around from the suitcase. "What did you say?"

"Don't sell to Devon Booker. He doesn't have the best repu—"

"No, not that. What did you say about promise?"

She shrugged. "You know, new beginnings and all that." She looked up at the cracked ceiling. "I mean it needs work and all, but you could make a real go of it if you wanted." She dropped her gaze to meet my eyes. "What's wrong?"

My eyes avoided her glance. "Nothing, I guess. It's just that phrase you used, 'real promise for you.' That's exactly what Maeve had said to me in her will when she bequeathed the property to me."

"Well, that's kind of cool, huh?" Libby replied with a smile. "Maeve and I think alike."

I made one of those awkward nods of my head; you know, the kind that you give when you're actually uncomfortable? Yeah, one of those. "Makes sense."

Except it didn't. That suitcase flipping to the ground with such a bang happened right when I said out loud that somebody wanted to buy Maeve's place from me. Aunt Maeve had specifically requested in her will that this place stay in the family. And then there was that thing with the bobcat and her voice ringing in my head. *"It'll be okay. Trust me."*

I straightened and looked around the room. Was this another message from my aunt? The funny thing was, I wasn't frightened by it. If anything, I *hoped* she was still around.

When I smelled the scent of her favorite perfume, my eyes widened.

"Do you smell that?" I looked over at Libby.

"What, Jack Daniels and wine? Yup."

I shook my head. "Never mind. Must be my imagination, but I thought I smelled flowers."

FOUR

The next morning, my eyes tried to creak open at the gentle rub on my shoulder.

"Shannon?"

"What?" I jerked upright, staring into Libby's puffy blue eyes. Beside her, holding two mugs of coffee was Mary-Jane. It came back to me in a flash—staying up until three in the morning as we drunkenly reconnected. The jolt of pain in my right temple was another poignant reminder.

Mary-Jane handed me a cup of coffee. "Here. You probably need this as much as I do." Her mess of curls looked like a bird had made a nest there.

Libby forced some pills in my other hand. "This aspirin will help." She blinked some sleep out of her eyes and then yawned. "I can't remember the last time I was awake after midnight. But it was worth it."

I washed the pills down with a healthy swig of coffee and then threw the covers back. "What time is it?" It was hard to tell with the overcast sky outside.

Mary-Jane's smile faded as she sat on the end of the bed to finish her coffee. "After ten. I hate to be a party pooper but I've got to get going. Saturday night is pretty busy at the restaurant, and I've got a ton of food prep to do. But I'll call you later to see if you need anything."

"That's okay. I think I have everything I need. I'll probably finish unpacking, and then I'm going to make an inventory of what needs work around this place." I definitely needed to get started on that if I was going to stay there for any length of time.

Libby smiled and extended a hand to help me get to my feet. "I can stay for another hour or so. I'll call Kevin to help us unload the U-Haul. He's got a job at the grocery store, but he doesn't go in until four. Besides which, I'd like you to meet him."

Mary-Jane smirked. "Kevin is definitely number-one son."

Libby turned on her. "He's a good kid! Okay, maybe he's more serious than the others, trying to fill his father's footsteps. But that's not such a bad thing."

"I'm teasing! He is a good kid." Mary-Jane rose and led the way out of the room. "Roy texted me about ten times already wondering when I'd be home, so I guess I'd better fly." She turned and looked at me before she started down the stairs. "Come over to the restaurant tomorrow for dinner. My treat."

I nodded. "Maybe I will. If what you served last night is any indication of the quality, I'm in for something special." I followed MJ down the stairs, leaving Libby as she texted her son Kevin.

"For sure! Even I can't resist." Patting her generous hips, she laughed. "As if you couldn't tell. But come Monday, it's back on the diet treadmill for me." She grabbed her oversized handbag from the coffee table and ambled toward the front door. Turning, she gave me a one-armed hug. "Don't work too hard, sweetie. You need to rest, especially after staying up half the night. Maybe go for a walk along the lake. Reconnect with nature and all that happy horseshit."

"Got it! Actually, I probably will do that. I'd like to check the cabins, even if I don't do anything with them right away." At the sound of Libby coming down the hallway, I glanced back at her. "Did you contact Kevin?"

"Yup! He'll be here in fifteen minutes." The pride in her eyes shone through when she answered. Yeah, Kevin really was her number-one son and it showed.

"Okay, you two, I'm outta here. Talk at you later." Mary-Jane waved her hand as she walked to her van.

I closed the door and turned to Libby. "We have time for one more cup of joe before Kevin gets here, right? I need something to help get my ass in gear." As I poured two more cups for us, I smiled. "That was fun last night! I can't remember the last time I laughed so much. It's been awhile, let me tell you. Mary-Jane's still a hoot."

Libby took the mug from me and then wandered over to sit at the table. "She is when she's away from Roy. But that doesn't happen too often. Don't get me wrong; they work hard, and the restaurant is thriving, but it's thanks to MJ." Her eyes narrowed, and she looked at me quizzically. "Do you remember Roy Matthews?"

When I shook my head, she continued, "I wouldn't say this if I didn't love Mary-Jane but...Roy's not that nice a guy. He certainly doesn't deserve her."

My stomach dropped as I looked at her. Oh no. Not another impending marriage breakup...and to one of my best friends. Men! "He's screwing around on her or what?"

"No, no, nothing like that." She snorted. "Who'd have him besides Mary-Jane? No, he tries to be funny, but his jokes and ribbing really aren't all that funny. He's continually berating her about her weight and how she's not all that smart." Her eyes narrowed as she stared into her mug of coffee. "That restaurant wouldn't be half as successful if not for MJ. People like her and she's a great chef. I think practically everyone in town tolerates Roy because of her."

"Shit! That totally sucks! Trust me, I know what being underappreciated is like. But to be berated? She's too nice a person, and way too much fun for her to have to put up with that."

"I think that's part of the reason he picks on her. It's like he wants to keep her under his thumb, keep her down so that she thinks she'll never do any better than him. To make matters worse, he dotes on their kid Zoe to the point that she's turned into a spoiled brat. Don't get me wrong. My Jack's rebellious, but he doesn't talk to me the way that Zoe talks to Mary-Jane. Roy just laughs about it."

I thought of my own two kids. "That's gotta be so hard on Mary-Jane. My daughter, Jess, is like me in lots of ways. She'd never do or say anything to hurt or show disrespect to either Alex or me. She's no doormat but she's kind to people. Now, Thomas...he's more pragmatic. He can be super sweet, but there's usually something in it for him. I think he was more concerned on how the divorce is going to affect him than what it's doing to the rest of us."

"And they're twins? That's odd, I guess. My daughter sounds a lot like yours. Dahlia brings home every stray animal she finds. I think she's going to be a vet. If you come to my house, which you will, of course, ignore the smells you might encounter. She may have a pet skunk in her room."

"You're kidding me!" A skunk? In a *house*?

She laughed. She keeps threatening to do it! Especially when she finds a stray cat or dog! She says it could be worse; she could bring home a stray skunk next time."

I chortled. "That apple didn't fall far from the tree considering what you do for a living. I can't wait to meet your kids and to introduce you to mine."

I jumped when the honk of a car horn sounded.

Libby stood up and peeked out the window. "Kevin's here." She gulped down the rest of her coffee and started to cross the room. "We'd better make hay while the sun shines, girlfriend. We've only got him for a little while."

When I stepped outside, I did a double-take. The young man standing next to the little Honda Civic could have been his father, Hank, standing there. He was the spitting image. I could understand why Kevin was Libby's favorite.

"Shannon, this is my son, Kevin. Kevin, this is Mrs. Walker."

I reached for his hand to shake it. "It's just Shannon. Pleased to meet you, Kevin. Your mom told me so many good things about you."

He actually blushed a bit when he murmured, "Nice to finally meet you...Shannon. My mom said some nice things about you too!"

I laughed, "All lies! But that's okay. You ready to show me the muscles she was bragging about? I've got a U-Haul to unload." I led the way to the back of the trailer. "If you can manage the grand piano, I'll get the box of dishes." Seeing the shock in his eyes, I tapped his shoulder. "Kidding! There's no piano, believe me!"

"Uh...good?" He reached for the nearest box when the door was lifted. "Do you want these in the kitchen or living room?"

For the next hour we worked getting the trailer unloaded. I had to say that without his help it would have been at least ten times harder, especially taking boxes up to the second floor. I was still feeling the effects of our reunion the night before, and Libby didn't look as bright-eyed as she was last night when I first arrived.

Finally it was done! Libby and her son paused at their vehicles before taking off.

Kevin spoke, "If you need help with that grass, I can come over this week to cut it. Our lawn mower fits in the back of this beast."

"Great! I'll pay you, of course!" It would be good to have a lawn again, the way Aunt Maeve had kept it. Plus, I wasn't sure if the lawnmower she had still worked.

"Not necessary. Consider it a housewarming present." He smiled before getting into his vehicle. "Mom? You coming now?"

"I'll be right behind you." Libby stepped over and gave me a warm hug. "I hate that you went through this shit with Alex. I think your aunt would be happy to know she was able to help you when you needed it most." Her hug took on an extra squeeze as she said, "But I'm happy to have you home."

I gasped. There was that word again. *Home?* Seriously? Yes, I spent many, many summers here, and yes, no matter where life took me, I always looked back at my days in Wesley as the best times of my life.

But even the years when I came here, it was only for a couple of months at best! I had lived my own life far, far away from Greene County, New York. I went to college. I met a man I truly loved and bore our children. Home? Seriously?

Nevertheless, in a way, Libby was right. Seriously. I always felt *something* when I passed the exit on the New York State Thruway for Wesley. It wasn't a Hallmark moment; not at all. I barely noticed when I had felt it. But it was there. I had felt it again and again back in those halcyon days of my adolescence and ever since, every time I passed that sign. I had felt it in my teens then, and I've felt it ever since I arrived back here.

I was truly where I belonged.

And if that's not "home"...what is?

"Home," I said aloud and burst into tears. Again.

"Yes," Libby replied. "Home."

I'd been able to hold my feelings in check when I was alone or with strangers, but the love I'd been shown since hitting this old town broke the dam. I blubbered my reply, "Thanks for all your help, Libby. I'm happy to be back with you and Mary-Jane." I saw her son wheeling the car around to head back down the driveway. "And thanks for lending me your son! He's as handsome and kind as his parents. You should be proud."

There were tears in her eyes when she pulled back. "I am proud. I'll call you tomorrow, but don't hesitate to call me if you need me." With that she slipped away and got in her car.

After waving to her as she drove down the driveway, I turned and looked at the old homestead. This was it. It was time to begin my new life.

FIVE

After working for four hours straight, I stepped outside. The sky which had earlier threatened rain was now clear and warm enough to go without a jacket. I'd packed a thermos of Jack Daniels cut with some ginger ale for my hike around my aunt's property.

Correction...MY property.

I wandered past the compact cabins perched on cinder blocks as protection in case the lake flooded over from the mountain's snow melt. Originally the small houses had been painted white, but now the paint had faded where it wasn't entirely missing in spots. The windows were still intact, no vandalism thank goodness. But the shingles on the rooftops were curled and bare of the gravel that normally coated them.

I continued on the dirt road that connected the ten cabins. To my right the buildings were well spaced out, hugging the shore of Eccles Lake, while on my left were fields bordered by thick stands of evergreens and maples. Veering to the left would take me down the paths where I'd raced with my friends, playing hide-and-seek and catching fireflies. It was all familiar but waaay overgrown with dense underbrush.

Finding a fallen log, I took a seat and poured a healthy cup of the bourbon. A monarch butterfly bobbed and danced by me while overhead a flock of migrating geese honked their passage. The sun was warm on my face as I looked up, inhaling deeply the fresh earthy air. It was so peaceful. If only things would stay this way.

I don't know how long I sat there, recalling summers past, my Aunt Maeve, and how simple life had been. It was a surprise when I poured the last of the thermos into my cup. Holy Hannah. That sure had gone down smooth. Still holding my drink, I rose and continued on, dodging rocks and trees until I came to a clearing. There I was, drink in hand, tipsy tripping through the woods.

I continued down the wooded path, the shore of the lake disappearing behind me. As the winding trail took me deeper into the woods, a sense of peace began to drift over me. It's hard to put into words, but I truly felt that I had come home.

"I belong here," I said aloud. That surprised me—not the talking out loud to myself, I do that all the time. No, what surprised me was that powerful sense that welled up in me and how, when I spoke it aloud, it felt so...so *right*. "I really do belong here," I added.

I rounded another bend in the trail and stopped dead in my tracks and stared blankly.

I blinked a few times at what I saw. It was the wishing well in my aunt's photo! It sat off to the side in a twenty-foot circle of vibrant green grass. I smiled, seeing the familiar limestone base and the wooden roof topping it. There was even a wooden bucket and rope to lower it. I looked around at the space where it sat, thick trees bordering a grassy oasis.

It was weird, but all of a sudden a stillness had settled over the woods. Not a bird or cricket or even a fly moved in the circle ahead of me. I took a tremulous step, my foot sinking into the soft loam under the lush grass. I was hardly aware of walking over to the well until I peered down into its depths. I could just barely make out a glint of water at the bottom.

I had thought I'd been through every square foot of Aunt Maeve's property during my younger years. I *know* I'd traipsed the trail in the woods dozens of times. But I never saw this well before. I took a step away to look it over. Thick moss ran around the base of the limestone wall, with lichens going up the sides. The wooden timbers that supported the cedar roof were dark with age. The bucket, attached to a spool of rope wrapped around a wooden axle, was also stippled with moss. It hadn't been used in quite some time, but still looked pretty sturdy.

There was no question this had been here for years and years, but I'd never come across it before. And why would there be a well in the woods with the lake so close by? I snickered. "It's a wishing well, silly!" I told myself aloud. Of course. I fished in my pocket for a coin to toss in so I could make my own wish, but my fingers only found a ball of lint.

I sloshed the dregs of my bourbon and ginger ale in my cup. Well, there's more than one way to make an offering, right? I tipped the cup holding my drink, pouring out the remnants, listening for the splash when they landed. How deep was that well anyway? And I made my wish—that my kids be healthy and happy and for me to resume a pleasant and prosperous life.

"Thank you!"

I jumped back so fast, my ass bounced on the ground! What the hell? That was a voice! It had sounded like it belonged to a woman! Was someone down there? I scrambled to my feet and peered down the dark hole, searching for a body, a person, or any sign of movement.

"Hello?" It came out as a whisper so I tried it again, only this time louder. "Hello? Is anyone down there?" My heart thundering in my chest was the only sound that reverberated in my ears.

But I'd definitely heard a woman's voice from deep in that well! But now all was silent from the dark depths. My gaze darted around at the stand of trees wondering if there was someone there, playing some kind of trick on me. But the only movement was the soft rustle of leaves and boughs swaying high above.

"Is anyone out there? Come out and show yourself! This is my land you're trespassing on!" I tried to inject a sense of authority in my voice despite the fact that my knees were knocking. But again, nothing.

I backed away from the well, scanning the area for anything and everything! A raccoon, a teenager...or more importantly, anything threatening. When my foot snapped a twig, I almost had a heart attack. Turning, I walked quickly back through the trees, trying to ignore the temptation to break into a full-out run.

Thank you. I could still hear that voice in my head as I scrambled back down the path. It hadn't sounded panicked but rather matter of fact, the way you'd thank someone who brought you a coffee. What the hell?

Finally I saw the dirt road and the rooftop of one of the cottages. Taking great gulps of air, I made my way until I collapsed on the step of the verandah of my house.

"That couldn't have happened. Could it?" In my haste to leave the odd little clearing with the well, I'd dropped my cup and never even given a thought to the thermos. Small loss. Maybe I should have stuck with just ginger ale and skipped the Jack Daniels. But I wasn't drunk, let alone even feeling tipsy. With the adrenaline coursing through my veins, I was certainly sober now!

Oh my God. Was I losing my mind?

SIX

I closed my eyes and counted to ten. Whatever had happened back there was over. If it had even *happened*. It was time to go inside and take a long hot shower to clear my head. When I rose to go into the house, I noticed a small white card wedged in between the door and the frame.

Plucking it out, I peered at the photo of a fortyish man. Dark hair combed back from a broad, smooth forehead above smiling eyes and a sculpted jawline with a hint of beard shadow. He wasn't hard to look at, that was for sure!

Devon Booker
Mountain Planning and Development
537 964 8999

I flipped it over but there was no handwritten note, just the card. I snorted. Well, he didn't waste any time getting in touch with me. Steve Murphy had been right about him salivating about buying up land on the small lake. I kind of wished I'd been there when he visited, if for nothing else than to hear what kind of money he was offering.

After setting the card on the kitchen table, I raced up the stairs to my aunt's bedroom. I peered at the photo of the wishing well. For sure it was the same one! There'd been more moss on the rocks than I'd seen earlier, and the wood had darkened, but there was no mistaking that circle of grass and the trees bordering it.

I turned the frame over and loosened the pegs holding the photo in place. When I managed to slide it out from the frame, I turned it over. There in my aunt's loopy handwriting were the words, "Witching Well September 1972."

My mouth fell open. *"Witching Well?"* Was that a joke? Why would she write that?

The chords of Mambo #5 filled the air while my cell phone in my pocket vibrated against my hip. Jess! I sighed, feeling another lump of guilt settle in my gut. In the excitement of seeing Libby and Mary-Jane again, I'd forgotten to text her that I'd made it safe and sound.

> **Mom! Where are you? If you don't call me or text me back in the next ten minutes I'm calling the police. Please, I'm worried sick.**

I hit the icon to place the call. She picked up on the first ring.

"Mom! Are you okay? Where are you?"

"I'm sorry, Jess. My cell phone was upstairs and I didn't hear it. I meant to call, but my friends had a surprise welcoming party here, probably why I never heard you ring. I'm okay. I'm here at my aunt's house in Wesley."

"Thank goodness! I tried to get you a bunch of times with no answer." She paused. "How is everything there?"

I took a deep breath. Where to start. "It's fine! The place needs some work but nothing major...at least I don't think so. My friends got the electricity turned on, and there's internet and heat, so I'll be okay. It's a nice spot right on the lake. Hey! I've already been approached by a big developer who wants to buy it." A little stretch of the truth, but I wanted to ease any worry from her mind.

"Oh yeah? Maybe you should sell it. That would take care of any money problems." Jess sounded relieved at that piece of news.

"I'm not sure what I'm going to do, to be honest, although

I'm leaning in the direction of staying here. It's been fun reconnecting with my friends."

"Mom? I saw Dad yesterday."

My attention was immediately yanked away from the photo. Since Ass-hat had walked out, he had barely communicated with the kids. In the last six months, he'd only spoken to Jess twice as far as I knew. When he'd walked away he felt his obligations to them ended with the checks he'd cut for their education—an amount which would have been less until I fought him on it. For him to show up out of the blue at her school was odd, even if it was long overdue. Bastard!

I couldn't help sniping when I answered her, "That's big of him. What'd he have to say for himself?" I could just imagine him making excuses and trying to play some kind of victim card.

She huffed. "That's just it. He wasn't here to see me. When I went into the caf for lunch, he was sitting there with Alicia McDonald. Alicia's also a freshman, living in my dorm. Dad didn't see me until I was standing next to their table. He looked like a deer in the headlights when I said hi."

"What the hell was he doing there visiting her and not you?" My forehead tightened as I gripped the small phone. This made zero sense. Who *was* this kid?

"Oh, he wasn't alone. Alicia's mom was there too. When Alicia asked me how I knew her stepfather, I almost shit! I said he's my father. Then she goes, 'What? Alex has been seeing my mom for the past two years. When he moved to Philly six months ago, he moved in with us!'"

For a few moments I sat there in shock, unable to say a word. He'd been seeing some woman for *two years* behind my back? All those so-called business trips out of town! He'd been at *her* house! How much of our marriage had been a lie? Was this his first affair?

"Mom? Are you still there?

"Yeah. What happened next? Did he say anything, the little weasel!" I could picture the scene and how shocked Jess must have been. And *hurt.*

"He said that there'd been problems with the marriage for years before he finally left." There was silence for a few moments before I heard her sniffle. "I understand that people drift apart and get divorced, but did he have to divorce Thomas and me too? He's got a whole new family now."

"Honey, I'm so sorry that this happened to you." My heart actually hurt as I pictured her alone in her dorm room. I'd give anything to be there with her, holding her, trying to end the hurt. "I don't know why your father did this to you and Thomas. But it's him that's at fault, not you, not Thomas. You did *nothing* to deserve this kind of treatment. I hope you realize that."

"Neither did you, Mom. He's an asshole! He can have his new family for all I care! I never want to see him again!"

"I don't blame you for feeling like that, Jess. But never is a long time. There may come a day that he will want you back in his life." It was a total platitude that I was spewing, more to help my daughter than defend the Ass-hat.

"I debated whether to even tell you about it, Mom. It was so awful!" Her voice broke as a fresh set of sobs claimed her.

"Oh, honey, I feel so bad for you. I'm sure it was a nightmare, Jess. What the hell is wrong with him to show up at the same school you go to? Why didn't he let the woman go alone? That was senseless and cruel." Even though I tried to keep my voice level to comfort her, my fist was so tight that my fingernails in my free hand bit into my palm! If he were here now, I'd rip his face off for what he was doing to our kids.

"Alicia's mother never said a word. But I'd seen her before, Mom."

"Where?"

Jess's voice cracked. "At his office! He said she was from Philadelphia, opening a satellite office or something...now he's *living* in Philly! They're both dirty rotten liars, Mom. They told Alicia that Dad lived in another city until he moved in with them."

A well of brand-spanking-new rage filled me. He had been

having an affair with someone from work? And not just an affair, but he'd left his family to be with her! The rage coursing through my head made me see double!

"Did he even take you aside for a few moments, Jess? Give you a hug and say he was sorry?" I'd bet not! The prick!

"He didn't get the chance. I told Alicia I hoped he was a better stepfather than he'd been as a father to me. I left him sitting there with his new family."

That was one good thing. At least Jess had gotten her licks in. "Does Thomas know? Did you speak with your brother yet?" I could only imagine how he'd feel. It was one more cheesy thing about the divorce that he'd have to deal with. A new family would totally skeeve Thomas out.

"Not yet. What's the rush? It's not like Dad's going to get to him first. I'll tell him at some point though. He has a right to know the truth."

"Why don't you both come here for Thanksgiving? I'll pay for your plane tickets. I miss both of you so much! I love you, Jessica." This time it was me who swiped a few tears from my cheeks. All of this was so unfair to my children. They should be spreading their wings and enjoying college, not dealing with a father who didn't give two shits about them.

When had that happened? Why hadn't I noticed him distancing himself from the kids as well as me? I thought Alex was going through some problems at work that he'd become so aloof. Now I knew the source of those problems.

"I've got to get going, Mom. I've got to do some research for an English paper that's due next week." She snorted. "That's one plus of being swamped with reading and papers. I don't have time to think of Dad and all this shit."

"Yeah. I hear you. I'll call you in a day or so to see how things are going? You take it easy and try to have some fun. College is work, but it's also supposed to be fun. Remember I love you, Jess."

"Love you too! And you try to have fun too, Mom. Don't kill yourself fixing that house up. See your friends and go out to dinner or something."

"Will do! Bye, hon."

When I clicked off the phone, I sat there shaking my head. I'd been angry with Alex before this, but it was nothing compared to what I felt now. He and that woman were a pair of skeeves. I hoped they had a big argument for each and every time they'd sneaked around and lied. Maybe she'd find some other idiot to glom onto and hurt him like he'd hurt so many people.

And if he became impotent, that would be A-OK too. Damn right!

SEVEN

The next day, I climbed out of bed when the alarm on my phone went off. Shit! It was almost nine, and it felt like I'd only just got to sleep. That conversation with Jess had stirred up a hornet's nest of emotions. I'd ping-ponged between rage at the ex to bouts of tears for my kids and me. It was only after having half a dozen shots of Jack Daniel that I'd finally been able to drift off.

But I wasn't going to live in that space anymore. Worrying, reliving what had happened and letting anger claim me would ultimately do me more harm than Ass-hat and his skank. Besides, if I didn't take care of myself, I wouldn't be much help to my kids getting through this. They needed me to be strong if I was going to help them work past this life crisis.

I needed to be strong for ME, as well.

A half hour later, with my list of the supplies I'd need to start peeling wallpaper and lift the old linoleum, I headed into town. If I could get the kitchen in decent shape, it would make the whole place more livable. After a quick stop at the U-Haul office to drop off the trailer, I continued on to the hardware store. I spied a parking spot a few spaces away from the Mountain Homes Hardware on the main street and flipped my turn signal on. Just as I was about to wheel the truck into the spot, a red Honda SUV appeared out of nowhere and darted into the empty space.

My mouth fell open as I watched her park the car. Today was definitely *not* the day to mess with me! Not after what I had learned yesterday from Jess and spending a restless night! I rolled the window down and yelled at the matronly redhead who got out of the SUV. "Hey! Didn't you see my signal?" In Pittsburgh, a stunt like that could end in a few choice F bombs, if not an outright brawl.

"Snooze, you lose." She gave a perfect cheesy grin as she flounced her way across the sidewalk.

"Bitch. I hope that flaming-red car goes *up* in flames!" I muttered and slammed the steering wheel with my hand. It was another two blocks before I saw an opening to park the truck. More reason to snarl about that bitch who cut me off.

By the time I walked the couple blocks to Mountain Homes Hardware, the redhead was just leaving the drugstore next to it. She purposely didn't meet my eye even though I gave her the coldest look I could muster, staring right through her. Weasel!

When I entered the store, a bell hanging over the door tinkled loudly announcing my presence. It was an old-school establishment; dark hardwood floors creaked under my feet as I entered, and a mellow aroma from the paint area lingered in the air. It was warmly lit too, not the dazzling fluorescents like in the big-box stores. A real country hardware store.

"I'm coming!" The voice that called from the back of the store was familiar. When Steve Murphy ambled up the aisle wiping his hands with a speckled paint rag, I smiled.

"You work here?" But from the beige apron with the company logo on its bib, it was pretty obvious he did.

"Naw, I just come in to mix paint and hustle pretty shoppers when it's slow." He laughed and tossed the rag onto the counter next to him. "I own the joint actually. How's the house? Ready to pack up that U-Haul again and head south? You'd have better weather at least."

"The house isn't as bad as you said. Don't get me wrong, there's a ton of work, but I think I'll be okay." I folded my arms across my chest. "That Devon Booker left a calling card on my door. I was out for a walk in the afternoon and missed him."

"Hmmm." Even though he looked down at the floor, he couldn't hide the smirk that danced on his lips. A lock of hair brushed his eyebrows when he shook his head.

It hit me once more how damned cute Steve had become. How was that possible when he'd been so gorky as a kid?

He continued, "Told you so. He's been after me for years, but he needs your spot to make his dreams come true. I can see it now. A whole subdivision of oversized log homes, in what would probably be a *gated* community around the lake."

"Yuck. That would change the character of the area entirely. I remember when vacationing families filled my aunt's cottages over the summer." I sighed, thinking of all the people who'd worked all year for their time at the lake in the mountains. It would be a shame for just a select, affluent crowd to have that privilege.

"I hear you, although it would mean money in *my* pockets." He smiled at me. "So Libby and Mary-Jane were there to greet you when you arrived? That must have been a fun night. I saw their cars there when I drove by."

"Too much wine and whisky but a total blast. I felt it yesterday, let me tell you." I pulled the shopping list from my purse. "But now it's time to get to work. I thought I'd tackle one room at a time, starting with the kitchen. I want to get the wallpaper off and lift the floor covering to see what's underneath. It might be worth refinishing if it's decent wood."

He took the list I extended and was quiet as he read through it. "There're a few items that you might want to add, to make the job easier." He glanced at me as he stepped to the front of the store to roll a shopping cart toward me. "You probably could use a large garbage container for all the stuff you're ripping out."

I followed him as he grabbed scrapers, pry bars, a steamer, and a ton of stuff not on my list. "So, I heard that you've got a son. The girls said he's a pretty nice kid."

He met my eyes, and there was a big grin on his face.

"Yeah, Byron's all right. He's with his mom this weekend, which is why I'm working today. We share weekly custody, so he won't be around for a few more days." He resumed plucking items from the shelves, wheeling the cart to another aisle with me close behind. "How about you? When will your kids be here to visit you?"

Considering the size of the town, he probably knew I had two kids and also knew about the divorce. "Maybe for Thanksgiving. I know that's not for another couple of months but I'd like to get the place in better shape before they get here."

"You might want to get a load of firewood in before it gets much colder. It's always nice to have a backup source of heat in case there's a power outage. You've never been here during the winter. It's damned cold with a ton of snow. I can give you some names of guys with seasoned wood that won't cost you an arm and a leg. I'll help you split and stack it, if you want."

"Will that be on my bill or is that your welcoming gesture?" I grinned at him to let him know I was teasing.

When he turned to me, he winked before a slow smile lit his face. "Taking you out to dinner is my *welcome* gesture. Making sure you're warm this winter is just being a good neighbor. But if you'd like to pay me, sharing an evening next to your fireplace with some wine and dinner might cover it."

My cheeks and neck were infused with heat, and it had nothing to do with the prospect of the wood. It was the way he looked at me that shot a jolt of warmth through my core. I couldn't remember the last time a guy, especially one this gorgeous, had openly flirted with me. For a moment my mouth went dry and words failed me.

But then I remembered, I'm single now! I even had the divorce papers to prove it! If a hot guy was coming onto me, then that was okay. Better than okay—it was awesome! I still had it, even in my forties, despite carrying a few extra pounds.

"That works for me! I'd gladly cook dinner if you want to give me a hand with the firewood." Even though my tone was light, I couldn't help wondering if dinner and snuggling by the fire would turn into something even hotter...upstairs. The tingling in my stomach told me that my hormones were still kicking around even if they sputtered like an old car every now and then.

"My pleasure. But before you think about using that fireplace, you should have the chimney checked. It hasn't been used in years so there may be a blockage of leaves or a dead animal. I could stop by on my way home some evening to check it out. You'll soon want a fire to take the evening chill out before your furnace is going twenty-four-seven."

"It was cold in Pittsburgh, but I guess you get a lot more snow. Sure, if you'd like to stop by, that'd be great." Something told me that the term "neighborly" could be a euphemism for...something more? Not that I minded that prospect. I was a free woman with needs. I wasn't ready for any kind of serious relationship, but maybe he wasn't either. Friends with benefits? Hmmm. My neck infused with warmth at the thoughts tripping through my head.

Or was I reacting to Ass-hat's screwing around and now living with some woman? But noticing the dimple nestled in the stubble of Steve's beard, and the way his blue eyes twinkled when he gazed at me, was a total contradiction of that thought. Nope. If you Googled sex appeal, Steve's picture could claim the screen.

"About dinner this week... I was thinking Tuesday or Wednesday if that works for you. I have Byron on Thursday." He looked over at me after he picked another item from the shelf.

"Tuesday sounds good. Around seven?" I was doing more dining out in one week than I'd done in Philly for a month. But I hadn't felt like going out even if I wasn't watching my budget. Mary-Jane had said that dinner this evening at her restaurant was her treat. I'd figure some way of paying her back, even if it was just baking her some cookies.

"Tuesday it is." He did a quick inventory of the items he'd collected. "That's a good start for you, Shannon. If you need anything else, just ring me and I'll drop it off on my way home."

When he stepped away, I grabbed the shopping cart and wheeled it to the counter. "Thanks for your help with this, Steve. Everyone has been super friendly and nice to me since I arrived here. I mean, aside from the bitch who cut me off from the parking spot in front of the store. It feels good to be back in Wesley."

His voice became even warmer when he started ringing things through. "You make it easy to be nice to you, Shannon. Even when we were kids, you were always a blast to be with. Of the three of you gals, you were my favorite." The look he shot me bordered on being shy, reminding me of the awkward kid he'd once been.

I smiled. I'd always known that little Stevie Murphy had a crush on me and for him to say what he'd just said, was as close to that admission as it got. "I'm looking forward to Tuesday night, Steve. I want to hear all about your son and how life has treated you these many years. We can trade war stories."

"If that's a challenge, I think I've got you beat. But after your evening with Libby and Mary-Jane, you probably have the dirt on what happened in my marriage. But just so you know, I'm over all that stuff. I'm happy I have Byron. My life is pretty good, but I'm looking forward to dinner...reconnecting as well." His gaze lingered on my face for a few moments before he handed me the bill for my supplies.

Well, the shy teenager was gone, that was for sure. This guy was a lady-killer now.

At that moment I knew that he had given more than a passing thought to our dinner together. *Reconnecting?* He'd been a gawky preteen when we'd known each other, while I was years ahead of him, flirting with guys my own age. But he'd transformed into an Adonis in the years since I'd known him.

Reconnect? Another euphemism like *neighborly*? I could feel my heart beat faster and my cheeks flush with visions of how we'd reconnect. Actually, I should be thankful that I'd heard the news about Ass-hat living with the saleswoman. If there'd been the slightest iota of any emotional connection to my ex, that had totally broken it. Especially after what he'd put our daughter through.

"Where you're taking me...is it casual, or should I wear something fancy? I'm not familiar with what's around here anymore." Not to mention that it had been eons since I'd been asked out to dinner by a guy. Correction. A gorgeous, totally ripped guy. "I'm kind of out of practice with going out, Steve."

He ran my card through the debit machine and chuckled. "As for what to wear...business casual I think is the term they use. And going out, dating? It's like riding a bike, Shannon. You never forget."

"Maybe getting thrown from a horse is a better analogy." Shit. Here I was trying to be upbeat, instead coming across as Debbie-Downer.

"You know what they say about *that*, don't you?" This time he peered at me closely, barely keeping the grin from spreading.

"You get back up and ride him again?" As soon as the words were out of my mouth, my cheeks flushed. Why'd I say that?

Pretending not to notice the smirk playing on his lips, I took the bags he handed over. "I'd better get going. I've got tons to do before I go to Mary-Jane's restaurant for dinner."

"That's where *I* was going to take you. I guess you'll see for yourself about the attire. Do you need a hand getting this stuff to your car? Are you parked nearby?" He started to come around from behind the counter.

"No thanks. It's a couple blocks but I'll be fine." I adjusted the bags so that the weight was equally distributed. "I'll see you Tuesday, Steve."

"Looking forward to it. Don't work too hard, Shannon."

And with that, I left the store. My cheeks still heated up when I relived the conversation with Steve. How many times had my mind drifted into getting down and dirty as we'd talked? Hell! It had been a *long* time since I'd been laid. My hormones had certainly kicked into overdrive being around him—not that there was anything wrong with that. I may be a little past prime, but I wasn't dead. As I walked to my truck, I smiled looking down at the sidewalk.

"Excuse me?"

My chin rose, and I saw that same face from the business card left for me: Devon Booker. Oh shit! What was in the water in this town? Were all the men who lived here handsome as hell? He was even better looking than his pic, if that was possible.

EIGHT

I bet you're Maeve Burke's niece, aren't you? I know practically everyone in town and I've never seen you before. I stopped by your place and left my card. I'm Devon Booker." He made a move to extend his hand in a handshake but then seeing my hands full with the parcels, he took a couple from me. "Let me get that. Where are you parked?"

"Yes, I'm Shannon. Thanks, but that's not necessary. I can—"

"Nonsense! What kind of a gentleman would I be if I didn't at least offer to help you?" He fell into step beside me, and I couldn't help but notice how tall he was! There had to be at least a foot difference in our heights.

"I'm just on the next block—the red Toyota pickup truck." I sneaked a glance up at him. He wore a button-down shirt and tan Dockers. Like Steve, he was in pretty good shape but he was more lanky, like a swimmer or long-distance runner.

"I'd like to sit down with you and talk about your aunt's estate, Shannon. I'm a property developer. I think you'd be interested in how I could help you with that old place. It needs so much work, I'm surprised you're roughing it there and not enjoying the comforts of a hotel."

His blue eyes took in my jacket and worn jeans as well as the faded pink T-shirt. Yeah, I'm sure he was surprised all right. Wearing these old work clothes, I was the opposite of a pampered tourist at the Four Seasons. "I'd like to hear what you have to say, but if you're hoping I'll sell, you may be out of luck, Mr. Booker. My aunt's place has a lot of sentimental value to me. As you can see, I'm trying to fix it up to live in it."

"Please call me Devon. Mr. Booker is my dad. We're closer in age than that. Where'd you live before coming to Wesley? I can't detect any accent, like Boston or the Bronx, and you're definitely not from the South."

"Pittsburgh." When we came to my truck, I lowered the tailgate and hoisted my bag onto the bed.

"How about we meet for coffee sometime this week?"

When I just looked at him blankly, he went on, "I have some great ideas about your property that I'd like your opinion of." His smile was a perfect combination of boyish shyness and man about town all rolled into one. How the hell did he manage it? "I promise no pressure, but I think you'll like what I have in mind." He set the bags he'd carried in the truck bed. "How about Wednesday morning, ten o'clock at The Bear's Claws?"

"I remember that place!" I pointed farther downtown. "It's still in business, huh?"

"Yep. For me, the worst thing that can happen is I get to have coffee with an attractive woman. Sounds like a win to me."

Ignoring the blatant flattery, my mind went to the fact that by Wednesday, I would have all the wallpaper off and be ready to paint. I could kill two birds with one stone and stop by Steve's store. "Sure. But I warn you, I'm probably not going to sell my place."

"Fair enough. Just hear me out. That's all I ask."

"Thanks for helping me with the bags." I shook his hand. "I'll see you Wednesday."

"Ten o'clock it is, then." He held my hand for an extra second or two.

As I pulled away, a glance in the rearview mirror showed that he stood there watching me drive away. Even though he had the slickness of a salesman, he didn't seem like "bad news" the way Libby had described him. Still, it wouldn't hurt to keep my guard up. There was no way he'd persuade me to sell, not even for a million dollars. But five million? Would I sell if that were his offer? I'll see; I'm not counting any chickens here.

I had just about reached the outskirts of the small town when I spied a fire truck parked on the road while a billow of black smoke plumed in the air beside it. What the hell? A fire? I slowed down and waited for a firefighter to wave me through to the other lane to pass by.

Being a total gawker and not giving a damn that I was, my jaw dropped, seeing the red-headed woman standing off to the side while her red car was being hosed down. Holy cow! Her car had caught fire?

Ha! Letting out a hoot of laughter, I slapped the steering wheel! It couldn't have happened to a nicer person! Talk about karma in spades! I scratched my head as my grin faded. Karma never usually worked for me. I'd seen it work for lots of other folks so I didn't doubt that it happened...just not for me. Hmph. And after I'd wished that something awful would happen to her hot little red car.

Like going up in flames. Wait, that's exactly what I wished would happen! Wow. I got some hot karma today!

I was just about at the drive to my house when my cell phone beeped with a text message. I fished it out of my purse and glanced at the screen. Thomas. I'd sent him a text the night before to see how he was doing, and he was now getting back to me.

After I parked the truck, I tapped the screen to read his message.

> I'm doing fine, Mom. School's keeping me on my toes and that's just the parties! LOL Glad you made it there ok. The pics you sent of the lake look nice but the house? Maybe you should do yourself a favor and rent a bulldozer. Seriously. I can't imagine you living there after our house in Pittsburgh. Maybe you'll find someone crazy enough to buy it...that'd be the best I think. Then you can return to civilization.

My spirit fell lower as I read my son's text. Not the most encouraging message or even the most sensitive. But that was Thomas. I'd think about what I'd come back at him with...when I wasn't feeling the sting from his words.

Besides which, I wanted to get at least two walls cleared of paper before I had to stop and get ready to go out to dinner at Mary-Jane's restaurant. I unloaded the truck and then found a playlist of songs from my cell phone to listen to while I worked.

***

Just before six that evening, I stepped out of the bathroom from my shower. Humming a tune as I walked into my bedroom, a glance at my bed stopped me in my tracks. The photo of the wishing well was propped up against my pillow.

My heart leapt into my throat. I hadn't put that photo there, so who did? I clutched the bathrobe tighter to my body as I wheeled around. Oh my God! Had someone come into the house while I was in the bathroom? I raced to the top of the stairs, looking down at the hallway and living room. My voice came out as a croak when I called out, "Hello? Is anyone there? Libby? Mary-Jane?"

When there was no answer, I raced back into my bedroom and grabbed my cell phone. As I tried to tap out 9-1-1, my hands were shaking so badly I hit 9-1-2, then 8-1-1, then 9-1-1. "Come on. Pick up!"

My gaze was caught once more by the photo. I gasped! The photo rose up from the pillow, all on its own! My eyes were almost on my cheeks watching it go higher, inch by inch. The breath froze in my chest. How was this even possible? I stumbled forward when my knees turned to water. Everything started to go black...

The last thing I heard after the cell phone thudded onto the floor was a faint whisper, *"Shannon? Holy doodle. Now I've done it."*

NINE

It was pitch black in the room when I opened my eyes. It came back to me in a rush—the photo rising in the air. I must have fainted from the shock of it! Who wouldn't? I started to sit up and grope for the light switch and froze in place.

I was draped with a comforter. I ran my hand over the surface in the darkness, feeling the complex stitching. This wasn't just a comforter. I reached over and threw on the light and looked down.

Maeve's quilt, the very quilt that I saw my first day here; the one I actually had helped her with when I was a child was covering me from my chest to my feet. It was as snuggly-cozy as I remembered it so many years ago.

Waitaminute! I had fainted onto the floor, and now I was tucked in bed? What the—?

"Auntie Maeve?" I whispered.

Of course there was no answer. No, let me rephrase that: thank God there was no answer. If I had heard anything other than the sound of my breathing right then, I promise you, I would have had a stroke.

So naturally, I did it again.

"Maeve?" I shouted.

Again, nothing.

I sat up in bed and looked around the room. Yep, there was my cell phone on the floor. Piece of crap—I couldn't even dial 9-1-1 with it, and on top of that, it didn't ring, chime, or anything when Jess had tried to call and text me all those times.

I took a deep breath and slowly, really, really slowly looked around the room.

The breath went out of me when I saw the photograph. It was sitting right on top of the dresser where it belonged. Not on the bed where I saw it, not floating in the air...

Dammit! I did see it floating in the air!

Right?

Or was I going nuts? I mean, seriously; I wouldn't blame me, okay?

Look—in the last three days, I moved hundreds of miles from Pittsburgh, Pennsylvania to the middle of nowhere in the Catskill Mountains of New York. I hadn't been in this area in almost a quarter of a century, okay? And here the hell I was!

On top of that, my daughter had just informed me that my ex, who walked out on me six months ago and cornered me into signing off a no-contest divorce, wasn't actually going through male menopause. Noooo. That stinking bastard spent the last two and a half years tomcatting behind my back with some chippie! He left his own wife and children to begin a new damn life with another woman and *her* damn children!

On top of that, my freaking change of life was driving me up the wall with an acute case of the horns! On top of the damn hot flashes! Stephen Murphy, a kid I wouldn't look at twice has taken up residence in the bedroom of my imagination, and furthermore, I got Devon Booker waiting in the wings for a second romp of fantastic fantasy thunder bumping!

I threw Maeve's quilt back and sat on the edge of the bed.

And promptly buried my face in my hands.

And what the hell about that freaking well in the woods? I'd spent every damn summer here from the age of seven to nineteen! For three months of the year, I traipsed through every square foot of Maeve's property more than a few times without ever—EVER seeing that stupid well. And the day I find it, it...it talks to me?

Oh! Excuuuuse me! It's not just a damn well! I hopped to my feet and yanked that picture off the dresser. I examined it. Sorry...it wasn't just a damn well—it's a damn "Witching Well"!

Whatever the hell that means.

"Shit." I tossed the picture onto the bed beside me. "Shit shit shit!" I flopped back down onto the edge of the bed and ran my hands through my hair.

Yup. I was going crackers. Full steam ahead to bonkers.

"Wait a damn minute!" I jumped to my feet.

I got this.

I never allowed myself to grieve. All my life, I never allowed myself to really engage with grief. From the time I was a girl, I'd gloss over stuff, pretending everything was A-OK rather than confront the crap life threw at me.

My mother didn't just *let* me go visit Aunt Maeve, she shunted me off! Every summer I spent here, Mom never, ever so much as phoned to see how I was or even sent a letter! Never bothered me; I took it like a damn trouper, grateful for the break.

My goddamn husband exhibited *all* the signs for the last three-plus years he was fooling around. The last-minute "important meetings" out of town? The credit card bills that didn't come in the mail every couple of months? I snorted. "He really began to look after his appearance about three years ago, didn't he, dummy?" I said aloud.

And only *now* am I pissed off like hell at him!

Aunt Maeve dying? I never so much as shed a tear for the passing of the woman who was a true lifeline for me at the most vulnerable stage of my life. I took her death as just a fact of life! That's what I actually said when I found out: "Well, she had a good life, didn't she? Life goes on."

I've kept so much bottled up inside of me for so long, no wonder coming back to the place of my childhood joys opened this crazy emotional Pandora's box!

And my terminal case of the horny forties? That's just hormonal changes coupled with a bad dose of rejection, that's all. My self-esteem was so shot to hell that any half-baked, friendly look from a man was like cool water in a desert, that was all.

I wasn't going crazy. I'm there already.

But not with any "Boo" or other ghosty crap, okay? I'd been slammed by life itself! No wonder things were off kilter! A couple of visits to a therapist and I'd be right as rain, that's all.

Did they have headshrinkers out here in the boonies?

Shit.

Except…

That damn well *did* damn well talk to me. And that framed photo *did* damn well float in the air before my eyes! I heard and saw those things happening as clear as day, dammit.

"Okay then, Shannon," I grumbled, "then you are truly off your rocker."

"I know what I know!" I yelled.

Oh, this is going wonderful! I'm seeing things and talking to myself! I'm right as rain!

I looked beside me on the bed and fingered the edge of Maeve's quilt. How the hell did this damn thing get in here from Maeve's bedroom, then? Should I add sleepwalking to hallucinations to my list of crazy?

I let out a deep sigh. This was too much.

"Holy Doodle indeed, Maeve," I huffed. "Yeah, you really went and did it. I'm officially losing my mind. Thanks!"

My mouth fell open as I lay there. Only one person I'd known had ever used that corny expression Holy Doodle. "Aunt Maeve?" This time, my voice was a tremulous whisper. If I expected an answer, there was only silence.

Again.

I held my right hand out in front of me, palm up. On the one hand, I'm an emotionally repressed middle-aged woman, reeling from an out-of-the-blue divorce, going through menopause, who is having just a few, tiny hallucinatory experiences brought on by life's crises.

I held my left hand out the same way. On the other hand, my house is haunted, and there's some kind of magic well on my property.

I stared at my hands, my eyes flitting from one to the other and back.

I shook my head. "I'm *not* crazy!" I yelled. I began to giggle maniacally. Every insane person thinks they're fine.

I made up my mind. I clapped my hands together. "Okay, Maeve!" I said. "Feel free to stop by anytime, okay?"

Holy shit. First I heard her in my truck. Then that piece of luggage falling over my first night here. That had to be her too! She was still in this house even though she'd died. It was her house, so why wouldn't she want to stay here? I took a few deep breaths processing the fact that my aunt was still with me. It should make me happy, right? I'd even said that to Libby the other night.

My fingers touched the soft fleece of my bathrobe. I'd been getting ready to go out to Mary-Jane's restaurant for dinner. Mary-Jane! What time was it? She'd be worried when I didn't show up! I grabbed my stupid cell phone. Shit! It was almost eight o'clock. I'd been out for two hours. But after what had happened, that was understandable.

I dialed Mary-Jane, and she answered on the second ring; Mary-Jane's words came out in a rush. "Hello, Shannon? What happened to you? I tried calling but it just went to voicemail."

I held the phone away and stared at it, enraged. Cheap plastic piece of crap! Putting it back to my ear, I took a deep breath so I could answer her. "I'm sorry, MJ. I-I worked so hard around here that I took a nap and I just now woke up." There was no way I was telling her what had really happened. We might be good friends but that would worry her even more. She'd think that I'd totally lost it. Hell, I probably had lost it.

"No worries. We can do it another night." She was quiet for a moment before asking, "Are you okay, Shannon? You sound out of breath or something."

Out of breath? How about out of my mind? "Yeah, I know; I woke with such a start! I never take naps!"

The sound of a car engine and then a door slamming caught my attention. "Hang on, MJ. I think someone's here." I got up and headed for the stairs.

"That'll be Libby. I told her I couldn't reach you on the telephone and asked her to pop over to check on you."

"You guys! What'd you think? That I left town or—"

"You could have fallen off a ladder and hurt yourself! Excuse me for caring!"

Dammit, she was right. "I'm sorry, Mary-Jane; I think that nap has me kind of out of sorts. Thank you for giving a damn."

I heard her chuckle over the phone. "You're welcome. I'm glad you're not dead."

"Me too?" I asked, making my voice small. We both had a laugh and I rang off.

I gave my head a shake and opened the front door. "Nurse Libby to the rescue." Libby had just been about to knock, but she smiled, seeing me standing there.

"You're alive and well, I see." She stepped into the house and slipped her jacket off. "Mary-Jane was worried about you when you didn't answer. It was a good excuse for me to get out of the house for an hour or so."

I led the way into the kitchen and took the bottle of wine from the fridge. "I worked like a Trojan today getting all this wallpaper off. Then I flaked out. Want some wine?"

"Sure." She looked around the room and then ran her fingers over the plaster. "Still some glue here, hon. You'll need another scrub down before you paint." When she turned to take the glass I extended, her eyes narrowed, looking at me. "You're pale as a—"

"Don't say it!" I gulped down half a glass of the wine and then wiped my mouth.

"Whoa, you're pretty jumpy for someone who just woke up."

"Sorry." I shrugged and made a face. "I'm having a day."

54

She sat at the table. "What's up?"

Where to begin? Ass-hat? Hormones? I sighed and took a seat. "Remember when we used to sit around a big bonfire scaring each other with ghost stories?"

She nodded. "Mary-Jane always told the creepiest ones, but yours were pretty good too. Why? What's that got to do with anything. Shannon, you really are quite pale. I think you may have overdid it today."

"Do you believe in the afterlife? I know we tried to scare the pants off each other as kids, but...for real, do you believe in ghosts and that kind of thing?"

"You're asking a woman who lost her husband in a senseless car accident if I believe in ghosts." She looked down for a few moments. "I want to believe in ghosts. I'd give anything to see Hank again, talk to him. But life's not like that, you know?"

My stomach fell as I watched her smile fade. I probably shouldn't have brought this up with her, but now that I had, I carried on. "I think my aunt is still here, Libby. The other night when my suitcase tipped over for no reason, I think that was her."

Libby leaned closer, putting her hand on my knee. "That was odd, yeah." She sat back and stared at me. "What's going on, Shannon?" When I just stared back, she said, "There's more to this, isn't there? You look upset. What else happened?"

I took a deep breath. Libby had always been sensitive to other's feelings, a trait that probably led her into a nursing career.

"Promise me that you won't think I'm crazy or imagining things. And most of all, this is just between us, okay? I love Mary-Jane, but she would really be freaked out. Hell, I miss dinner and she sends the cavalry to check up on me."

She nodded with a smile. "I get what you're saying, and I promise I won't say a word. Now, tell me, Shannon. What happened that has you convinced that your aunt is still here. I mean the suitcase thing was odd, but there's something more."

I stared at her for a few moments deliberating on how much to actually tell her. But Libby was smart. She'd know if I was holding something back. I finished my wine and poured another glass for liquid courage before spilling everything, starting with the near miss with the bobcat and hearing my aunt's voice before she yanked the steering wheel, then the voice at the well, and ending with being tucked into bed by my dead aunt.

She was silent for a few moments peering at me. Finally she spoke, "Can I see this photo? In all the time we roamed these woods, hiked the trails, I've never seen this well. I can't remember anyone ever mentioning it either." Libby stood up and plugged the kettle in. "I have to limit the wine, as I'm driving. Get this photo for me, will you?"

By the time I went upstairs, carefully checking to see if anything else was amiss, got the photo and returned, Libby had opened a can of soup and had it heating on the stove.

She turned when I entered and smiled. "You missed dinner and you need to eat. I figured if you're going to drink your supper, it might as well include soup."

"Thanks, Mom." I handed the photo to her and watched her closely when she examined it. "I can't help but think that my aunt wanted me to visit that well. And she didn't want me to dismiss it out of hand. Why else would she put it on my pillow and then make it levitate?"

"I've never seen this well. And... I agree. Your Aunt Maeve wanted your attention." Her lips twitched into a smile when she asked, "She actually said, 'Holy Doodle? That's so like her. She's here watching over you, Shannon. You're lucky, although a lot of people would be creeped out by that."

I stopped for a moment and looked at her. "Why aren't you?"

She looked at me puzzled. "What do you mean? It didn't happen to me."

I made a quick wave with my hand. "I know that. Why are you so quick to believe me? I mean, before you showed up, I was up in my bedroom going back and forth trying to figure out if I'd lost my mind. I mean, I think I'm *not* going crackers, but I give you a quick rundown and you're all in. How come? I mean, you're a nurse, for God's sake! You do medical stuff all day—science-y kind of stuff, right? So why don't you think I'm loony tunes?" I could hear my voice stretching higher as I talked to her.

She looked away for a moment. "Yeah, I should be all worried over your mental health, shouldn't I?"

"Are you? Are you just humoring me right now? You really do think I'm crackers, don't you?" My voice was wire-thin now. "Am I? Am I nuts?"

She was still looking off into the distance. "I don't think so."

"Why?"

"Saint Francis of Assisi."

"What? What the hell does some saint got to do with it?"

"No, not *the* Saint Francis of Assisi. It's the name of a nursing home I worked at. When I was still a student nurse, I had to work on a ward for six months. I ended up at St. Francis nursing home." She tipped her head at me. "On the night shift. It's a pretty big institution, you know—more than fifty beds of palliative care, one hundred assisted-living units and another two hundred retirement residents. I mean, almost four hundred elderly people, right?"

"Okay. I don't know the place; I mean I just moved here, right?"

She nodded. "Well, on a pretty regular basis, someone would pass away. It was usually in the palliative care section, sure. But also people would pass away in assisted living, or even every once in a while someone in the retirement residence would die."

"That sounds depressing."

She nodded. "It was at the beginning. I mean, I was only eighteen when I started nursing school. I wasn't even twenty years old when I did that rotation." She sat back. "I had to either leave nursing or else accept that death was a part of life." She looked away again and wiped her eyes. "Maybe that's what kept me from going crazy when Hank was killed."

I stayed quiet.

She looked back at me. "In those six months of training, I saw a lot of people pass on, Shannon. And they all died peacefully. Some were afraid, but they all passed away." She looked up at the ceiling. "And during those times, there were enough things that happened when the person died that I came away knowing full well that there's a lot more to the universe than"—she patted her arms and legs—"than this body we're packaged in."

"Oh? Like what?"

She waved at me. "I'll tell you my spooky nursing stories another time. Let's just say that it's not a stretch for me to believe you at face value, all right?" She looked around the room. "You going on about what's happened to you? I got to tell you, hon, it just sounds *right* to me or something. I'm good."

"Really?" I squeaked. "You're not just saying that, are you? You really really believe me?"

"Yeah. So I guess we're both 'crackers' huh?" she said with a wide, genuine, loving smile.

I burst into tears and clutched at her. "Thank you! Thank you, Libby! OhmyGod! I was afraid you'd think I was crazy!"

She held me and stroked my back. "No, I think you've had some serious shit get dumped on you. But you're rolling with the punches, Shan. You're not crazy." She took me by the shoulders and looked me in the eye. "Maeve's not ready yet."

"Ready for what?"

She rubbed my head. "For whatever. Not ready to move on, maybe? Or not ready to appear to you? I don't know. But when she's 'ready,' you'll know; how about that?"

We hugged again.

Who cares whether there were any headshrinkers out here in the boonies, anyway? I got Libby! She's either the best counselor you could ask for, or as crazy as I am, and I don't care which one it is.

When I calmed down, I took the photo from her and then

got a bowl down from the cabinet. The smell of chicken noodle soup made me remember that I hadn't eaten since when I returned from Steve's store. Which prompted my next comment, grabbing her arm.

"I forgot to tell you! It might be nothing, but then again, it might mean something. I found the well, yesterday, right? So today, when I went to town to get tools to strip the paper, some woman cut me off from getting a great parking spot right in front of Mountain Hardware. It pissed me off, and I remember wishing that her flaming red car would go up in flames."

"So?"

"On the way home, it happened! There was a fire truck dousing her car's engine that had caught fire."

Libby paused as she was pouring soup into the bowl, staring at me. "That's a weird coincidence, for sure. But we can't jump to conclusions with this, Shannon. That's all it might be, right?" She set the bowl on the table and then brought her tea over.

"It had better be a coincidence for Ass-hat's sake!" This led to another long story, telling her about Jess's phone call and his visit at her school. And how I wished he'd become impotent, among other things.

She burst out laughing. "I know it's not funny. What he did was reprehensible to you and your kids. But if it's true that somehow what you wish for comes true, he's in a world of trouble. But we can't know that for sure. If you want to test your theory, you could wish for me to win the lottery! I'd like that test."

"You and me both!" I finished the soup and poured more wine. After the day I'd had, I deserved it. And I wasn't driving. "Maybe I'm jumping to conclusions because of what Aunt Maeve called the well. Witching Well? Do you suppose that she was a secret witch?"

"I don't even know what the hell that means. What's a 'secret witch'?"

"That she was a witch for real, but didn't tell anyone!"

"Well, I haven't a clue. To me, she was a wonderful person, the farthest thing from being a witch that I can think of." She looked into my eyes. "Maybe you could take a break from all your renovation work and show me this well."

I don't know why, but my gut clenched tight at the thought of taking Libby there. It wasn't just that the voice in the well had totally creeped me out; it just didn't feel right for me to do a show-and-tell. Although I'd already done all the telling. But taking her there?

"Not yet." It popped into my head as clear as if someone had spoken the words aloud, startling me. I peered at Libby to see if she'd noticed my eyes flash wider or anything weird, but she had picked up the photo again.

"I'm not even sure I could find it again. You're welcome to visit me and we could try, but not Tuesday. I've also got a date with Steve Murphy that day and I'll need time to get ready for it. I'll probably lose five pounds trying to wrestle the Spanx on."

For whatever reason, even though I loved Libby to pieces, it wasn't the right time to show her the well.

Weird.

Libby's eyes widened. "Steve Murphy? You're going on a date with him?" A wide grin spread on her face as she bobbed her eyebrows. "You go, girl! I am going to want all the dirty details starting with when he brings you home. I know more than a few gals in town that would kill to get next to Steve."

Thank God for small favors. The idea of Steve Murphy took the idea of the well off the table. Even so, I could feel my face grow warm before I answered her, "It's just a date, Libby! Between friends. His welcoming gesture, although he also offered to stack some firewood for me some evening."

"Are you kidding me? He adored you when we were younger! This is probably his wet dream come true—to finally go out with you—and more. Stacking wood, huh? There's some stacking he wants to do, and it ain't got nothing to do with firewood!"

Her insinuations and teasing really had my cheeks flaming.

"What about you, Libby? It's been years since Hank...You could be dating too! I bet there's some hot doctor at the clinic who'd love to do a pelvic exam on you!" Okay, that was downright dirty, but she started it.

Her eyes widened, and it was her turn to blush. "I have no interest in dating until my kids are grown and gone. Even then, it's questionable. No one would measure up to Hank." But immediately a small smile lit her eyes. "Not that I haven't been asked, mind you. And it's not a doctor. You might have noticed a handsome fireman when you passed that burning car. Stan Jones has been asking me out for years."

"Get out! You should go! A hunky fireman! Maybe I'll start a chimney fire just to meet this guy!" When she shot me a dark look, I added, "Kidding! I wouldn't do that. But it seems to me there may be a burning fire deep in you that he could take care of."

"Stop it!" Her lips tried to form a frown, but the curl at each end betrayed her. "How did we go from talking about ghosts to dating and guys?"

"Girlfriend, we're pushing fifty! We're not 'talking about guys'! We're talking about getting laid!" The gasp from her was priceless.

I laughed, "Some things never change, do they? Except that now the guesswork about sex is long past. Two frisky, middle-aged women with men raining down around us." Again, I wondered about the water in that town that the guys were so hot.

"Oh, I almost forgot!" I added. "Speaking of raining men, I'm meeting Devon Booker for coffee on Wednesday. He's going to try to talk me into selling."

BANG!

We both almost jumped out of our skin at the noise coming from upstairs. It sounded like a door slamming. This time it was Libby who blanched.

I pointed at the ceiling. "See? I'm sure that's Aunt Maeve. She doesn't want me to sell."

TEN

When Tuesday afternoon arrived, I was so ready to get out of the house and talk to another adult. It had rained for two solid days while I continued working in the kitchen, listening to my tunes. Even though a few times, I had directed a comment to Aunt Maeve, she'd been totally silent. The funny thing was that there was the odd moment I would swear I'd smelled her flowery perfume and felt her nearby. It was a blend of lilacs and primrose, one I'd never forget.

Before I climbed the stairs to shower and change into something nice for my date with Steve, I paused, gazing out the picture window at the lake. So much rain had fallen that the dock was almost completely submerged, and the shoreline had crept up closer to the house by about a foot or so. There was still thirty feet of overgrown sodden grass between the house and the lake so I wasn't worried that I'd be flooded out, but I'd never seen the water so high.

Ten minutes later I stood in the shower, lathering my hair with shampoo, feeling the knots in my muscles finally let go from the hot water. A loud gurgle from the drain bubbled up, and I swiped the soap from my face to see what was happening. The water from the shower pooled around my feet even though I hadn't put the stopper in to close the drain.

"Shit!" Why wasn't it going down the way it was supposed to? There had to be some kind of clog in the pipes leading out to the septic system. The house hadn't been lived in for a while, and maybe with water now going through the plumbing, some buildup had dislodged? I was no plumber, but it was the only thing I could think of.

I finished rinsing and then got out of the old claw-foot tub. There was now about six inches of sudsy water standing in it. After drying off and getting my robe I knew this was a problem that couldn't wait for another day to get fixed. There was the sink and toilet that would also start backing up if there was a blockage. To make matters worse, I couldn't remember seeing a plunger anywhere in the house to try to fix it myself.

I grabbed my cell phone from the vanity and hit Steve's number from my contact list.

Instead of a hello, he groaned. "You're not canceling on me, are you? I know it's lousy weather but—"

"No, I'm not canceling, but I may have to postpone our dinner. I've run into a problem with my plumbing."

When there was no response, my face heated up realizing what I'd just said. I quickly added, "My bathtub, Steve! It won't drain!"

"That sucks."

"Well, if it sucked, it'd be okay, wouldn't it? It's a lack of sucking that's the issue. Do you have a plunger I could borrow until I get to the store to buy one? If I can fix this in the next hour, we might be able to salvage our dinner." It was probably wishful thinking, but I'd really been looking forward to going out.

"I'll be there in ten minutes with a plunger and my plumbing snake. Don't worry, Shannon, we'll get you fixed up in no time." With that the connection was broken.

I threw my ripped jeans and sweatshirt on and then scooped my hair up into a loose bun. It was not exactly how I'd pictured my outfit, the blue scoop-neck silk dress and high heels when I greeted him at the door, but that was life. When I went downstairs, I went into the kitchen to watch for him out the window. But a glance at the sink as I walked by made my shoulders sag. Any water that had managed to seep down from the bathtub was now pooling in the stainless steel.

"Shit and double shit!" Headlights flashing in the windowpane caught my eye and I rushed to the front door. When I opened it, a dank smell hit me full in the face. I stepped out onto the veranda, sniffing while my face screwed up. That was a sewer smell.

When Steve got out of his truck, he was a misty blur moving fast in the torrential downpour. When he pulled his equipment from the vehicle, he paused for a few moments before racing over to the shelter of the overhang.

His eyes were wide, and rain dripped from his chin when he stared at me. "I don't like that smell, Shannon. It might not just be a blocked drain going on here. I hate to tell you this, but you may have problems with the septic bed or the tank. With all the rain we've had, if there was a problem before, it just got worse.

I sighed. "I smell it too. This is the first I've stepped outside all day. Would the septic bed screw up so fast like this? The drains here are slower than what I'm used to, but I thought it was just that they hadn't been used in a while, that it would come around the longer I'm here using it."

As I watched him shake his head and then look out at the side yard where the septic bed probably was, a lump formed in my gut. What a way to start a date with a superhot guy! He gets out of the truck, and the first thing he smells is sewer gas and sludge. I was really swinging for the bleachers, all right.

He turned, and his mouth pulled to the side. "I don't mind trying to plunge the tub for you, but I think you'll need a plumbing contractor in. It could be just that you need the tank pumped, or worst-case scenario, you might need to replace your weeping tiles."

My eyes closed for a moment. This had leap-frogged from awkward to a potential HUGE expense. I had some savings from the sale of the house, and I got a modest monthly income from Ass-hat, but this was probably going to take a serious bite out of all that.

"Let's go inside and I'll give plunging a try, Shannon. It can't hurt, and it'll smell better than out here." He opened the door and waited till I had passed through before stepping inside.

When he took off the yellow rain slicker, he also wore an old plaid shirt and jeans. He'd come prepared to work so I nodded. "Sure. But if it doesn't work right away, don't waste your energy. The kitchen sink is also filling up with the bath water."

His eyes narrowed and he walked into the kitchen. "That tells me that if it is a blockage, it's between the sink down here and the outside pipes. I'll start here."

I watched him plunge the sink for about five minutes, the water sloshing over his arms and onto the floor before I stopped him. "Enough. Don't spend any more time on it, Steve. It looks like it's totally screwed."

"You can't stay here, Shannon. You could stay at my place until you get it fixed. I've got three bedrooms. You'll have to put up with a rug-rat half the time but it's cheaper than a motel." He grabbed a few paper towels, and his head tipped to the side gazing at me as he dried himself.

"Thanks, but Mary-Jane would be livid if I didn't stay with her. When I first contacted them that I was coming back, she tried to talk me into staying with her while I decided what to do with the place. Plus, you've got your son. You only see him half-time so you don't need me hanging around." I forced a smile trying not to think of the financial sinkhole that was outside.

"Look! Pack some things in a bag and come to my house. I can see the worry on your face over all of this. It might only be for a few days, and it's basically a place to crash, right? I'm five minutes away, and you'll still be able to come here during the day to keep plugging away at your renos." He looked around at the walls. "You've done a good job so far, you know."

When I was about to object, he put his hands on my shoulders and forced me to turn, prodding me along to the stairs. "Don't worry about MJ. She'll understand, and if she doesn't—tough. As for you being a wet blanket when my kid's there, I don't see it that way at all. He'll love you. Now, git! I'll wait for you down here, and then we'll take two vehicles."

As I walked up the stairs I tried not to think of the financial outlay that I could possibly face. I really didn't have the emotional reserves to argue with Steve about staying at his house. He was right. If Mary-Jane was miffed, she'd come around. It was only going to be for a couple of days at most. If it looked like it would take longer to get this fixed, I could take her up on her offer.

When I went into my room to pack some toiletries and clothes, I looked at the photo of the Witching Well on the dresser. "Aunt Maeve, what am I going to do if I have to replace the septic system? I can't afford that, not with my income and savings."

"Go to the well, child." I jumped back, staring around me. Had I just heard her answer me? It had been like when I'd been talking with Libby! That voice had sounded in my head! What the hell!

A calm quiet flooded through me as I stood there. This would work out okay. I'd go to that well tomorrow afternoon, after my meeting with Devon Booker. Even though Aunt Maeve had signaled her disapproval of me selling, I couldn't take that option off the table—not with the potential problem of the septic.

***

When I got out of the truck at Steve's house, with the rain still pelting down, my feet flew, going up his walkway to a two-story structure. He waited at the door for me and then held it open. When I stepped inside the entry, immediately my eyes were caught off guard by the enormous room. It was totally awesome. There was a kitchen off to the left, dining area on the right, while behind it was an expansive living area, with windows that spanned two floors.

"Wow! This is gorgeous, Steve! Did you build it? I can't

remember it from when I was staying with my aunt." I wiped my feet on the mat and hung my raincoat on the hook by the door before wandering into the living room, gawking up at the cathedral ceiling, the giant fanlight suspended and the fieldstone fireplace on one wall.

"I kind of did. I mean, it was a cabin initially that I kept building and adding onto. The only thing that's original after all that, is the fireplace." He stood off to the side from me with his thumbs hooked into the pockets of his jeans. The look of pride in his eyes shone through. "There's a big deck just outside where I have my morning coffee, gazing at the lake."

"You've done an amazing job here. This place is right out of a magazine!" I noticed the bookshelf with a stack of children's board games and puzzles, the only thing indicating that he shared this home with his son.

"I think we both need a drink, Shannon. We can still go out to dinner if you'd like, but it'd have to be someplace real casual, maybe the burger joint. Or, I can pop a pizza in the oven and toss a salad. You decide." He was already walking to the kitchen area.

"Pizza sounds great! As for a drink, make it a double Jack Daniels and I'm in." I joined him in the kitchen area watching him grab a bottle of vodka and the whisky from the cabinet. For just a few moments, my problems were the last thing on my mind as I watched the tanned muscles in his forearms and the dimple that teased the corner of his lips.

"I'll show you your room after we have a drink. I'll get a fire going and we can sit in the living room for a bit"—he looked over at me—"or are you hungry? Do you want me to start dinner first, and then we'll veg out?"

"No rush. I think I'd rather sit for a bit. It's nice to be in a home where I'm not tripping over buckets or wallpaper scrapers." I took the tumbler of whisky and ice and followed him into the living room. It was heaven sinking down into the comfy leather sofa and slipping my shoes off. And watching Steve squat next to the fireplace to get it going wasn't hard on the eyes either.

"I had a look around at what you've done to your place while you were packing your things. You've got a lot done in a short time, Shannon. I took a peek under the linoleum, and the floorboards look like they're maple. You mentioned you might want to refinish them." He lit a match, and the fire started spreading and crackling in the grate.

"And I suppose you rent floor sanders or know of someone who'll tackle that job." I squeezed over closer to the armrest when he took a seat next to me.

"Of course. I don't mind lending you a hand, but something tells me you'd probably tackle that job too. Are you sure you majored in English in college? I think you hung around with Bob Villa or apprenticed on *Holmes on Homes* or something." He laughed and took a long sip of his drink.

"I'm good with my hands, I guess." When I saw him shoot me a quick look, I added, "Will you stop? Are we doing the double-entendre thing again?"

He turned to me and grinned. "Sorry, I'll stop. It's so much fun to joke around with you. You're easy to talk to."

I couldn't help smiling at him. "Nice save, Steve. It's fun for me as well, when I'm not opening my mouth to change feet. And yes, I totally had a huge crush on Bob Villa."

"Yeah, me too. You got to love the way he fills a tool belt." His eyes glinted when he smirked at me. "But seriously, I'll give you the name of a plumbing contractor I know. He's not cheap, but he knows what he's doing and he's honest."

"That's what I need." Rather than go down this train of thought, I decided to lighten the conversation. I rose to examine the photo of his son that was perched on top of the bookcase. He must have inherited his mother's fair skin tone with a splash of freckles over his nose.

"Eight is a fun age. I remember when my kids were that old. We'd actually do things as a family even if it was the annual trip to Disney. Now they're both in college. I wish I'd brought them here to meet Aunt Maeve and see this place." I wandered back to the sofa and sat down. "My son wants me to sell the place, and my daughter just wants me to be happy."

He gazed into my eyes. "And what would make Shannon happy? I know this past year has probably been a challenge."

I took a sip of the whiskey, thinking of his question. Of course I wanted my kids to be healthy and succeed in school, but what did I want for *me* to be happy? And as angry as I was with Ass-hat's lies and treachery, revenge wasn't the answer. "As crazy as it sounds, I haven't thought of anything specifically that I'd like. For sure, I want to have peace and freedom from financial worries. I don't have to be wealthy, just comfortable. I'd hoped that restoring my aunt's house and property would lead me there."

He looked down into his drink, swirling the ice cubes. "Would you ever remarry? Do you see that in your future?"

I looked at him, wondering if there was more to his question than simple curiosity. "I'm not sure, to be honest. Being tied down in a serious relationship with a man isn't in the cards for a long time. That's not to say I don't want to start dating again. I want to live my life on my terms and that involves having fun. The divorce and betrayal knocked me on my ass, and I'd be lying if I said I'm not angry as hell. But I read a good saying in one of these self-help books: 'Get better, not bitter.'"

"Good advice. I think that applies to all of us dumpees. You got dumped when he walked out, and I got dumped when Amy left me for Suzanne." He shook his head before getting to his feet. "I'm going to freshen these drinks and then put a frozen pizza in the oven."

I stood up. "I'll join you and throw a salad together. It's the least I can do after you putting me up for a night or two." As I followed him, I asked, "So do you and Amy get along? Are you civil with each other?"

"Yeah, we are. At first I was devastated that she left me, and for a *woman*? It messes with your head, let me tell you. But then I just gradually accepted the fact. In lots of ways I admire her. It took guts to come to terms with her sexuality and make such a change in her life."

I accepted the romaine lettuce he extended and stepped

over to the sink to begin the salad. "According to Libby you could have your pick of single women in town, so I can't imagine your marriage breakup shook your confidence *that* much." It was a weak probe to see how much of a revolving door his bedroom had become.

He propped his butt against the oven door after popping the pizza in. There was a smile on his face when he gazed at me. "It did at first, as I said. I dated lots of women to prove something to myself. But then I realized it was not only shallow, but I didn't have to prove anything. Now I know it's more important to be able to have a conversation and some laughs with a woman than having sexual flings. Sex is easy. It's the other parts that aren't."

Speaking of parts, I could feel my breath become shallow while my heartbeat kicked into overdrive. My hand slipped on the knife, nearly nicking my finger when he finished talking. After what he'd said on the sofa, that he liked laughing with me, this admission was pretty clear. As Libby had said, back when we were younger, he'd adored me. And some part of him still did. It was flattering and...tempting.

His cell phone dinged and I felt a wave of relief. Even though my body was ready to go down this dangerous path, or more specifically up the stairs to his bedroom, my head wasn't there. Not yet.

"Hang on." He slipped his phone from his pocket and murmured when he looked at the screen. "It's Byron."

"Go! Talk to your son. I'll finish in here." I watched him wander over to the living room and stand at the large patio door as he spoke. I couldn't help but notice laughter and affection in his tone. He may be hot as hell in the ripped jeans that hugged a tight ass, with broad shoulders that strained the flannel fabric of his shirt, but he also sounded like a pretty good father.

I couldn't help but think of Ass-hat and how he'd practically abandoned our kids when he'd left. But even before that, I couldn't recall any time he'd shared a laugh that didn't hold a little barb for one of them. Nothing like what I was eavesdropping on from the other room with Steve and his son.

I finished the salad and rummaged in the fridge for dressing and Parmesan cheese. It was well stocked and organized much like everything else in Steve's house. By the time he was finished with his phone call, I had the table set and the pizza out of the oven. He was still grinning as he walked over to the table.

"That kid! He was bragging how he's reached seventy-four thousand in Pitfall while my best score is sixty. The little monkey's got game all right." He took a seat and looked over at me. "Good timing though. You got all this done and even have us eating at the table. I normally eat in the living room watching TV."

"We can move in there—"

"No! It's nice to sit across from each other and talk. It's not the Cat's Whiskers with Mary-Jane's culinary skills, but it's more civilized than what I'm used to when I'm here alone."

For the next couple of hours, Steve brought me up to date on what had happened to other kids that we used to hang out with, while I shared some fun stories about my kids and memories from college. We both avoided talking about our exes while treading on the thin ice covering the sexual chemistry sparking between us.

It was close to eleven when he showed me to my room. After he set my knapsack down on the queen bed, he stepped over to me and extended his arms. "Let me give you a hug! It's been a rough day for you, and I don't want you to worry about the problems at your house. It may be a simple fix."

I stepped into his arms, smelling the faint aroma of aftershave mingled with his own magnetism. It felt good to snuggle close, feeling his breath on my hair and the warmth of his arms around me. We stood there for a few moments, just being together, before he pulled back and his fingers tucked a strand of hair behind my ear. When his gaze became softer and fell to my lips, I felt a warm tingle flutter low in my body.

At first the brush of his lips against mine was as light as the wings of a butterfly, barely there as our warm breath mingled.

His palms cupped my face and his kiss became bolder, sending a bolt of pure longing that I hadn't felt in a very long time. When he pulled away and smiled, I felt like my knees had turned to jelly.

"We'd better say good night now, Shannon. If we keep doing this, I'm going to carry you over to that bed." His gaze met mine, and I saw my own longing mirrored there.

"Yeah." It came out as a breathless whisper as I tried to reclaim my voice. "We'd better." My words warred with the burning desire coursing through me. I gulped when he took a step away, heading for the doorway.

"Good night, Shannon. If you need anything during the night, I'm just down the hallway." He winked and then left, closing the door behind him.

Oh God. I let out a long breath, practically stumbling to the bed for my knapsack. If I had any sense, I'd take a pass on staying even one more night at his place. Especially since his son wouldn't return until Thursday, and it would be only us here, alone again. I wasn't sure that we'd be able to show such restraint again.

I flopped down on the bed. It had been a long time. Too long. Would it be so bad if something did happen?

ELEVEN

By the time I rolled out of bed the next morning, Steve was gone. He'd left a note telling me he'd pick up steaks for dinner, and had written the name and cell number for a contractor to look at my septic. When I took my mug of coffee to the big picture window with a view of the lake, the sun showered rays of diamonds across its surface. No more rain. Thank goodness.

A call to Mike's Plumbing resulted in voice mail. I practically pleaded with him to call me back, that it was an emergency. Shit! I deliberated whether I should cancel the coffee with Devon Booker in favor of exhausting the search for a contractor, but decided there probably wasn't a glut of them in Wesley.

After showering and donning a pair of yoga pants with a long white blouse, I headed out to my appointment. I'd have just enough time to pop by the house for a few minutes to see if that god-awful smell was still there and to see evidence of damage to the septic bed. I knew it was at the side of the house because when Aunt Maeve had been planning a vegetable garden, she'd mentioned she couldn't put one in the east side because of the weeping tile.

When I stepped outside of my truck, I headed to the side of the house, sniffing the air like a hound dog. It wasn't as bad as it had been the day before but there was still an odor lingering. The ground was completely sodden and my feet sloshed in the grass before I realized I actually had no clue what I was looking for. Better to leave this to the professionals.

I went inside and immediately checked the kitchen sink to see if there was still water standing there. But it had cleared overnight. I crossed my fingers and closed my eyes, wishing that the problem had somehow resolved itself.

I smiled thinking of Libby asking if I'd wish a lottery win for her the other night. I'd skip the lottery if I could have this plumbing issue resolved. That might be a good test to see if that well actually granted wishes.

Right.

A glance at the clock showed that I had better get going if I was going to be on time for my meeting with Devon Booker.

Fifteen minutes later, I strode into the Bear's Claw coffeehouse, where the smell of cinnamon and pumpkin spice filled the warm air. Devon Booker was seated at a table near the picture window overlooking the street. He snapped his laptop shut and rose, smiling at me.

"Good morning, Shannon! How are you today? You're right on time." He held the chair out for me, and I took a seat across from where he'd been sitting.

"Hi." The smile fell from my lips. "I almost canceled this meeting. I'm having a plumbing emergency at the house. I think all the rain we had over the last couple of days has played havoc with my septic bed."

"Oh no! I hope it's not the weeping bed. If you have to replace it, it could cost you a pile of money." When the waitress appeared at the table, he paused.

"I'll have a dark roast coffee and"—I noticed the pastry sitting next to Devon's computer. I pointed to it—"and one of those."

The waitress, a middle-aged woman, nodded. "A bear claw and a dark roast, coming up."

Devon smiled. "You won't be disappointed. These things are addictive." He leaned over the table, pushing his small laptop to the side. "So, did you contact anyone to fix your plumbing issue? If not—"

"I left a voice message at Mike's Plumbing, and I'm waiting for him to call me back." I cleared my throat, waiting for Devon to make his pitch. This was why I was here, and I'd just as soon not waste time, especially now that this new problem had popped up.

His eyebrows rose and he sat back. "Maybe I can solve this plumbing issue for you, along with any other financial problem." He opened his laptop and spun it till the screen faced me.

I squinted a bit, seeing the drawing of a bunch of houses, every one a McMansion-sized estate, dotting the ten acres around half the lake that I owned. My aunt's house wasn't on it, so I'm sure the plan was to demolish it. "Eccle Lake Estates. Hmmm." There had to be twenty or so of these monster houses. My stomach sank, seeing the montage of suburbia he wanted to introduce to the picturesque lake.

The waitress set my coffee and pastry on the table and topped up Devon's mug. When she left, he started right in with the sales pitch. "People in New York and Albany are lined up looking for homes in small towns where they can raise their children in a safer, more wholesome environment. With the internet, more and more families can work from home. Many times, they only need to go to the office once or twice a month. Your property would be ideal for them."

I took a sip of coffee and nodded. "I agree the demand is probably there. But I'm not a big fan of changing the character of the lake. I like it just the way it is." Which, of course, was absolutely the truth. But I also wanted him to start talking about money. I may not want to sell, but it could be an issue of *having* to sell if I encountered many more problems.

"I grew up not twenty miles from Wesley, Shannon. I totally understand your appreciation of the beauty here. But times change, and it's better to be ahead of the curve rather than behind it." His gaze never left my face when he continued. "I know you are recently divorced with two kids in college. This is an opportunity for you to turn your life around. You could visit your kids more...hell, travel all over the world if you wanted."

My jaw tightened as he talked. He had done his homework enough to know my circumstances but that didn't mean he *knew* me. Not by a long shot. "How much are you offering, Devon? Let's cut to the chase here."

His eyebrows rose while his fingers played with the edge of the placemat. "Half a million. Invest it right, and you'd have a nest egg to last you quite a while."

I took a bite of the pastry, chewing it while my eyes never left his face. He had to be joking with an offer like that. The silence stretched like warm toffee between us. There was an old adage that I'd heard once. "He who speaks first loses." Besides, the pastry was delicious.

After a few long minutes, he finally ventured a comment. "I might be able to offer you more...maybe as much as three quarters of a million. But that's as high as I could go and still make a profit. I'm a businessman first and foremost."

I slapped the table and sat forward. "If you're offering three quarters, then that land is easily worth double that. But I'm still leaning into staying and renovating my aunt's house. Besides, she requested in her will that the house stay in the family or at least eventually go to someone who loves the spot."

He laughed. "*I* love the spot, Shannon. I've had my eye on that land for quite some time. I've even spoken to Steve Murphy about him selling his land to me. Between the two of you, you pretty well encompass the lake. Think of the families who will love the lake, and the town."

"Well, you've heard my counteroffer. Although, even if you agree, I probably won't sell. The place is worth more to me than just money. The best summers of my life were spent at that lake, along with scores of families vacationing from New York City and Albany. Reopening the resort isn't off the table either." I wiped the sweet crumbs from my lips with the napkin and finished my coffee.

"Wait. Don't go yet. I just want you to give this some

serious thought, Shannon. As I said, I hate pressure put on me, and I hate the thought I might be applying it. I could help you with your septic issues. That's not something you can delay. I could call my plumbing contractor to take a look at it this afternoon. Whether you sell or not, that's the least I can do. Neighborly, you know."

His head tipped to the side, and his eyes had kind of that earnest puppy-dog look. As if the neighborly comment wasn't enough, he even looked the part, dressing down in jeans and a white denim shirt.

And I still hadn't heard anything from the contractor who Steve had recommended. I sighed. "I really have to get this fixed. As it is, I stayed the night at a friend's house and I'd like to get back to my own home."

He leaned forward, folding his hands together. "Look, I'll go with Eric when he visits your place this afternoon. He's good at what he does and he charges accordingly. But he owes me a favor or two. If you decide to get him to fix it, I'll see that he gives you his best rate. You have to stay on top of some of these guys, you know."

I grabbed my purse to pay for the coffee and bear claw but he shook his head. "My treat. I write this off anyway, Shannon. Besides, it's only coffee. Maybe we can do this again, but make it dinner."

Even though I'd pretty well shut him down about buying my place, he still wanted to see me? I peered into his eyes, but the laugh wrinkles at the sides had deepened, and his smile seemed genuine enough. Still, I wasn't sure. I stood up. "We'll see. For now, I've got some errands to do before I go home. Thanks for the coffee and bear claw."

He stood up and reached for my hand. "My pleasure, entirely. I'll see you around two at your house."

His handshake was firm and warm. I left the coffee shop feeling a little lighter even though the bear claw was heavy in my stomach. I usually tried to avoid pastries, sticking to lighter breakfasts that didn't stick to my thighs and hips. If I could get this damned septic issue resolved sooner rather than later, I'd be a happy camper. I didn't want to think about the cost and whether this would influence my decision as to selling, but I had to be practical.

My cell phone dinged, and I pulled it from my purse before starting the truck. It was Thomas. That was odd. My son didn't usually initiate a call and wasn't always prompt in returning them.

"Hello?"

"Hey, Mom. I just got off the phone with Jess. I heard about Dad's visit and his new family."

My eyes closed, and I let out a long breath. I'd been expecting this. He sounded angry as hell and who could blame him? I was still livid about what Ass-hat had done. "I'm sorry for all this, Thomas. I know how hurtful—"

"That bastard! To show up like that with some skank he was banging to see *her* daughter and not Jess! It's all so skeevy. I called him, Mom."

"What? What'd he say?" I could only imagine how that convo went! Ass-hat deserved every iota of Thomas's anger rained down on his head.

"He actually apologized! It's been months since I spoke with him, and it was me who had to reach out, so I really let him have it. He said he thinks he made a mistake. That he misses me and Jess. He's flying out to see her this weekend."

I blinked, feeling my world tilt off its axis. Wait! This totally didn't sound like Alex. For him to do a one eighty to now apologizing to the kids was definitely not him! Even when we'd argued and he'd been completely in the wrong, he would never apologize. That wasn't his style.

"Mom? Are you there?"

"Yeah. Sorry. I was just trying to digest that." Now the pastry churned like a lump of lead. "Well, it's about time he apologized to you and Jess. He and I may not be together but you're his kids. It was absolutely unfair when he cut you out of his life."

"He said the exact same thing to me. He said he wants to spend Thanksgiving with Jess and me. He'll fly out here to

California and pay for Jess's flight. He mentioned renting a beach house for the week."

California? My jaw dropped while it felt like that bear claw was now tearing my guts out. "But *I* asked Jess to *my* house. She was going to talk to you and the three of us would spend that weekend together! If there's snow, you might even get skiing!"

"I know. She mentioned that to me. But Mom. I'd really like to reconnect with Dad. I think he really is sorry for everything. Maybe we could spend Christmas together. That would be more fun anyway. Can we get together then?"

My eyes narrowed even though my heart hurt, hearing Thomas's eagerness to see his father. "He reminded you that he's the one footing the bill for college, didn't he?" It was a snide, cheap shot, but it was out before my brain could censor it.

"Yeah. That came up." Thomas sounded matter of fact. His pragmatism was on full display again.

"You do whatever you want, Thomas. I'm not going to tell you what to do. But extend that same courtesy to your sister, okay? Come to my place for Christmas, and if you change your mind about Thanksgiving, you're always welcome." Even as the words came out of my mouth, I wondered if I'd even be there at Christmas or Thanksgiving. It all depended on what the contractor said later.

"Okay. That's fair. I'd better go, Mom. I have a class in ten minutes. You know, the weather in California's pretty great! Why don't you sell that place and get a house out here? I'd see you a lot more often."

I closed my eyes, counting to three before I answered. *Another* voice in the choir singing for me to sell. "We'll see, Thomas. There's a few things I have to deal with right now. In the meantime, get to class and study. I'll talk to you later."

I sat there for many minutes reliving the conversation with my son. Shit! I should have asked him if Ass-hat was bringing his new family with him when he went to LA for Thanksgiving. He'd apologized and now wanted to get together with Thomas and Jess? Could there be problems in paradise already?

My mouth fell open at the next thought. I'd cursed Alex after Jess told me about him showing up at her school with his new family. I'd wished *impotence* on him! Also, for their happy bliss to be flipped to constant battles. I tapped the phone to call Libby.

I didn't even say hello, bursting right to the point: "It happened, Libby! At least I think it happened!"

"What are you talking about, Shannon? Are you all right?"

I relayed the conversation I'd had with Thomas. "I think I might have totally screwed up Ass-hat's life! It's the only way he'd do such a reversal and try to make amends with the kids. I think he's having problems with the skank."

"I never want to get on your bad side, Shannon. If this is true, then you've got some kind of weird magic going on. But how can it be true? We're probably jumping to conclusions here."

"I guess I'll never know because I'm never speaking to that ass again!" But my gut was telling me something else. I knew he was having problems because I'd wished it on him. The same way I'd wished the flaming red car would go up in flames. This was all because of that Witching Well!

"Give it time, Shannon. Maybe he'll let something slip in front of the kids—"

"He's certainly not going to broadcast that his dick isn't working!" I snorted, picturing it.

"No, no, but they may not be getting along. That was part of your curse, wasn't it? If he doesn't bring the new family to LA, then that's a sign, I'd say."

"Yeah. Maybe. Look, I've gotta go. My septic tank is quite literally in the crapper. I'm meeting a contractor at the house at two. I may need to get the damned thing replaced! Oh...and Devon Booker offered me three quarters of a mil for the house and property." I rolled my eyes.

"That's it? It's worth twice that, Shannon! Good luck with the septic. Maybe it only needs to be pumped out. Did you call

Mike's Plumbing? They're pretty good."

"Yeah, but he hasn't returned my call. No, it's Eric something or other that Devon Booker's recommended. I'll let you know after I talk to him." I left out that Devon was going to be there too, knowing Libby's low opinion of him. And the fact that I'd spent the night at Steve's and more importantly— the kiss. There'd be time for her teasing later when I was more in the mood to hear it.

"Okay. I've got to go too. I'll call you later."

I glanced at the time before I put the phone in my purse. I had just enough time to visit the hardware store to get the paint and supplies. I had to think positively about the problem of the septic. Maybe it was a glitchy thing and an easy fix. I was going to carry on with the renovations even though Thomas had taken the wind out of my sails with his wish to spend Thanksgiving with his father.

My eyes rolled thinking I'd put this curse on Ass-hat. It was a horrible thing to wish on any man, even if my ex deserved it. Maybe... I'd reverse it...in time. But for now, if it were true, then he could suffer for a while. He hadn't thought anything of how he'd made Jess suffer.

Fifteen minutes later, I walked into Mountain Homes Hardware. I didn't see Steve, but the saleslady, Mona as her name badge showed, helped me with mixing the paint and grabbing all the supplies I needed. I was just leaving when Steve walked through the door.

"Hey, Shannon!" His eyes lit up, and a wide grin formed on his lips. "Too bad you hadn't shown up half an hour ago, I would have bought you lunch! Did you get in touch with Mike?"

"It's *me* who should be buying you lunch for putting me up last night." I glanced at the saleslady who was now walking to the back of the store. "I had fun." My face warmed up, along with other parts, remembering the kiss.

"Me too. I'm looking forward to a rerun." His voice had dropped, and he stepped closer to me, taking the gallon of paint from me. "I'll help you to your truck with this."

As we walked out, I looked up at him. "With any luck I may get my septic problem fixed soon. A contractor is going to have a look at it this afternoon." I'd already decided that another night at Steve's wouldn't hurt. I wouldn't mind sampling more of that kiss from the night before. The hormones were waging war with cautious logic, and I couldn't care less.

His eyebrows rose high. "Great! You'll like Mike. He'll be straight with you and he's a hard worker." He swung the paint can over the tailgate and turned to take the other parcels from me.

"Nope. Not Mike, although I tried him first. I left a voice message but I haven't heard back from him. Devon recommended a guy and we're meeting at two."

His eyes narrowed and he shook his head. "Cancel it, Shannon. If he's got anything to do with Booker, I don't like it. Wait for Mike to look at it." His arms folded across his chest as he blew out a long breath. "You can't trust Booker, Shannon. I thought I made that clear."

My chin rose and I peered at him. He had gone beyond giving me advice to actually telling me what to do? And maybe he was a bit jealous that I'd met with Devon and that he'd offered to help me? "Yeah, you made it clear what you think of Devon, Steve. But you know? It's *my* house. This is *my* problem, and I need to get it fixed or at least know how much it's gonna cost."

"You're not *desperate,* Shannon. You can stay at my house for as long as you need. If it takes Mike a day or so to get to you, it's worth it in the end. Don't commit to anything with Booker's guy. Do you need me to go out there with you?"

I blinked a few times as my head fell forward. Had I heard right? Steve was acting like I had no idea what I was doing, offering to come out to oversee this visit. I'd been told what to do all through my marriage. Now I was on my own, starting fresh, and I certainly wasn't putting up with *that* anymore.

"I'll handle this, Steve. I think I'm a pretty good judge of character. I'm not going to get snowed by some sleazy contractor. And for the record, Devon presented his case for buying my property but there was no pressure. He wasn't nearly as bad as you and Libby make him out to be. Even *after* I'd turned his offer down flat, he still wants to help me with this septic crap."

He put his hands up, palms facing out. "Okay. Have it your way. It's your house. I was just trying to help." But the twitch in his jaw muscle told me I'd ticked him off. He took a few steps away and then turned. "How long are you working at the house? I just need to know when to expect you for dinner."

At that point the thought of going to his house had all the appeal of a cold shower. I couldn't believe how miffed he'd gotten that I wasn't following his "advice." I totally didn't need that attitude, not now and not ever.

"I think I'll work late. Mary-Jane called me." A white lie, but whatever. "I'm going to stay with her tonight." My heart pumped hard against my ribcage while my fingers clenched into fists. "You know? I'm not into guys telling me what I should do. Not anymore. I know you mean well, and I appreciate that, but, maybe we're rushing things. I need to stand on my own two feet for a while, not get involved with a guy. Staying at your place just complicates things."

"Suit yourself, Shannon. I'll drop off anything you left at my place in case you need it. I just wanted to be friends, that's all." With that, he strode down the sidewalk to his store.

TWELVE

As I drove to my house, my eyes narrowed thinking about what I'd said to Steve. Getting angry and actually stating my case wasn't something that I was used to. Had I been too hard on him? He'd been kind, putting me up last night and trying to help me with this problem. His bossy attitude grated my last nerve; I'd been enough of a junior partner in a relationship, and if he thought for one minute that I'd be putting up with it now, he was way, way off the mark. If he can't handle me as an independent woman, then this relationship wasn't going anywhere.

When I parked the truck at the house, I pulled out my phone to call Mary-Jane. First things first, and making sure she was fine with me staying a night or two until this was fixed was priority one.

"Hey, stranger. I was just thinking about calling you." I could hear the background din of a restaurant kitchen with pots and pans clanging in the background.

"Hi, Mary-Jane. Sorry I didn't call you earlier, but I've run into a major snag out here. That's why I'm calling right now."

"What's wrong? What can I do to help?"

I took a breath and explained what had happened with the septic, leaving out the part that I'd stayed at Steve's the night before. "Can I stay with you for a few days? I'm hoping that this contractor can get to work right away but who knows?"

"Sure! I'd love that."

"Roy and your daughter would be okay with that? I could stay at a motel if it's not convenient. I know you're pretty busy with the restaurant." I crossed my fingers. It would be nice to meet her daughter and catch up with Mary-Jane's life. Besides, a motel would cost money that I would need to get this problem fixed.

"Are you kidding me? Of course they'll be fine. I'll make sure the bed's made up in the guestroom with fresh sheets. Will you be here later today? In time for dinner?" She sounded happy that I'd asked.

I gazed ahead at the verandah and the house. "Don't go to any trouble with dinner, MJ. I'll probably grab something here and work until eight or so."

"Suit yourself. Just text me as you're leaving and I'll be sure to be there. Wednesday's slow at the restaurant anyway. Debbie is working tonight and she can handle things here."

"Will do. I'll bring some wine. Thanks, Mary-Jane."

After I clicked off, I stepped out of the truck and started bringing my paint and supplies inside. I was just about finished when a white contractor's van and a deep-burgundy Mercedes SUV pulled into my drive and parked. Devon stepped out of the Benz and flipped his sunglasses up to the top of his head.

With a charming smile he said, "Good timing on our part. Let me give you a hand." He strode over and took the bag from my hand. "I guess I'm destined to be your delivery guy."

"Thanks. But I'm afraid the only tip I can give you is to stay out of dark alleyways." I smiled and then watched a heavyset guy in overalls and black boots walk over to us.

Devon turned. "Shannon Burke, this is Eric Anderson. There's nothing this guy doesn't know about plumbing and septic systems."

Eric extended his hand. "Pleased to meet you." His grip was firm before he pulled back and made a show of inhaling. "Yup. I can smell some problems here. I'll get some tools from the van and poke around a bit. You can just carry on with whatever you're doing." He smiled before turning to go back to his vehicle.

Devon nudged me, and his voice was low, "Eric's good at what he does, but he's kind of quiet and standoffish. That's just his way. He usually works alone."

"As long as he can fix this or tell me how much it's gonna cost, I'm good with however quirky his personality is." I glanced at the plumber hefting a big spool looped with a heavy metal cord. "C'mon. I'll give you the fifty-cent tour of the house that you're so eager to buy." As we walked up the steps, I peeked over at him. "Have you ever been here? Did you know my Aunt Maeve?"

He snorted a laugh. "It's a small town. It would be weird if I *didn't* know your aunt. But what you really mean is did I ever talk to her about selling, right?"

I nodded. "Yeah. I'm curious to hear what your reception was when you asked. Did she toss you out on your ass, or did she give it any consideration at all?" If I were a betting woman, it would have been the former that I'd put money on. Aunt Maeve was a sweet woman but you didn't want to rile her up.

Devon reached to open the door as we neared it, but after a quick try at the handle, he pulled his hand back. "You locked it? Folks around here don't usually lock their doors."

My eyebrows pulled together before I tried it. I'd made two trips into the house already and I sure as hell hadn't locked it when I was right there in the yard. But he was right! Somehow the dead bolt had been tripped on my last trip outside. "Hmph." I fished the house keys from my pocket and slipped it into the lock. "I'll have to check that because I didn't lock it. I certainly don't want to accidentally lock myself out."

I opened the door and paused for a moment, flicking the deadbolt handle a few times to see if it was loose or something. But it seemed okay. Weird. Just in case, I slid my keys back into the pocket of my jeans.

Devon followed me down the short hall and into the kitchen, commenting as we walked, "I've never been inside this house. When I talked with Maeve, we stayed on the verandah.

She didn't order me off the property, but she was pretty firm that she'd never sell."

When he stepped into the kitchen and gazed around, his smile fell. "She would have been quite comfortable in the luxury apartments I built on the other side of town. This had to be hard for her to maintain at the end, before she was forced to go to the nursing home."

I took the package from him and set it on the table. "My friends Libby and Mary-Jane took turns coming out a few times a week to check on her. We stayed in touch by email and Facebook." I led the way to the living room, glancing at the fireplace in the corner. Would Steve still want to check that out and help with the wood after our last conversation? Probably not.

Standing at the picture window, I saw that the lake was still swollen, rising higher up the bank. I looked up at Devon who now stood next to me. "What happens to that lake when the snow melt hits in the spring? Do people around here get flooded out?" Not that I wanted to borrow any more problems, but it would be good to know.

His eyebrows bobbed high. "Hasn't happened yet. I think there are underground springs that take care of that. But the rains we just got were pretty bad for this time of year. You can hardly see your dock." He smiled when his eyes met mine. "So you spent your summers here with your aunt. That had to be fun, swimming and hiking through the forest with your friends."

I nodded. "Every summer from when I was seven until I left home for college. It was a blast." I wandered into the dining room that still contained my aunt's buffet hutch and enormous table. I think the only times we'd ever sat at that table was when she was putting together a giant puzzle. I looked over at Devon who was inspecting some curios in the cabinet. "How about you? You said you grew up not twenty minutes from here. How is it that I never ran into you during the summer?"

I turned when the door opened, and Eric strode into the

kitchen. But as Devon had said, he was quiet, just going about his assessment, wanting to be left alone to do the job.

Devon turned and flashed a wide grin. "I was probably helping my parents! My dad had a huge market garden. Guess who got to do all the weeding? It was a relief to get a job working at the grocery store when I turned sixteen."

"I'll bet! I helped Aunt Maeve with her garden and it wasn't even all that big. It's backbreaking work in the sun. But I still had tons of time to swim and hang out with my friends."

"You were the lucky one, then! But hard work never hurt anyone, I guess. That's what my old man says and he should know! He's still living in the same house. I moved back in with him as he's getting kind of forgetful."

"I hear you. Getting old totally sucks." My smile fell as I thought of my aunt's descent into Alzheimer's. The last few years she'd had to be cared for in a nursing home because of that horrible disease.

"Yeah, well staying with him isn't optimal but so far it's working." I saw a melancholy look flit across his face for a moment. It didn't take a mind reader to tell that his father's decline weighed on him. There had to be strong family ties for him to put his life on hold moving back home to care for his dad. Again, this side of him was at odds with what Steve and Libby had said.

Devon wandered out of the dining room and looked up the staircase.

"Come on! I said I'd give you the tour, so let's go up." As we headed up, I said, "There's just the three bedrooms and a bath up here." At the top, I stopped short before passing by my aunt's bedroom. The door was closed. I was sure I had left it open. Was Aunt Maeve making her presence known once again? I opened the door and looked around, just in case it hadn't been her and someone had come into the house.

Devon stepped into the room and wandered over to her dressing table. "You don't see these anymore. This is a real antique." He picked up the photo of the wishing well.

What the hell? It was now back in its frame and once more

in her room? She'd put it there and now Devon was staring at it!

"No."

The word came out of nowhere, sounding in my head! And it wasn't a casual comment but more like a command! I blinked a few times and swallowed hard. It was Aunt Maeve's voice, and it was because Devon was holding a photo that meant a lot to her! I probably shouldn't even have opened her door for him to step inside.

I stepped over to him and took the photo, setting it back on the table. "That photo has sentimental value. I'll show you the rest of the upstairs, and then we should see how Eric is making out. How does that sound?"

He smiled and then nodded. "Lead on. This house is kind of homey, even if it does need a lot of work. I can appreciate the claim it has on you."

I looked over at him. That was an odd way of putting it. A claim? "Yeah. There's so many fantastic memories here." I shrugged. "Didn't you feel that way when you moved back in to look after your father? It was the house you grew up in, right?"

He crinkled his nose. "Maybe a little bit, but I'll be honest. I had a sweet condo that I'm now renting out. I was ready to move out when I did when I was younger, and moving back home kind of felt like I was moving backward in my life."

"Backward?" He sure hit a nerve with me on that, because comparing Maeve's property in the boonies with the chic house in the gated community we had in Pittsburgh...yeah, I've come down a few notches in status.

"Yeah...I mean, I love Pop, but it was a kick to the ego." He snorted. "Try online dating and telling women that you're forty-six years old and live with your dad, y'know?"

"I'm surprised women haven't been more concerned that you're single. Have you ever been married?"

He shook his head. "Nope. I'm good with being a bachelor."

I made a rueful half smile. "Well, that sounds better than an ex-wife."

He looked at me sharply. "Whoa. Don't say that."

"Why? It's the truth."

He shook his head slowly. "No it's not. You're a mother. Call yourself 'a divorced mother' if you want, but by saying you're some guy's 'ex-wife'? No." He tilted his head at me. "Unless you're still carrying a torch for him, of course, hoping you two could fix it."

I guffawed. "Not a chance in hell! Are you kidding me?"

"Then own it more. Shannon Burke's nobody's 'ex' anything. Language counts; it shapes the way we look at things."

This was getting a little too heavy for me. "Okay. Well, Devon, if this real-estate thing doesn't work out for you, you've got a great future in therapy," I said lightly.

"Yeah, that's me, Mister Touchy Feely." It got kind of quiet between us, and he said, "Can I see the rest of the place?"

"Sure!" When I stepped into the bathroom, I was relieved to see that the bathtub had drained, and things looked pretty well normal. That might be a good sign that the septic problem was resolving itself. Hey! That was what I'd wished for. Maybe it was working! But I wouldn't get my hopes up, not until I talked to the contractor.

As we headed back downstairs, Devon asked, "So that's it? Would you like that fifty cents for the tour now, or wait till the next time I see you? That offer of dinner is still open, you know. Just name the day. Your friend Mary-Jane is a terrific chef. Lots of times I pop by and pick up dinner for me and Dad. He loves her Chicken Marsala."

I turned to him, noticing when the light highlighted his face, the wrinkles in his forehead and at the corners of his eyes. He was holding up pretty damn good for a guy approaching middle age.

Smiling, I answered, "Can we make it sometime next week?" It could be fun to get to know Devon better, but for now, most of my brain was snagged around the thorny subject of the septic. "The tour is complete and you can keep your fifty cents. Consider it your tip for carrying my parcels."

We stepped out onto the verandah and then spotted Eric with some kind of meter, walking at the side of the house over the weeping tiles. He looked up when he heard our footsteps and then slowly wandered over. From the way his gaze fell to the ground and the slump of his shoulders, I had the feeling this wasn't going to be good news he was about to convey.

I folded my arms over my chest, trying to steel myself for some bad news. "What's the verdict, Eric? Can you fix this, and how much is it going to cost?"

He glanced at Devon before he started talking. "You've got broken drainage pipes underground; my meter's picked that up. So instead of your septic system dispersing your wastewater into the ground, I'm guessing that instead it's leaching over into the lake."

"Oh no!" Devon shook his head. He shot me an alarmed look. "You're lucky that the Health Department doesn't know this!"

Eric nodded. "For sure. As it is, you'll never be allowed to replace it...not in that spot so close to the lake. No, if it could be fixed that'd be one thing, but we're talking about a whole new weeping bed. You'll have to put it where your driveway is to get approval now."

All the while he talked, I could see money flying out the window. But adding that I'd lose my driveway and have to put in another access from the road running by the house, almost made my heart stop. My mouth had gone completely dry when I eked out the burning question again, "How much?"

Eric took a deep breath and his head tipped to the side. "Forty thousand. Maybe thirty-five, if you're lucky. That's for a whole new septic system."

"Oh my God! Are you sure?" I almost stumbled, taking a step so that my back was against the wall of the house. It was hard to breathe, hearing that number! That was over half of what I had in my savings account! And that wasn't even taking into account a new driveway! So much for my wishes getting granted!

Eric peeled his work gloves off and sighed. "I wish I was wrong, Shannon. But I've been doing this work a very long time. Don't use the sinks or toilet, not until you've replaced this. Technically, I could condemn your house and probably should in all good conscience. I'm licensed with the state so I have obligations in reporting."

Devon shook his head and put his hand on Eric's shoulder. "No, no, no, don't do that, Eric. At least give Shannon a few days to decide what to do. That's a lot of money. You're sure it can't be fixed rather than replaced?" Eric shook his head before walking back to his truck with Devon.

As I watched them talk, with Eric giving an exasperated look before nodding, I slid slowly down with my back rubbing against the weathered boards of the house. This was a disaster. I would be sinking almost all of my savings into the septic and the driveway. There'd be practically nothing left to do any other improvements to the house, not to mention that it was scary not having some kind of fallback for emergencies.

I closed my eyes when I felt the sting of tears threatening to fall. How could I stay here? My dream of living a simpler life in the mountains was crumbling along with the tile bed.

I hardly heard the van start up and drive out of the driveway. What the hell was I going to do?

"Shannon? I'm really sorry that this has happened."

Opening my eyes, I saw Devon take a seat next to me. "Are you? It looks like I may have to change my mind about selling. I'll be honest, Devon. I can't afford to do all the things that Eric suggested." I snorted. "Not suggested! Told me I HAD to do, or this place would be condemned."

He reached over and patted my knee. "Believe it or not, I really feel sorry for you. I know you want to stay here. I could lend you the money, if that will help."

My mouth fell open and I peered at him, trying to see if he really meant that! He stood to make a ton of money if I sold him the property, yet he was extending help for me to stay? And the sad expression on his face and in his eyes were either a really, really good act or he was being sincere. "Why would you do that, Devon? You just met me."

His head tipped as he fixed his gaze on my face. "I can tell you're a decent woman, I guess. Don't get me wrong, I'd still prefer to buy this property, but if you're determined to stay, I could help and still make a little money in interest. I'm a businessman after all."

I shrugged. "True. But I don't want to borrow money from you for this. I'm just not sure what I'm going to do. I've got a lot to think about, Devon."

"I asked Eric to put a hold on everything. He knows you won't make the situation worse by using the water and septic here. Hell! I'll even lend you one of my porta-potties if you want to stay here and keep doing renovations while you mull over your options."

"You own porta-potties?"

"I rent them when I have projects going on. Right now I have two subdivisions going up. I can have one dropped off anytime."

My face screwed up. "Ugh. I can't stand those things. Besides which, I'd still need to shower and use water in the kitchen. I think I'm going to take a pass on working at this place for a few days anyway. Why am I killing myself, if it's going to end up being sold? I just need to think about all this."

Devon squeezed my knee gently. "If I can do anything that will help you stay here, let me know. It's crazy but I can see how much this place means to you. It's kind of like my dad insisting on staying in our old homestead instead of moving to a comfy apartment. I respect that. It's why I've moved in with him to help him spend his last years there."

I watched him stand up and then extend a hand to help me to my feet. "Thanks. I appreciate your offer, but this is something I have to take care of myself. I'll be in touch next week with my decision about the house."

He nodded and then walked over to his SUV. "Shannon, if you need anything, please call me."

***

When I went back into the house, I looked around at the kitchen walls and all the work I'd done stripping them of the old wallpaper. Once more I felt my stomach sink. Now, it might all be for nothing, a pipe dream. I turned to go out to the truck and leave this mess as it stood.

I gasped. The photo of the Witching Well was now on the counter! My gaze darted around the kitchen. But everything else was as I'd left it. "Aunt Maeve?" It had to be her who had moved that photo from her bedroom. My heart pounded fast in my chest as I picked the ornate frame up. "What are you trying to tell me?"

My jaw clenched and I barked, "Dammit! I know you're here! I know you don't want me to sell but what choice do I have? I can't—"

"Go to it, Shannon."

My eyes almost popped out onto my cheeks. This time it hadn't just blared in my head. I'd heard her—for real. Either that or I had totally lost my marbles!

"Go now. Trust me."

I felt a brush against my cheek, and the smell of lilies drifted around me. For just a fraction of a second the air next to me shimmered, like the wavering heat waves above pavement on a hot summer day. A sense of peace flooded through me. The next thing I knew I was at the front door, racing across the verandah.

For whatever reason, I had to go to this well. I felt lighter than air as I ran down the dirt roadway. Aunt Maeve was still around watching over me! I had no idea how visiting that well was going to help but I had to trust that it would. The sun was almost at the horizon as I wandered along the roadway and then cut over, going into the darkness of the forest.

I looked for anything familiar that would confirm I was going along the right pathway. But it all looked the same: dense thickets of brush connecting the tall pines and maples on each side. A high-pitched yowl to my left made the hair on my arms spike high.

My heart leapt in my throat as I looked around. There,

framed by two birch trees, golden eyes stared back at me. A bobcat! Shit! I took a step backward, keeping my eyes fixed on the cat. But it made no move to attack, just blinking slowly as it calmly watched me. It was then that I noticed the ear. One of the ears was missing its tip!

My jaw dropped and I paused. That was the same bobcat that had jumped out onto the road when I'd driven to Wesley, the one I almost hit! It couldn't be, could it? But how many bobcats around here were missing an ear? And what was it doing just sitting there looking at me like a tame housecat? I was no expert on big cats, but even I knew that they normally avoided encounters with people.

In a flash the cat turned and disappeared into the underbrush. Just like that first time I'd seen it.

"The well, Shannon. Trust me."

Her voice yanked me back to the present. As I continued along, I couldn't help but think that the cat and my aunt were connected. This was the second time I'd seen it, and like before, her voice followed. My mind was scrambled from the roller-coaster ride of emotions I'd experienced in just the last hour.

Again, it came back to that weird well. I hardly dared to believe that it would solve my problems, but what else was there?

When I came to the clearing in the grass, I let out a yelp of joy. I'd found it! Even though the trees around the area cut the fading light, I could still make out the well off to the side. I raced over and clung to the rough, damp stone, peering down the opening.

"I'm back! Aunt Maeve sent me!" There was nothing but darkness as far as I could see in the depths. Even though it felt kind of silly to be standing there talking to nothing, she'd sent me here for a reason. This thing could possibly grant my wish, that the septic problem would somehow fix itself. I sure as hell didn't have the money to replace it as well as put in a new driveway! Or maybe I could win a lottery and be able to do both. I don't know...just make that problem go away.

With not even a drink or a coin with me to toss into it, my fingers shot to my pocket, and I scooped out the set of house keys. I toyed with removing the green four-leaf clover from the ring but decided to leave it. It hadn't been all that lucky.

I held the front-door key to my lips, silently wishing for a solution to my problem. "Here you go! I can only offer my house key. If you don't help me, you might as well have them." I dropped it in, feeling really stupid, but also hopeful.

It took a moment before I heard the small splash.

"Thank you."

I'd been half expecting the voice again, but it still made me jerk back. My hands practically shook when I grabbed the rocks again and peered over the edge. "You're welcome?" I don't know how long I stood there waiting. Everything was deadly still, exactly like what I'd experienced the first time in that weird little glade.

Now what? There was no other choice but to go home again and hope and pray that somehow this had worked! I crossed the fingers of both hands as I retraced my steps, leaving the little clearing and going back into the thick of the forest.

I kept an eye out for that bobcat, but there was no sign of him as I retraced my steps going back to the house. Soon I passed the cottages that stood empty, going back up the long dirt roadway.

When I rounded the bend and could see the house, my forehead tightened. There were two trucks parked in my driveway beside my vehicle. And one of them was Steve's.

THIRTEEN

What the hell was he doing? He'd said he would drop my things off but what was with the other vehicle? As I neared the driveway I saw "Mike's Plumbing" on the side of the silver truck. My mouth fell open and I stormed over, seeing them both at the side of the house where my septic was. The nerve of him! He couldn't trust me to meet with Devon's contractor! He had to be the hero. Well, he'd soon find out.

"What do you think you're doing?" My words were cold and clipped. I ignored the middle-aged, rail-thin guy standing next to Steve.

He turned and when he caught a look at my face his smile faded. "I'm trying to get you an honest assessment of the problem, Shannon. This is Mike Tappas. Where were you? We've been here for the past hour."

"I already had it looked at."

Steve crossed his arms. "Oh really? By who?"

"Uh... Eric somebody or other."

Steve cocked an eyebrow and looked over to his buddy Mike. "Eric Anderson was here, man."

Mike snorted. "Betcha' he said she needs a new system!"

Steve looked back over at me. "He came with Devon, didn't he." He wasn't asking. When I nodded, he added,

97

"Figures."

Mike turned to me and smiled. "I'm glad I made time for you today." He shook his head and walked into the house.

What the hell? They had made themselves quite at home in my house while I'd been gone! Coming and going like they owned it or something? "Hey!" I called after him. "What are you doing?"

He stopped and turned. "Just getting my gear. Job's all done. I'll send you a bill."

"What?" I turned back to Steve.

"Whoa!" He held up his hands. "When we got here, your front door was wide open, with a note on the door that said, 'Do what you mote.' I figured that you stepped out for a minute or something."

"What note?" I went to the front door.

Yep, pinned to the door with a quilting needle, was a note. Scrawled on it in pencil were the words, "Do what you mote." "What the hell does 'mote' mean?" I asked.

"I didn't write it! I figured you were saying 'must'!" He was behind my shoulder.

I had closed the door behind me when I left to go to the well. And who the hell wrote this note? My breath stopped.

Maeve. My jaw dropped.

"Hey, you okay?" He put his hand on my shoulder.

I closed my eyes and nodded. "That Eric guy *did* say I needed a whole new system. He said I might be leaching sewage into the lake."

"You don't need to replace the septic system, Shannon. Your problem is, or rather *was,* a blocked line. Mike snaked everything and took out a root ball almost eight inches wide. It happens more than you'd think. Now do you see what I mean about Devon and anyone he's associated with?"

"Wait! Are you sure? Eric had these meters and he said he found busted tiles. He thought that my weeping bed was actually draining into the lake. He wanted to condemn this place!" I searched Steve's face for any sign that he was aware of this. If his guy was that good, how could he miss it?

I looked over when the door opened. Mike's face tightened as he wheeled a giant spool with a motor attached across the verandah. He looked over at me, "This is the machine that snagged your root ball. It's a mechanical snake I threaded into your sewage pipe. I don't know what I'd do without it."

"Let me give you a hand with that, Mike!" Steve went over and helped him get the clunky thing down the set of steps. "Eric Anderson told her she needs a new septic system! Can you believe that?"

Mike sucked his lips into his mouth, trying hard not to laugh before he spoke. "It doesn't surprise me. He'd say anything to stay in Booker's good books. He's not the sharpest knife in the drawer either. The guy would be broke if not for Booker."

As I watched them, I felt the pressure that had weighed heavily on me about the house dissolve. Could this be true? When they were passing by me to put the big spool back in the truck, I spoke, "You fixed it? For real? I don't need a new system?"

Mike stopped and ran his fingers through red hair that was getting pretty thin on top. "If you don't believe me, take a look at the root ball. I left it at the side of the house for you to see. But it wouldn't hurt to get your tank pumped out. I think the rain we had forced an issue that would have cropped up later."

Steve grimaced. "Better fixing this now than when it's minus ten and covered with snow." When Mike grabbed the machine once more, Steve went back to helping him, muttering over his shoulder to me, "You're *welcome*, Shannon."

Oh God. I felt every ounce of blood rush to my face. I'd been so rude to both of them, and they'd done me a serious favor. Hell, they'd saved my house!

And then it hit me! I'd been to the Witching Well! The problem looked like it was resolved! I stood there with wide eyes, blinking slowly. It had worked! And Aunt Maeve had sent me there! I turned back to the door. Yep, the note was pinned with one of her quilting pins. The handwriting was terrible though.

Now this is what I call ghost written! I thought to myself. "We're going to need to have a chat, Maeve," I said under my breath. I pulled the note down and put it in my pocket and went over to where the guys were.

Mike stood next to his truck with the door open. "If you want your tank pumped, I'll get to it Friday. I'll hold off sending you the bill if that's the case."

I raced over to his truck and extended my hand. "Thank you so much for coming out here and fixing this problem! Please, do the tank on Friday! I honestly thought that I'd have to sell the house to Devon. You've thrown me a lifeline, Mike."

He shook my hand. "I knew your aunt, Shannon. You remind me of her. But don't thank me. Thank that jerk over there! He practically kidnapped me from a job that I was up to my elbows in. I'd better get back there, or there'll be hell to pay."

With that, he got into his truck and drove off, leaving me alone with Steve. My chin dipped down as I gazed over at him. "Thanks. But please don't say I told you so. I really don't want to hear it, even if it is true."

"You have a bit of a mess to clean up in the sink from Mike snaking the line. It looks like you'll be able to stay here tonight." He walked over to his truck. "Good luck with the renos, Shannon. I'll probably be seeing you when you come into the store for more stuff. Have a nice evening."

My gut twisted as I watched him get in the truck and back out of the drive. This had been another thing I'd wanted that day, to have more space and not get involved with him.

It looked like I'd gotten that wish too.

Which totally sucked now.

FOURTEEN

When I went inside, I texted Mary-Jane to let her know that I wasn't going to need to stay at her house. Her reply was immediate.

> Want some company? I need to get away from this place before I go crazy.

Oh shit. That didn't sound good. Libby had hinted that there were problems between Mary-Jane and her husband. Now it was her who needed a break at least for one night. It was turning out to be a good thing that Steve and Mike had fixed things for *her* as well as for me. Oh God. I hoped that she and Roy didn't have a fight over me staying with them?

I typed out my answer.

> Sure! I haven't eaten yet, so have dinner with me. Stay the night if you want.

She replied immediately:

> See you in twenty minutes.

As I set the phone back on the table, I remembered Libby saying that Roy constantly criticized Mary-Jane. Maybe she'd had enough and finally blew her lid at him. I would soon see.

I set about cleaning the sink and counters from the splatters of Mike's work. At least with MJ to talk to I wouldn't be dwelling on what an ass I'd been to Steve that day. Plus, I had reason to celebrate! My problem was fixed and I could stay here! Which prompted my next thought, making my jaw clench tight.

I'd tear a strip off Devon and his contractor the next time I ran into him! He wasn't getting off scot free. I had to give him credit though. He'd set me up perfectly and I had fallen for it. Shit! I'd even considered having dinner with him! And all the time he'd had this all cooked up with his buddy, Eric. Oh yeah, there was a score to settle with that creep.

I went over to the table to turn some music on. I jerked back when I saw what was next to the cell phone. My house keys, still on the ring with the green four leaf clover tag, lay in a puddle of water! Oh my God! How did they get there?

My mouth was suddenly dry, but I forced the words, looking around the room. "Aunt Maeve? Did you put these here?" Duh! Of course she put them there! Who else knew about the well and its power? "You sent me there and my wish came true!" I scanned the room, searching for the shimmer I'd seen before. But there was nothing, not even a whisper in reply.

"Thanks for leaving that note!" I said to the air. "And what the hell does 'mote' mean, by the way?"

Still no reply. I snorted. She always took a nap in the late afternoon, and she'd been one busy little spirit today.

This was all so very weird. It felt like I'd stepped into an episode of the *Twilight Zone*—a mysterious bobcat, a magic well that granted wishes, and my dead aunt hanging around looking after me? The weird part was how okay I was with it. I stared down at the floor as the next thought popped into my frazzled brain.

Ass-hat.

He probably *was* having problems in his sex life because of my wish! This magic-wish stuff was really powerful and it was actually happening. At some point I'd have to recant that wish from Ass-hat, but I'd leave it for a little while longer. It wasn't like I'd wished death on him or anything really painful.

It was his dick. No big thing.

I snickered.

I was going to have to censor my thoughts and wishes a lot more. No way was I going to indulge myself with thoughts of revenge on Devon. I could cause some *real* damage. Sure, I'd like to give him shit or even embarrass him—if he were capable of that emotion—but that was as far as it went. To really damage someone? No, that wasn't who I was.

"Aunt Maeve, I know you're here. If you don't feel like talking, that's fine. I need some help with this magic stuff. I don't want to hurt anyone, but I also don't want to get pushed around and taken advantage of." I gazed around the room. "How did it work for you? I know you used it. Is there some kind of owner's manual or something? I mean, can I wish for a million dollars and then I win the lottery? How does this work? Are there rules?"

Thud!

I just about jumped out of my skin at the bang that came from the dining room! I crept across the hallway and peeked in there. What the...My mouth fell open, seeing a black, leather-bound book dead center on the dining room table. I flipped the light switch so that I could read the title and edged closer to the book.

The lock securing a fold-over flap on the cover caught my attention even before the swirling imprint pattern in the worn leather. I picked it up, and my fingers toyed with the lock as a musty smell wafted up from it. With no title or any marking to tell me what kind of book it was, I'd guessed it was some kind of journal. In all the summers I'd spent there, I'd never seen this thing before. But it had appeared when I'd asked for guidance with this wishing thing.

I held the book higher, trying to pry the sides apart a little to see the pages, but the lock was a damned good one. Some of the gold edging on the pages rubbed off on my fingers. Nope, I had to find the key or else rip it open.

Headlights of a car shone through the window and I

scooped the book up again. Mary-Jane was here! I slipped the book onto the seat of the nearest chair tucked under the table and then took a deep breath. For the first time, I kind of regretted that MJ was visiting and I'd have to put off more investigation of this book. I looked around the room and whispered, "Thank you, Aunt Maeve."

At the light tap on my door I rushed from the room. When I opened the door, Mary-Jane stood there with a bottle of wine in one hand and a white plastic bag of take-out food in the other. From the reddish tinge of her eyelids and their puffiness, I knew she'd been crying.

I let out a long sigh, opening my arms and stepping over to her. "Oh, sweetie. What's wrong? Come in and tell me." I hugged her and then taking her arm, I led her into the kitchen.

"I'm a mess, Shannon! No. Correction. I'm an obese mess." Mary-Jane set the wine and food on the table before practically falling into the chair.

"What? Where is this coming from, Mary-Jane? What happened?" My face tightened at her words. Whoever had done this to her, had really punched below the belt. She'd mentioned wanting to lose weight the last time I'd seen her but this seemed excessive. *Obese?*

She slumped lower in the chair. "I had my annual visit with Dr. Morgan. She tore into me about my weight again. That whole forty, overweight, and gallbladder thing that runs in my family. Shit! I know I have to lose some weight or I'm staring at diabetes or worse."

I nodded and pulled up a chair to face her when I sat down. Poor Mary-Jane. Before I could question her about the visit, she continued, really on a roll now.

"When I got home from the visit, I told Roy that I want to lose weight. Well, he started teasing me about all the diets I've tried over the past fifteen years. And to make matters worse, when Zoe came home, she and Roy started wagering on which diet I'd try and fail with next."

My mouth fell open. "Teasing you? After what your doctor said? That's serious, certainly nothing to joke about."

"I didn't even get to tell them what the doctor said before they started in on me." Her lips tightened for a moment. "That's why I'm here. I'd had enough of their 'teasing.' Maybe it's their way of shaming me into it, but I've heard it all before. I will start my diet but *not* tonight! Tonight, I'm going to have my last feast. After the awful day that I had, I deserve it."

She smiled and began opening the plastic parcel of food. "I brought Tso Chicken, egg rolls, fried rice and ribs as well as chocolate cheesecake." Her gaze left the package of food and darted over to me. "Do you have ice-cream? There's nothing better than cheesecake and ice cream."

I stood up and grabbed the bottle of wine. "Yes, I think I have some vanilla ice cream. But let's have some wine first." Under her defiant façade, I could see she was scared to death about the doctor's prognosis. She needed something to calm her down. She also needed support at home rather than them trying to be funny at her expense. Mary-Jane was no shrinking violet, but this issue—her weight—was her Achilles heel.

Even though I was practically shaking with anger that she'd had to endure this teasing, I kept my voice calm when I commented, "That sounds very hurtful, Mary-Jane. You shouldn't have to listen to that, not from *anyone,* let alone your husband and daughter. It's *your* body! I can't speak for what the doctor said but—"

"But I'd really like to shed these pounds, Shannon. It's not only unhealthy but I hate looking like this." She let out a long sigh before she looked over at me. "Yeah, let's have some wine and get drunk. I'm taking you up on that offer to stay tonight. Roy will have to get Debbie, my assistant, to run the kitchen tomorrow. It'll serve him right."

I took the wine and poured two generous glasses. "Just so you know, I think you're beautiful, Mary-Jane, both inside and out." As I handed the glass to her, I asked, "How much weight does the doctor want you to lose?"

She snorted. "Forty pounds. Only the weight of a small child! I've tried every diet but if I lose ten pounds, twenty will find its way back to me." Rolling her eyes, she added, "It's not easy being around food all the time. And who has the time to exercise between work and keeping the house going?"

"I hear you, but it doesn't sound like you have much choice on this one, Mary-Jane. You have to make caring for yourself a priority. As for Roy and Zoe, they need to support you, not tease you about this. You need to have a serious talk with both of them. If they knew the risks to your health, I'm sure they'd support you. You need to make them understand how serious this is." I took a long sip of my wine, looking at her over the rim of the glass.

It certainly was a shock to me knowing what her doctor had advised. Mary-Jane had to win this battle with her weight. Hmmm. Maybe I could help her out. Even though I hadn't read the journal that Aunt Maeve had left for me, Mary-Jane's weight loss was for a good cause. It was worth taking a chance.

As I stared at her, I yearned for her success in her diet plans, visualized the excess pounds melting from her body. I felt a buzzing in my head as words formed. *However this works, please help her make time for exercise. Let it bring her such pleasure that it's practically orgasmic! And most of all, that she'd stick up for herself more. And her daughter and husband need to support her efforts.*

"Why are you looking at me like that? Your eyes are kind of glassy, Shannon. Are you okay?" She leaned closer, peering into my eyes.

The buzzing in my head stopped before I stammered, "I-I'm fine! My mind just wandered a bit, I guess. I hate that this is happening to you but I'm glad you're here. I have a good feeling that things are going to turn around for you."

Her forehead tightened for a moment before she grinned. "Weird, but I feel better just getting this off my chest, talking to you. I'm glad I came out to see you too!" She raised her wine glass in a toast. "To the new me when I shed these pounds! It's going to work this time."

I touched my glass against hers. "No doubt in my mind, MJ!"

When she swallowed a few mouthfuls of wine, she looked over at me. "Now, tell me what happened here. You ring me that you need a place to stay, and then the next thing I know everything's fixed! How'd you pull that off, Shannon?"

"Pull that off?" My mouth went dry for a moment staring at her. But there was no way she could know about the well or my brushes with magic. Hell, I couldn't explain it when I didn't understand it myself!

I took a deep breath. This was just my paranoia. For the next ten minutes I brought her up to date on the day's events, leaving out the visit to the Witching Well, of course.

"That bastard! I never trusted Devon Booker even if he *is* a good customer at the restaurant. Thank God Steve went ahead and called Mike. You might have sold the place and we'd never see you again if not for Steve." She started taking Styrofoam containers out, filling the air with the scent of food.

I set cutlery and plates on the table, murmuring, "Yeah, thank goodness for Steve's persistence. But I don't want to dwell on Devon. He wants this property pretty bad, but he played his card and lost. He's not worth another wasted thought."

"Hmph, you're kinder than me, Shannon. I'd string him up by his balls! So, you stayed at Steve's house last night? How'd that go? Was his son, Byron, there?"

"No, I didn't get to meet his kid. It was nice being with Steve. We laughed and talked about our lives. I feel bad that I was so harsh with him this morning. With any luck he'll get past it, and we can be friends again."

As tempting as it was to give that a nudge with a wish, something stopped me. Until I have a better understanding of all this wish stuff, I'd better ease back on more "wishes." Aunt Maeve had guided me to the well to make that wish and it worked. But was there a limit to how many wishes you could do in a day? I might even be pushing my luck making those wishes for Mary-Jane.

Besides, wishing for some kind of relationship with Steve didn't seem right. Would I want to get involved with someone because of some kind of magic influencing them? Nope. That wasn't a good idea.

Mary-Jane opened the containers and picked out bits of beef and vegetables, not even bothering with the rice or sweet, glazed chicken. "So Byron wasn't there? That sounds cozy." She smirked at me. "How cozy did it get, Shannon? You're single. He's single, not to mention built like a Greek god."

"We slept in separate rooms, if you have to know." I couldn't help the slow smile from spreading on my face. "He kissed me goodnight though. That was downright hot and not at all cozy. If he hadn't stopped, I'm not sure I could have."

"Why would you even *want* to? If it were me, I would have been all over him. Hell, I'd probably still be there!"

I shook my head, laughing. "Poor Steve wouldn't know what hit him. It's a good thing you're married!" When I looked over at her, I noticed her smile fade.

"I kind of envy you right now, Shannon. You're free to come and go as you please and you don't put up with shit from anyone...not anymore." She got up and poured a tall glass of water after setting her wine glass in the sink.

As I ate the Chinese takeout she'd brought, I watched her push her half-eaten plate aside. Holy Hannah! Could my wishes for her welfare be taking effect this soon? She'd switched to water and had hardly touched the meal. I wiped my mouth with a napkin, studying her. "You left room for that cheesecake and ice cream, right?"

"Ugh." Her cheeks puffed out and she burped. "I think if I eat any more, I'm going to puke. Nope. I'm good." She started closing the containers of food and tidying up.

I blinked a few times just watching her set the cheesecake and leftovers in the fridge. When she took the plates and started to rinse them, I stood up. "Hey! Let's leave that for now. Come on and sit in the living room where it's more comfortable. We can catch up."

She smiled and set the dishes in the dishwasher. "Okay, if you insist."

When I walked into the living room, my eye was caught by the glow of the moon shining down on the lake's surface. "Isn't that gorgeous, MJ? Why would I ever want to sell this place to Devon Booker? My aunt lived here for almost fifty years. I totally understand why."

She paused, standing next to me. "I'm glad to hear that. Yes, the full moon tonight is amazing. It looks like it's just a giant ball hovering above." Giving my sleeve a little tug, she stepped over to the sofa. "Now tell me about your kids and the jerk you married. Libby said he visited Jess at her school?"

I took a seat next to her, tucking Aunt Maeve's throw over our legs. Tonight would have been a good night for the fireplace but that would have to wait. After I finished filling in the details that Libby had missed with the Ass-hat story and subsequent Thanksgiving hijacking of my plans to have Thomas visit, I turned the conversation to her daughter.

"What about Zoe? You mentioned the first night I was here that she's a kid in danger of going astray, getting in with the wrong crowd?"

Mary-Jane took a deep breath, squaring her shoulders. "Zoe used to be the sweetest kid before she started high school. But this group of kids she's hanging out with now are rich snots. Can you believe she wanted me to spend almost a thousand dollars on her back-to-school clothes this year? As if I'd ever spend three hundred dollars on a pair of jeans! I told her no, but Roy…" She let out a long, slow breath.

"He gave her the money?" Oh my God! Sure, kids liked the name brands but that was nuts!

She nodded, swirling the water and ice in her glass. "He can't say no to her. And I look like the bad guy continually. Zoe needs some tough love. She's gotten away with far too much because of Roy. He indulges her like she's his ally. She takes advantage of that." Her eyebrows rose high and her smile was grim. "That stops as soon as I get home. It's time I set some rules and boundaries for her and her father." She sighed. "I love my daughter, but if I don't do something, she's going to screw up her life."

I nodded. "I sometimes think that dealing with my kids was way easier when they were toddlers. I don't mean Jessica. She's great. But Thomas. He looks out for number one. He's ready to make up with his father because Alex pays for his education costs and can rent a beach house for a holiday. He wants to spend Thanksgiving with him. He knows that Ass-hat was running around with some skanky business associate, but he's okay with all that."

Mary-Jane patted my leg. "There may come a time that Thomas will see what's important in life. You have to trust he will. That's all you can do." She rose to her feet. "Thanks for being my sounding board. I know normally I'd sit with you and talk until the wee hours, but, it's been a day. I need to turn in and get a decent night's sleep for a change."

My eyes almost popped out onto my cheeks for a moment as I looked at her. Was this my party-animal friend? But then I thought of the journal on the chair in the dining room. I now had the time to read it before I fell asleep.

"I understand. You should get some rest after the day you had." I set the wine aside and got up to make sure she had everything she needed in the spare room.

When I came back downstairs to lock up and turn off the lights, I went into the dining room to get the book. Bending to slide it from the seat of the chair, my fingers brushed against a loose metal object. When I pulled both objects out, my eyes opened wider, seeing a gold key. It had to be for the book! I slid it into the lock, and immediately there was a click. "Yes!" The book's flap fell open, revealing the first yellowed page.

It was going to be a long night.

FIFTEEN

When I was finally settled in my room with the door shut, I picked up the journal again.

Grimoire, Alice Hunter 1901

"Grimoire?" *What the heck was a Grimoire?* Below that, in a loopy handwritten scroll was,

Maeve Burke, 1968

So this was a book that my aunt had used. But who the heck was this Alice Hunter? I flipped a page and saw flowers and vines bordering some kind of weird symbol—a circle containing three leaf shapes, with the points touching in the center. If it had been a pentacle I wouldn't have been surprised, considering my aunt had referred to the well as the Witching Well. But this shape was odd.

I took my cell phone from the night table and snapped a pic of the symbol before doing a search to see what it was. When the search revealed the exact image, I clicked on the Wiki page link.

"Trinity knot, a symbol of white witchcraft or Wicca." I skimmed the *paragraph noting, "...the practice of folk magic for benevolent purposes, i.e. white magic."*

Holy Hannah! My aunt must have been one of these white

witches! My fingers flew to find the definition of Grimoire.

It was a book of spells! A "how-to" journal of magic spells that white witches used. I slipped my phone back onto the desk and flipped the pages of the book, admiring the calligraphy and sketches of plants. Considering the age of the journal, the color and vivid detail of the drawings were surprising.

Other pages were devoted to the phases of the moon, astrology, and a map of the area crisscrossed with intersecting lines. But it didn't line up with maps I'd ever seen of latitude and longitude. I squinted, holding the book farther from me, barely making out the words "Ley Line." Hmmm...more research for later.

I had to look really hard to make out the loopy handwriting, trying to find more guidance in using this magic. I may have broken some kind of rule with my wishes for Mary-Jane and even Ass-hat. Although his problems didn't worry me as much as what Mary-Jane might encounter.

Finally I found a page that had to be written by Aunt Maeve, since it was easier to decipher.

> *October 18, 1968*
> *My grandmother's locket which had been missing for the past two months turned up today! Last night, standing under the full moon, I wished for knowledge about its whereabouts. Presto! There it was on the hutch when I dusted today.*
>
> *October 25, 1968*
> *Testing what Alice Hunter had written about wishing for money, I bought a ticket on the Irish sweepstakes last week. The winners were announced and lo and behold I won $1000! So much for not wishing for more than you need to get by. All that hooey she wrote about Mother Nature providing what we need for food, shelter,*

our dreams and aspirations, is just that, hooey.

October 30, 1968

One of the cabins has termites! I went to check on all of them to winterize the lines and my foot went through the floor. I sprained my ankle and it's pretty bruised. That $1000 doesn't quite cover the replacement of wood and the treatment of the termites.

Lesson 1- Do not wish for riches. The universe will grant you the wish but immediately correct the imbalance you've created. Sometimes it will overcorrect, and you'll be worse off.

"Looks like you learned the lesson the hard way, Maeve!" I said aloud. I looked around for any kind of reply.

Nothing. I went back to reading.

November 4, 1968

Lesson 2 - Do not wish for ANYTHING in anger. Alice was right about this one. A simple problem mushroomed into an enormous one for me after I made a wish against the town's tax assessor. He wants to triple my property taxes! Yikes! I 'wished' for him to misfile his paperwork and forget he'd ever visited my house to make his reassessment.

It worked, but I can't believe how many crappy things have popped up in my life:

1. My car needs a new transmission

2. I learned that my younger sister ran away with some lowlife

3. My cat has disappeared.

So there's something to what Alice Hunter wrote that when you wish in anger, it will come back and hit you THREE times as bad.

I couldn't even try to revoke the original wish

with another one! Alice said when you make a
mistake and wish in anger, you can't wish it away.
I believe her!

My gaze lifted from the notes in the book. Twice, I'd been angry and had wished bad things on people. First, it was the woman in the flaming (literally) red car and then for Ass-hat to experience sex problems and fights with the skank.

Shit! If I'd felt bad about that before, it was nothing to the dread that weighed down my chest at that moment. What was worse, I couldn't revoke or counteract this wish with another wish according to what Aunt Maeve had written. But I had to figure out something that would fix things before it all landed back on my own head with a triple wallop! I'd deal with figuring that out tomorrow.

Turning back to the journal, I continued reading:

December 18th
I've been snowed in for the past three days. To
make matters worse, the electrical power went
down, forcing me to use the fireplace for heat and
cooking. With only a day's worth of wood left
between me and freezing, I ventured outside into
the blizzard. It was a tough slog through thigh-
high snow to get to the Witching Well, but
desperation is a great motivator.

It was exceptionally difficult to empty my mind
of the frostbite nipping my toes while the
blustering snow stole my voice, but I must have
been successful. True to Alice's writings to flow
with Nature's power to redirect and invoke the
energy, I must have stood there for hours before
the storm abated and the sun broke through. The
funny thing was that I could sense when the
Mother and my essence melded.

Lesson 3 - Mother Earth will provide and aid

those who seek her help with a pure heart in humility.

Would I have learned this if not for that storm and being isolated here with no one to turn to? Not likely.

I flipped through the pages remaining, seeing a number of other incidents she'd written. But my eyes felt like they were filled with sand and I yawned. The rest of the journal or Grimoire would have to wait till the next day to finish. I turned the bedside light off and rolled over, tucking the book under my pillow.

SIXTEEN

Thump. Thump. Thump.

At first I thought it was part of the naughty dream, the headboard of the bed banging against the wall, Steve Murphy's face above me. When it persisted, interrupting the Pornhub in my head, my eyes creaked open. The light filtering through the window was pale, while around me heavy shadows clung to the dresser and end of the bed.

Thump. Thump. Thump.

My forehead tightened and I sat up. It was coming from directly below me. Was it a tree branch hitting the house? Whatever was causing the thudding was annoying as hell! I threw the covers back and climbed out of the warm bed.

A glance down the hall to the guest room showed that it was wide open. Mary-Jane? Was she up already? God. It was hardly light outside yet. I plodded down the stairs and then stopped short, seeing Mary-Jane in the center of the living room.

I rubbed my eyes, barely believing what I saw. She was doing jumping jacks? Her arms rose above her head, clapping her hands together while her feet thudded on the floor each time she alternated between extending outward and closing again with a hop. Her face was fifty shades of tomato, broken only by the flash of white teeth in a wide smile.

"What are you doing, MJ? Are you all right?" I continued down the stairs, shaking my head as I peered at her.

"Oh! Hey, sorry. Did I wake you?" She slowed down a little but still persisted in her jumping, with boobs ricocheting up and down under the loose sweatshirt, while her thighs jiggled.

"Yes, you woke me!" I took a deep breath to keep from barking more at her. "Why are you doing jumping jacks in the middle of the night?" I so wanted to go back to bed and fall into that dream again.

She stopped and then extended her leg behind her, bending it to stretch out her quads. "I'm getting warmed up, Shannon! Remember! I said I would start my diet and exercise today. This is great!" Her eyes sparkled and even though she was winded, she kept that gaping grin plastered on her lips.

When her eyes closed for a moment and she bit her lower lip while her thighs clenched, my mouth fell open. I couldn't possibly be seeing what I think I just saw.

This was because of my wish! I'd wanted her to find so much joy in exercise it was almost orgasmic! From the looks of it, she was definitely reveling in some kind of endorphin rush! Or more. My neck grew hotter and I looked away.

"I'm...I'm glad you are having fun, but did you have to start this at the crack of dawn?" A glance at the clock on the mantel showed that it wasn't even six o'clock yet! *Be careful what you wish for*, resounded in my brain.

"What do you mean? The sun's coming up! I wanted to get a head start on my run into town. I figure I can be there by seven, in time to make breakfast for Zoe and see her off to school." She now switched it up to bending at the waist from side to side.

"Hold on, MJ! Have you *ever* jogged for exercise? Maybe you should take this slower, warm up to it. Maybe consider walking or even power walking?" This wasn't good. The poor woman would have a heart attack if she kept going at this rate. "Have a coffee with me and we'll talk about your exercise. I've run marathons, and this is something I know about, Mary-Jane."

She shook her head. "Nope. I can't believe how good I feel just warming up! No way am I going to sit down when I'm on this kind of high. Hello, muscles! Goodbye, flab." She laughed and swiped a bead of sweat from her temple. "I'm leaving my car. Can you drive it into town later and I'll give you a lift back? I really want to get going now."

There was no way I could talk her out of it. I couldn't stop her if I tried. She made a mad rush for the front door.

I hurried after her. "I'll drive your car into town on one condition. You promise me you'll slow it down to a fast walk, MJ. You need to build up your stamina before you take on a four-mile run. It isn't good to literally run before you can walk. It's dangerous."

She patted the pocket of her jeans. "I've got my cell phone. If I get tired, I'll call you to come get me. But don't sit by the phone, Shannon. I've *got* this!" She opened the door and bounced across the verandah and down the steps. She raised her hand in a wave and then ran down the driveway to the road.

There was a sinking feeling in my gut as I leaned against the doorframe watching her fade into the distance. This was the result of my well-intentioned invocation for her health. According to the Grimoire, I couldn't wish this away, but even so, I looked in the direction of the well. *Please, please let her be okay.* I closed the door and went back into the kitchen to make some coffee.

As I stood at the counter watching it slowly drip through, I smiled as the dream she'd interrupted flitted across my brain. My stomach fluttered, picturing the hot romp with Steve which ended waaay too soon. Yikes! My hormones were playing havoc with the best of my intentions to keep him at arm's length. How much did the unconscious play a role in this magic wish making? Could that raunchy escapade come true as a result of the dream?

I sat down with the Grimoire while I had my coffee. Aunt Maeve had never married but that didn't mean she hadn't dated. There'd been a few older gentlemen that she'd gone out to dinner with occasionally when I'd stayed with her. I couldn't recall any of them spending the night, but who knew what happened for the eight months of the year I wasn't there?

She might have written something about sex in her journal. At one time thinking of sex and Aunt Maeve in the same breath would have grossed me out, but now? I was too old for that priggy BS. She was an attractive woman who must have had her needs. So what?

After settling on the sofa with my coffee and the journal, I skimmed through the pages searching for anything that referenced sex. Sheesh. I kind of felt like a curious teenager finding a parent's *Cosmo* or *Penthouse* magazines, exploring the ins and outs. Hmph! I snorted at that. The ins and outs. Right.

When I came to a page with a sketch of a hibiscus flower nestled next to a calla lily, my eyes opened wider. How had I missed this last night? It was by Alice Hunter, which meant the words were almost impossible to decipher because of her spidery handwriting. But the picture she drew left little to the imagination. The stamen in the hibiscus could only be described as a golden, erect penis, while the delicate folds of the calla looked very much like a vulva.

I could feel my body heat up and it had nothing to do with the hot coffee! It was probably the result of being celibate for the past six months and being within a hundred miles of Steve Murphy. Even Devon Booker hadn't been hard on the eyes until he'd turned out to be a total turd.

Alice's penmanship was so full of swirls and flourishes, it was impossible to read. It might as well have been written in a foreign language. Dammit! I could only look for hidden messages in the artwork she'd framed the script with. Aside from the phases of the moon in the upper right corner and what looked like a blue pond at the bottom, there were only flowers and vines flowing between them. I narrowed my eyes to blur the effect to see if there was some kind of pattern not readily apparent.

It was only then that the image of a sleeping woman on a bed of grass seemed to pop out of the background. It was like looking at one of those mind-riddle sketches where examining the background, the negative space became something not readily apparent. Once you see past the intentionally obvious, it becomes impossible to *not* see the obscure. And from the look on this woman's face—kind of like MJ's when she was exercising!—she was having a pretty exciting time, surrounded by flowers with sexy parts.

I took a sip of coffee, gazing out the window to try to make sense of it. Alice lived in a time where sexual expression was oppressed, yet she'd camouflaged it in her drawings. So sex was important enough with this magic stuff to be drawn into her Grimoire. I snorted. Either that or Alice was a closet nympho.

And what about the moon phases? That might even be linked to menstrual cycles? Fertility? I knew the moon influenced the tides. And every nurse I'd ever talked to said that full moons brought out the crazies as well as an uptick in pregnant women going into labor. So the moon was really important with this witch stuff.

And sexual energy. If that were the case, I had that in spades! But with the writing indecipherable, I'd have to wait and see how that played out with Steve. Maybe MJ was right about having a no-strings-attached romp with him. How could it hurt?

Sighing, I rose from the sofa to bring my mug back to the kitchen. All this was interesting, but it wasn't getting me anywhere with the work to be done in the house. Plus, there was an errand that I knew I had to do later that day.

I had to find the woman in the flaming red car and see if I could make amends to her. Even if it meant giving her some money for a replacement vehicle. There was no way I wanted bad karma coming my way. I'd had enough horrible things happen in the last year.

***

It was almost three o'clock by the time I pulled up to the fire station in Wesley. Maybe the firefighters who had put out the blaze in the red car would know who she was and where she lived. With another bit of luck I might even get to see the hot guy, Stan Jones, who had hit on Libby so many times.

I got out of the car and wandered over to the open garage door in the brick two-story building. Inside, polishing the chrome of an enormous fire truck, a guy in his mid-forties looked over at me. He straightened, holding the blue rag in both of his hands, peering with ice-blue eyes that I swear felt like he could see right through me.

If this was Stan Jones, I could only wonder at Libby's sanity that she'd never gone out with him. With shoulders like a linebacker and ripped arm muscles below a face that was ruggedly handsome, he could be a model for a calendar. If they sold any with this guy featured, I would buy a dozen!

"Can I help you?" Even his voice was smooth as dark chocolate.

"Maybe." I strode forward, extending my hand. "I'm Shannon Burke. I just moved into my aunt's old place on Lakeshore Lane."

He smiled and his grip was warm and firm. "Pleased to meet you. I'm Lester Holmes."

This *isn't* the hot Stan guy? What the hell was with this town? I hid the disappointment that this wasn't Libby's guy and continued. "I'm trying to locate the woman who owned the red car that caught fire a few days ago. I saw the whole thing as I drove by on my way home. I felt sorry and baked some brownies to take to her, but I don't know her name or address. I was hoping that you could point me in the right direction."

His eyebrows rose high and he scratched his head. "I'm not sure—"

"Any problems here, Lester?" The guy who emerged from the darkness of the garage was even hotter than Lester, if that were possible.

There was definitely something in the water in Wesley to create such perfect male specimens. His hair was dark with a few streaks of gray near his temples, and there was something about his eyes. They seemed to laugh even though his face was deadpan, although totally gorgeous. He was taller than the first guy and more muscular, stretching out the arms of his T-shirt.

Lester turned and introduced me. "This is the chief: Stan Jones, Ms. Burke. She was asking about Ida Watkins. She saw the car on fire and wanted to take her brownies."

Stan shook my hand and my mind went blank! I even found it hard to speak. Libby had to be made of stone not to fall under this guy's spell. "Yes. Can you give me her address?" At least I had her name now, thanks to Lester.

His mouth pulled to the side and he shook his head. "Technically, I can't do that. Privacy and all that good stuff, y'know."

"I understand, completely. I told my friend Libby Walker you wouldn't be allowed to give out that information, but she said if anyone could help me, it would be Stan Jones. She couldn't say enough good things about you, Stan." It was a fib, but from the way his eyes bulged at Libby's name, it had been worth it.

"Libby said that?"

Lester winked at me and smirked before walking away. If he'd given me a high five, his wink couldn't be any clearer. I'd stroked Stan's soft spot in mentioning Libby's name.

I lifted the aluminum foil from the side of the plate, revealing double-chocolate brownies slathered with creamy icing. "Would you like a brownie? Libby wasn't kidding when she said you were totally buff. You must spend a lot of time lifting weights. I guess that helps when you're rescuing people from burning buildings."

I saw his face almost melt into a wide smile, beaming at me. "So you're a friend of Libby's? She's an amazing person, isn't she?" He took a brownie from the pan and leaned in. "If I was looking for Ida, I'd take a drive on Harvest Avenue. It's only a few blocks long and not many elevated bungalows have a red Ford Focus in the driveway. I hear she got it back from the garage where they fixed it all up, just this morning."

"You don't say! Maybe I'll take a spin down Harvest

Avenue. I'll be sure to thank Libby for putting a bug in my ear about you, Stan!" I turned and stopped after a few steps, looking back at him. "I've been working on fixing my aunt's place up. I was thinking that in a few weeks I might have it done enough to have a small party...kind of a get-to-know-my-neighbors type thing. Would you like to come? Libby will be there."

If I'd said he just won the lottery, he could not have looked more surprised or excited. "Well, sure! Let me give you my contact information and send me the date and time. I'll be there with bells on."

"Then I'll hear you coming!" I pulled out my phone and took his information. "Libby will be smoked when I tell her you'll be there." I looked past him at the truck. "Maybe smoked isn't a good analogy considering I'm at a fire station. Let's just say, she'll be thrilled."

"Wow! My day was pretty dull till you showed up, Shannon." He took a small bite of the brownie and then added, "Mmmm, I can't wait. Make sure you have plenty of these around."

"Count on it, Stan! I'll be in touch." I fluttered my fingers in a wave and then walked over to my car.

Now if the conversation with Ida Red-Car went so well, I'd be laughing.

SEVENTEEN

After circling the block, I finally saw the red car peeking out from under the branches of a large maple. And the house was a bungalow. It had to be Ida-Red-Car's place. I parked the car on the street and then sat looking at it, wondering how the hell I was going to open this conversation up without looking like a total whack job. Finally I could procrastinate no more.

I knocked on a white colonial door with a brass knocker shaped like a bear. Inside, the sound of footsteps made me suck in a deep breath. When the door opened, a woman in a blue sweatsuit peered at me. Yep, it was her. I let out a sigh; the feeling of victory from the other day was replaced with guilt. Yeah, she snatched my parking spot...but I then set her car on fire.

She tilted her head at me. "Hello, can I help you?"

"Hi. You don't know me, but I saw that you had a fire in your car a few days ago when I drove by. I've been thinking of how horrible that must have been and I brought you some brownies." I thrust the plate of brownies out in front of me.

Her mouth fell open, and she blinked a few times watching me.

"It's not much but..." My voice faded. *But I'd like to apologize for my ignorant use of magic?* Sure, and yes, I am totally nuts. I let the silence hang instead until adding, "I hope you're okay."

She looked down at the brownies and back up at me. "I'm great!" Her hand flew to her throat and she beamed. "Come in! Would you like a coffee or tea? I'm Ida Watkins by the way."

"I'm Shannon Burke. It's nice to meet you."

As I stepped inside, she continued talking, "My car bursting into flames was horrible and scary, let me tell you! But it turned out to be the best thing that ever happened to me!" She looked over at me and her smile seemed almost sheepish. "I'm prattling on and on, but I still can't get over what happened. Normally I don't air my private business but this is...well, it's *uncanny*."

My head was spinning. This was definitely not what I'd been expecting! She was happy that her car engine had been torched? I followed when she gestured for me to go into her kitchen. Her house was sparsely furnished and smelled of lemon cleaning products.

"What do you mean, uncanny? I'd freak out if my car caught fire." I set the brownies on the granite countertop of the island table and took a seat.

As she poured two mugs of coffee, she kept going, "I was on my way to do something that I would have regretted for the rest of my life. I'm not going to go into details, but I was fit to be tied that day, acting out of pure rage." She shook her head as she handed the mug to me. "Ironically, that fire gave me the chance to cool down. I can't imagine the hurt and pain that I would have caused if it hadn't happened."

When she slid cream and sugar toward me, I looked down, busying myself while I tried to make sense of this. I had wished that fire on her in anger and yet she'd *benefited?* "Well, I'm glad that it worked out for you. I guess it's true what they say that it's a foul wind that doesn't blow some good somewhere."

She took a sip and then nodded. "That's true in my case. It didn't even cost that much to fix my car either! Turns out there was a recall on a thingamabob on the engine! Which is a double blessing." She grabbed a couple of plates and dished out some of the brownies. "That was so thoughtful of you,

Shannon, to think of me and bring me these brownies. See! That's another good thing that happened as a result of that fire. I've made a new friend."

I smiled at her despite the tightness that gripped my chest. I'd caused her car to catch fire, and here she was acting like it'd been the best thing that had ever happened. "Yes. I'm glad I stopped by to chat with you. At least I know that it ended well."

Her eyes narrowed, peering at me. "You look familiar, yet I've never run into you at church or even the grocery store."

I smiled despite the sinking feeling in my gut, remembering how she'd cut me off from the parking space in front of Steve's store. Now that I knew she was pretty upset even before running into me, I could understand her dismissal of me that day.

"No. I just moved back here a week ago, to my Aunt Maeve Burke's place. I was on my way home when I saw your problem with your car. Did you know my aunt?"

Her eyebrows shot up as she smiled. "You're Maeve Burke's niece? Of course I knew your aunt! She was a lovely woman! She always donated to our bake sales even though she wasn't a regular at church." She lifted a brownie in salute. "I can see that you've inherited her gift."

My eyes popped wider at the word "gift." Ida, you have *nooo* idea of the gifts from Maeve I've come into! "I'd like to think so. You know, I'm thinking of having a party soon to get to know more people. Would you like to come to it?"

Ida grinned. "As long as I can bring something. Count me in!"

We finished up the visit after exchanging contact information. This had gone better than I'd ever expected.

***

When I arrived home, I was still puzzled by how things had gone with Ida-Red-Car. What I'd read in the book totally contradicted how my wish born out of anger had turned out. It was time to go to the source and see if I could make sense of this. There was also a tiny kernel of hope that perhaps the curse I'd put on Ass-hat might not have such devastating consequences. Look, I'll admit it, I was more concerned with the backlash it might have in my own life.

It took me about forty minutes, but finally I arrived at the clearing where the Witching Well was. The sun, once more, was low in the sky, and despite the blustery day, the glade was still as a tomb.

I strode over to the well and scowled down into the depths. "Hey! I don't know who you are and how all this wishing magic works but I want some straight answers. I know you have a connection to my Aunt Maeve and some woman named Alice, and according to what they wrote, I should never have wished something bad on that woman in the red car. So what gives? It turns out, I actually did her a *favor*! What's up with that, Well?" I could feel my cheeks grow even hotter, and I was glad there was no one around to hear me talking to a *well*!

"You just got your one free pass!"

I jerked back, and my mouth fell open, hearing the familiar voice. What the hell? Even though this thing had talked to me twice before, it was still a shock! *My one free pass?* So I'd wasted my one opportunity to screw up on a perfect stranger?

"The curse you put on Ass-hat will return to haunt you. In the future, be more cautious with what you wish for."

My heart was a racehorse galloping in my chest as I peeked over the lip of the well. It had read my mind about my biggest fear, that I'd pay in spades for what I'd wished on my ex!

It wasn't fair! What the hell was happening here? I practically barked when I asked, "Who are you? Did you speak to my aunt like this?"

"You have my Grimoire. Figure it out. Or not."

"Alice? You're Alice Hunter?" My hands shook, so I clutched the sides of the well, leaning over as far as I could to see any sign of life. But only blackness met my search. I stayed that way for a long time, waiting for her to answer. It had to be Alice Hunter! She'd admitted it when she referenced the Grimoire.

127

I backed away slowly, never taking my eyes from the well. I wasn't sure if some old woman or ghost would crawl over the lip but I wasn't taking any chances. When I came to the edge of the clearing, I turned and bolted through the woods, never stopping until I got to the road near my cabins.

If not for finding the Grimoire and the inexplicable things that I'd seen with my own eyes, I would have questioned my sanity. But this was real and happening to me!

When I came to my house, a surreal bout of déjà vu hit me between the eyes. Steve Murphy's truck was parked at my house again! What was this, a daily occurrence? I had enough on my plate trying to figure all this witchy wishing stuff out without him distracting me.

He saw me walking into the drive and then met me halfway. The look on his face was sombre and he stopped, folding his arms across his chest.

"Hi. What's up?"

"Do you ever pick up your phone messages or answer it? I've tried you at least a half a dozen times today." His eyebrows pulled together, and his eyes had a narrow, hard look when he glared at me.

I pulled out my phone and looked at it. Shit! There were seven messages and missed calls. What the hell was with my phone? I'd never even heard it ring. My teeth gritted together as I put it back in my pocket. Him showing up and making me look foolish was getting old.

"Sorry. What did you want?" I stepped by him, heading to my verandah.

When he grabbed my arm and spun me around, my head jerked back, gaping at him. Before I had a chance to slough away his grip, he spoke again, "It's Mary-Jane. Libby called me when she couldn't get hold of you. Mary-Jane fell and messed up her knee. A truck driver found her on the side of the road about two miles from here. She sprained her ankle and busted her phone!"

Oh my God! Mary-Jane! "Is she all right now?" My heart was in my throat as I stared at him. This was my fault! What if…

"They took her to the hospital and put a brace on. But she's still in a lot of pain." He glanced at her car still parked in my drive. "Why didn't she drive her car home? Why the hell would she *walk*?"

I closed my eyes and let out a long sigh. Thank goodness it hadn't been worse, but still…with her job, how was she going to manage? As a cook, she was on her feet all day. Shit. This was my fault. Again.

"I tried to stop her, but she insisted on starting her exercise program. I even asked her to start slowly, but you know MJ. She left here jogging." I looked up at him. "Come in and I'll make us a drink. I certainly could use one."

EIGHTEEN

Steve leaned his butt against the counter, nursing his Jack Daniels as he listened to what had happened the day before. When I'd finished telling him about her showing up and being so upset after her doctor's visit, the scowl dropped from his mouth.

But I left out everything about the well and visiting Ida-Red-Car.

Shaking his head he said, "She's lucky she didn't have a heart attack. But her knee? She's going to be laid up for a while, and that's if she's lucky." He waved me off when I offered more whiskey. "Thanks. I'll have just this one, and then I've got to get going. Byron will be getting home from karate class soon."

My head tipped to the side when I looked at him. "I'm sorry about being bitchy with you, Steve. This is the second time you've done me a favor, stopping by like this."

He smiled and it was like the sun coming out from behind a cloudbank. "Hey! You're one of my best customers at the store." His hand lifted and gently cupped my cheek. "You know I'm teasing, right? It's not just that you're a good customer or neighbor."

Just the touch of his hand on me sent a shiver down to my belly. Teasing? A flash of the dream I'd had the night before flitted through my mind. I had to look away when my heart skipped a beat and my knees turned to jelly. "I know." My whispered words sounded skittery even to my own ears.

He set the glass down, and his fingers tugged at my shoulders, pulling me into a warm hug. "Can we get back to where we left off when you stayed at my place? I'd much rather laugh with you than argue."

I could smell the slight woodsy scent of his aftershave as I snuggled into his neck. His arms around me and my body pressed against his felt soooo good. I looked into his eyes, and then my gaze drifted to his lips, full and upturned at the corners. "There's a lot of things that are better than arguing, Steve." Makeup sex or even just plain raunchy sex pulsed in my brain but I held my tongue.

His hand rose, and fingers threaded through my long, dark hair, pulling my head closer. His kiss was electric, sending a jolt of pleasure through my core. I could feel where our bodies met that the feeling was quite mutual. I pushed into him, abandoning myself to pure desire. I couldn't remember the last time that a kiss had turned me on like this. Man oh man, it's been a long, long time!

When he pulled back, it felt like my soul had poured out of my body, leaving me empty. My blood pounded so hard in my ears that I almost missed his whispered words, "I hate to leave but I'm afraid I have to. Bryon will—"

"I know." My finger crossed his lips, caressing the soft skin and reveling in his hot breath. "Maybe you can stop by when you have more time...when you can stay the night." I tilted my head toward the living room and grinned. "After all, my chimney still needs your attention."

He laughed and grabbed my fingers. "Stop it. You're killing me, Shannon! I thought I had it bad for you when we were kids, but it's nothing to how I feel now. You were gorgeous when we were kids, and you're even better-looking now. You're gorgeous and sweet *and* funny."

My lips curled into a flirty smile as I looked up at him. "Well, you've certainly grown up too, and absolutely for the better. That skinny kid has become totally ripped and in all the right places." My hands wandered freely over his shoulders and muscular arms before sliding inside his windbreaker and shirt.

He gripped my shoulders and eased away slowly, once more leaving my hands empty. God! This was difficult to stop! I wanted to grab the sides of his jacket and rip it right off. I was even breathing faster. Hell, who was I kidding? I was panting.

"How about I stop by on Thursday? I'll check your chimney and then we can stoke the fire? I'm pretty sure we can get it blazing." His eyes were hooded with heavy lids as he gazed at me, the corners of his mouth twitching in a slow smile.

"That fire is smoldering, just waiting for the right...fuel." My fingers traced a line down his chest and over rock-hard abs, going lower until he grabbed my hand.

"This is gonna be a looong week. Maybe some afternoon I should personally deliver some lumber and tools that you'll need. For the house, you know?" He chuckled and then kissed my forehead. "We'll think of something, Shannon. But I'd better go now."

I closed my eyes and let out a long breath. "Yeah. I don't think I want to wait till Thursday either. It's been a long time...too long." I took his hand and followed him to the door.

When I saw Mary-Jane's car parked there, reality hit me once more. "I have to call Libby and see how MJ is. Maybe she'll give me a lift home if I drive MJ's car into town." I felt kind of guilty for avoiding visiting her, but the thought of seeing her husband and daughter after the part I'd played in Mary-Jane's injury wasn't appealing at all. They probably would tear a strip off me for letting her run all the way into town.

It was like he read my mind. "She'll be okay, Shannon. Don't feel guilty. It was her decision to race off on her own." He pulled me in for one last hug and then edged away slowly. "I'll see you later this week and get you fixed up here."

"Can't wait!" I could feel the flutter of butterfly wings take flight in my belly at the thought of his next visit. On a whim, I added, "Don't forget you offered to cut wood for me! I'm partial to hardwood."

He turned around, and his eyes were wide above an face-splitting grin. "You are bad! If I didn't have my kid to tend to...Well, let's just say you'd be plucking splinters from your ass from the boards on that verandah, Shannon!"

I crossed my arms over my chest, lifting my chin high in the air. "Promises. Promises."

He wagged his finger at me before he opened the door of his truck. "You got that right! See you sometime this week!"

When I turned after watching him back out of the drive and head down the road for home, I hugged myself. My life was turning into quite a wild ride since coming back to Aunt Maeve's. It felt like I'd been sleepwalking up to this point.

I'd found a magic well, my Aunt Maeve still hanging around, and a guy I'd like to get naked with. Not too bad for an old doll like me.

As I walked back inside, the phone in my pocket buzzed with a text message. Now it's decided to work again!

When I saw the name on the screen, my eyes narrowed.

Devon!

NINETEEN

> How are you doing now that you've had a
> chance to sleep on things? I know I just saw
> you yesterday but I couldn't stop thinking
> about you. Frankly, I'm worried about you.
> Let me know how I can help. I'm serious.

Hah! What a bullshit artist! The only thing he was probably
worried about was how soon he could get my house and
property. I shook my head, barely believing the nerve of the
sleazy crook. When I went back in the house and poured
another drink, I mulled over what I'd say to him. He had
deliberately tried to trick me. Turnabout was fair play with
someone like him. My fingers flew, typing a response.

> It was a pretty restless night, Devon, even
> though I took almost a full bottle of sleeping
> pills. This whole thing is weighing down on
> me so much I don't know what I'll do. This
> place means so much to me and now that
> this septic situation has happened, I'm
> almost ready to give up. I wish I had
> someone to talk to.

I actually cackled when I hit send! The text may have
sounded like I had a serious case of what was once called "the

vapors," but I didn't care. Let him think I was at my wit's end. The bottle of sleeping pills was a nice touch. Maybe he'd worry that his lies had pushed me over the edge. Maybe but not likely.

I rolled my eyes wondering if I should have just told him to screw himself. But when the phone dinged with his quick reply, I smiled.

> Don't do anything foolish, Shannon! Nothing is ever as bad as it seems. I could stop by later if you need to talk. Both offers (lending you the money or buying your property) still stand. I really would like to help you out. I know I just met you but I feel a connection to you.

My fingers curled into a fist as I read his lies. I was going to let him have it right between the eyes but not like this, not in a text. No. He'd been nervy enough to lie right to my face, so I wanted to see his expression when I called him out.

> I appreciate your offer to help me. Maybe we could work something out. I'm at the house still trying to sort through this mess if you want to come out to visit.

When I hit send, I thought about my intentions and the Witching Well. It wasn't like I was wishing him harm. I just wanted to give him a piece of my mind like any other normal person would. Nothing magical about that. I was on safe ground with this.

> I'll be there in a half an hour. Hopefully we can work something out to take this burden off your back.

I clicked the phone off and then made myself something to eat. But knowing Devon was coming out and that I'd be having it out with him had my stomach churning. I pushed the sandwich away after two bites and just sat at the table ruminating about the day and the Witching Well.

Counting on my fingers, I summed up all my experiences with that well.

One: I'd gotten a pass in wishing bad to Ida-Red-Car, which was a good thing.

Two: Alice Hunter from the depths of the well (and afterlife!) told me there was bad karma coming my way from the Ass-hat wish. That was so not good.

Three: When I'd wished good for my friend Mary-Jane, she'd been injured. Again, not good.

Four: My erotic dream about Steve looked like it was about to become reality sometime in the coming week. I could live with that all right!

But try as I might, I couldn't see any sort of pattern or reason to how these wish things worked. Wish bad things, and it apparently comes around and bites you in the ass. Wish good things, and it still bites you in the ass. Wish for a fun romp with Steve, and that one looks promising. I was going to have to start writing my experience into that Grimoire and see if I could figure this out. What was the good of having this magic if the only thing I could count on was getting laid? I could have managed that much on my own.

It had become dark outside while I sat there lost in these thoughts. When headlights glared on my kitchen window, I took a deep breath and finished the dregs of my drink.

It was time to have it out with Devon Booker.

I threw my jacket on and went outside and stood on the top step of the verandah. I watched him park his Beemer and then get out.

"Hey, Devon! Notice anything different in the air tonight?"

He stopped short and looked around, taking a deep breath. "No. There's a nice breeze but that's about it. How are you doing—"

"I'm fine! And so is my septic system, for your information! You and your thieving plumber friend tried to trick me, Devon. Luckily I have friends who are honest and care about me. The only thing wrong with my septic was a root ball and that's been fixed, no thanks to you."

Even in the low light I could see his face harden and his eyes narrow. He called over to me. "Nuh-uh. Eric knows his stuff and I trust him. He's been doing work for me for years."

I went down the steps and walked over to him, stopping about five feet away from him. "Funny you say 'trust'! *You're* the one who's full of shit! You tried to manipulate me into thinking the problem was a *catastrophe* and that you would help me. Do you do that in all your business dealings?" Before he could say anything, I added, "My friends tried to warn me about you."

His nostrils flared when he took a deep breath, his mouth a straight, thin line. "That's not true. I'm respected in this town. Unlike your crazy aunt who people sniggered about behind her back. As for your septic, you have way more problems than you've been led to believe."

I leaned in, practically spitting my words at him, "It's not my septic that's overflowing with crap, Devon! It's you! I wanted to see your face when I told you that."

"Hey, lighten up here! I've just been trying to help!"

He's so full of shit. "Help, huh? By having your buddy tell me that I need to spend forty thousand dollars? You call that help?" I couldn't resist the next dig. "No damn wonder you're single!"

"Hey! You don't know anything about me!"

I was letting myself slip into fury. The hell with it. Enough crap's happened to me, and he's standing right there. He's lucky I didn't wish a meteor to land on him.

Look, I have a temper, but it takes a lot to get my fuse lit. I'd held it together for the last six damn months, and I was at my limit. Seething, I came down the steps to get right in his face.

"I know enough about you, you bastard. You got some big plans for this lake, and I'm in your way. You're a conniving one, aren't you?" I barked a laugh. "But you're so damn easy to see through." I jabbed a finger at him. "Living at home with your 'dad.' What sort of bullshit line is that?"

His jaw dropped. "Now you're bringing my dad into this? It

wasn't enough to slag my love life? What the hell's the matter with you?"

"With me?" Oh God, I wished I were a guy because I would have slugged him right then and there. "You tried to trick me out of my home, you bastard!" All bets were off with this bozo.

"I didn't! I tried to help you!"

"Yeah! Into the poorhouse or onto the street! I can't wait to spread the word around town about you!"

"Oh, really?" His eyes narrowed.

"Yes, really! I'll make sure to tell anyone and everyone what kind of a weasel you are!"

Now he glared back at me. "You know something? I can tell some stuff about you too." He looked over my shoulder. "There's stuff about your house, you know."

What the hell was he talking about? The well? No. Way. I decided to call his bluff and folded my arms. "Oh yeah? Like what?"

"I'll just tell Eric to make that ol' report to the Health Department about your place leaching wastewater into the lake." He pointed a finger at me. "You can spread all the rumors you want about me around town, Shannon. Big freaking deal. I'll just drop a dime to the Health Department."

He stepped over to his car and opened the door, pausing before he got inside. "You'll soon have no house to live in. The health and environmental people will be on your case from now on. You should sell me this property before it bankrupts you. And by the way, the offer I made to you just went down by fifty percent."

"Get off my property, Devon, and never, *ever* come back." I stood my ground with my arms across my chest watching him spin up some dirt as he peeled out of the driveway. I brushed my hands briskly, wiping any semblance of his BS off me.

"The rotten scoundrel! Grifter!" I muttered to myself as I stomped back into the house. I locked the door for good measure and headed into the kitchen to make another drink and try to eat the sandwich I'd made.

But what I saw on the table made me gasp. There, sitting in front of where I'd sat earlier was the Grimoire.

"Good job, Shannon."

My aunt's voice whispered close to my ear. I felt her touch on my cheek and I froze for a moment.

Tears filled my eyes as I looked around the room, trying to see that glimmer I'd seen before. "Aunt Maeve?" When there was no immediate answer, the adrenaline still spiking through my body made me add, "You *have* to help me, Aunt Maeve! I'm worried about this curse on Ass-hat, and now Devon is making threats so he can take this house! The Grimoire is almost impossible to decipher, and that voice in the well isn't much help either! Give me some clues on how to *handle* this!"

"You'll find your way. Use the Grimoire and follow the signs. Have patience."

Again, her words were so enigmatic as to be worthless.

TWENTY

I settled myself on the sofa with the Grimoire, my phone and a double Jack Daniels. Libby answered practically on the first ring when I called her.

"Hey, Shannon. I was just about to call you. Roy just texted me to let me know how she's doing. She's still pretty sore, and she'll be off her feet for a couple of weeks. But she's home resting, which is a good thing."

My eyes closed, and I took a deep breath thanking the stars for that piece of good news at least. "It's all my fault, Libby! When she showed up all bent out of shape about her health and wanting to lose weight, I made a *wish* that she'd stick with a diet and exercise. It worked! She insisted on running into town all the way from my house. And look what happened? She blows out her knee so bad, she needs surgery."

"Hold on! You didn't force her to do that! How do you know it was your wish that made her choose to run? For years, she's been talking about getting into exercise and losing weight. It might just be a coincidence, you know. Again."

I shook my head even though she wasn't there to see it. "I don't think so. I found this book...it's called a Grimoire. Originally it belonged to someone named Alice Hunter, but my aunt wrote in it too. It's kind of a journal or 'how-to' book of spells. They were white witches, Libby."

"What? Your aunt really was a witch? So now what? Since you went to the well and now have this strange book, does that make you a witch too?" She laughed. "You're really getting a jump on Halloween, girlfriend. How much have you had to drink today?"

Hearing her mock me rankled. I sat up straighter, and my voice became sugary sweet with venom. "Stan Jones sends his regards, *girlfriend*! I used your name when I met him to find out where Ida-Red-Car lives. He melted like butter when I told him how much you admire his body!"

"What the hell! You didn't! I'm going to strangle you, Shannon!"

"Hey! You'll have to take a number! Devon was just here, and I tore a strip off him for lying to me about the septic. He's threatening to go to the Health Department and the environmental people. Hell! He'd probably go to the *governor* too if he thought he could get me to sell this property."

"You're really making the rounds today, aren't you? But don't worry about Devon. It's just more of his BS. He can't do anything to you. It's ME you have to worry about! You actually told Stan Jones I admired his body?"

I snorted, enjoying her shock. "I may have said you're warm for his form. I don't know. He really is a looker, Libby. He's coming to my party because I told him you'll be here."

"*A party?* I can't believe you! You're so lucky I'm not there because if I were, I'd—"

"Relax! I didn't say warm for his form. But he *does* think he has a chance now with the ice queen. But I wasn't kidding about a party. Maybe in a couple of weeks." Then another idea hit me. "A Halloween costume party! You can be Nurse Goodbody and he's the hunky fireman."

"Well, you don't even have to *dress up*! You already are a witch!" She was silent for a beat or two. "But it could be fun, I suppose."

"Totally a blast! I even asked my new friend Ida-Red-Car! It turns out my wish for her car to ignite into flames was doing her a huge favor. The well told me it was my freebie wish.

Things aren't going to go so well with Ass-hat's though."

"Wait a minute. You went to the *well* again? Did it speak to you?"

"Yeah and it was more chatty today. Instead of just thanking me for my offering, it told me this other stuff. It turns out, it's Alice's spirit in that well. She even mentioned the Grimoire."

"Oh my God. I can't leave you alone for any length of time before you get into this even deeper. You need to take me to this well. I also want to see this book you found."

For a few minutes I deliberated whether to do what she wanted. But something about the well held me back. It just didn't seem right. "I'll let you see the book for sure! It's filled with calligraphy or something and impossible to read. There are some seriously naughty sketches in it you might like."

"Then I definitely have to see it. What are you doing tomorrow? I don't work until eight in the evening. I could pop by early afternoon."

Immediately, my hormones kicked into gear thinking that Steve might show up tomorrow. "Can I let you know around noon if that works for me?"

"Why? What are you doing? I thought you'd be busy tearing up the kitchen floor or painting."

I rolled my eyes before fessing up, "Steve might stop by with some firewood. He also wants to check my chimney."

"So? I don't mind if Steve is there. I like Steve. We can do our thing while he does his." She sounded totally surprised that this was a consideration.

"That's just it! *His* thing might include *my* thing. He stopped by to tell me about MJ, and well...we kind of patched things up between us." Kind of? If not for his son being at his house we'd probably have ended up in my bed!

"Oh. OH! *Now* I see." She started humming the tune to an old song, "Afternoon Delight."

"Okay! Okay! We're even with the Stan thing! Don't push it, or I will tell him you're not only warm for his form but you're smokin' hot for it. I'll call you around noon to let you know about tomorrow. I want to show you the book so you can help me figure this out."

"No problem. But at some time in the future, you have *got* to take me to that well, Shannon." She then changed the subject. "What about your aunt? Has she showed up lately?"

"A few times. She also made sure I saw the book. But when she's here, she speaks in riddles. I wish she'd leave Post-it Notes telling me what I should do." As soon as the words were out of my mouth I realized what I'd said—*I wish.*

Oh shit.

TWENTY ONE

The next morning, I made great headway with the painting in the kitchen, getting all of the walls done in a butter-yellow shade. As I cleaned the roller and brush, I looked at the clock on the stove. It was almost noon and I hadn't heard anything from Steve. Oh well, if he hadn't called by now, any "delivery" he wanted to make that week would have to be another day. After all, he did have a son to look after. I picked up my phone to text Libby.

My forehead tightened, seeing a new text message from an unknown caller. When I opened it, my head dropped forward as I gaped at the message.

> This "texting" thing is new to me but since you "wished" for more clarification, here goes. You must guard your thoughts and be especially vigilant with your spoken words. This is true for anyone, of course. Thoughts send out a signal to the universe, calling on forces which influence outcomes. The spoken word amplifies this by an order of magnitude that is a hundred times more powerful. That's even for so-called normal people.

For you, having made your offering to the Witching Well, this is a thousand times more powerful. Choose wisely because once the forces are unleashed, they cannot be stopped. Another side effect is that until you "know" what you are doing and can control this, unforeseen consequences will happen. The universe seeks balance in all things and your wishes upsets that equilibrium.

Study the phases of the moon. Go outside and meditate to discover how it affects your soul—your moods, energy, and body. Use that knowledge to help yourself and others. (Baby steps!)

Be aware of the mystical power of the triumvirate. Look for patterns in nature as well as within yourself. As your awareness increases, so will your power and control.

I am always here watching over you but this afterlife stuff is still new to me. I know that I passed on some time ago, but time works differently for me here. It feels like it was just yesterday you were visiting me as a child, and yet now look at you!

I don't want to get into too much mumbo jumbo. I'm just trying to say we're both still learning, Shannon. When I appear or physically influence objects, I am left drained, like an old battery. But using this text communication isn't so hard, although I can't figure out how to make your phone ding when I write.
Love,
Aunt Maeve

OMG! I collapsed into the chair at the table. I looked

around the kitchen, totally gobsmacked that she'd left this message. "Thanks, Aunt Maeve! You have no idea how badly I needed to hear from you." I hit my head with the heel of my hand. "Duh! You totally know."

I was beginning to see the light at the end of the tunnel. I could master this magic stuff with her guidance. I sat quietly for a few moments, thanking her and the universe that I'd come back to live there. Things were going to work out.

My phone buzzed and I grabbed it from the table, hoping it was her again. But it was Libby.

> Is it still okay to visit today? I don't want to interrupt your sexcapade with Steve but I WILL demand every lurid detail later.

My fingers practically flew, typing a response! I'd be able to show her evidence that my aunt was still around!

> The coast is clear. No deliveries today. I can't wait to show you the latest! Hurry!

After I hit send, it occurred to me that when Steve showed up this week, Aunt Maeve would be in the building. I rubbed the back of my neck trying to sort out how I felt about that. Much as I liked the comfort of her being in the house, I'd have to establish some boundaries, if that were possible. Her words in the message reverberated in my head, and I realized that perhaps just thinking it would be enough. This magic shit took a lot of getting used to.

I was about to get up to make something for lunch when a sound outside caught my attention. The slamming of a car door followed. It couldn't be Libby! Not that quickly.

When I looked out the kitchen window I saw a blue Suburban parked in my driveway and a guy in a dark-green uniform step out of it. I went to the door and stood on the verandah watching. The guy practically waddled over, his arms swaying out at the sides while his beach-ball belly led the way. When he noticed me standing there, he tipped his fedora-type hat at me and nodded.

"Shannon Burke?"

Alarm bells screamed in my gut, but I managed to keep my voice level. "Yes. What can I do for you?" The fact that his face was stone cold with eyes that didn't quite meet my gaze was another sign I didn't care for.

"I'm Wilfred Smith with the municipal office. I've had a complaint that your septic system is not functioning according to environmental standards. This is a pristine area, ma'am, and we need to ensure that our waterways aren't being contaminated. I'm here to take a sample from the lake to test it." He stopped at the foot of the stairs.

My teeth clenched together before I let out a fast sigh. "I'm pretty sure I know who made that complaint, Mr. Smith. It's the same guy who wants to buy my property and ruin this lake by putting in a subdivision. Now, THAT would wreck this pristine area. He and his lackey looked at a problem I was having—which has been FIXED—and made it sound like a catastrophe." That bastard Devon sure didn't waste any time in setting the authorities on me!

He looked around at the house and trees surrounding it. "I don't know who lodged the complaint, ma'am. But I'll just take a sample, and we'll take it from there, shall we?"

"Knock yourself out!" But how did I know that this guy, like Eric, wasn't in Devon's back pocket. "Wait! I'll grab my jacket and go with you. Hang on." I practically ran into the house to get my coat. When I returned, Wilfred was getting a small case from his vehicle.

As I walked with him along the side of the house, heading for the shoreline, I decided it might be a good idea to get on his good side. My aunt had always said you catch more flies with honey than vinegar. "There was a problem with roots from these trees sneaking their way into my septic lines. That's fixed, but just to be on the safe side, the tank's getting pumped on Friday. There's no way I'd ever want to pollute this lake. I love it here!" Well, not like one developer whose name I wouldn't bother mentioning.

"Ayup." He seemed out of breath from the short walk to the shoreline. When he bent and took a small bottle from his case, his face was a florid, rusty shade. If MJ thought she was in bad shape, she was an Olympic athlete compared to old Wilfred.

"How long until you get the results? Not that I'm worried, but it would be nice to have it confirmed." I watched him screw the top back on the plastic vial and then look up at me.

"Oh, I'll be out a few more times over the next few weeks to ensure the validity of the tests. We take this very seriously, Ms. Burke."

"Hello? Shannon?"

I turned at the sound of Libby's voice. I felt the knot in my stomach begin to loosen, hearing a friendly voice. I definitely didn't appreciate Wilfred's last question. Did he think I was some outsider trying to pull the wool over a local's eyes?

"Out here, Libby!" When she appeared at the side of the house, I breathed easier. In her jeans and suede jacket with her blonde hair flowing loose over her shoulders, she was a sight for sore eyes. I turned to Wilfred. "That's my friend Libby Walker. Do you know her? She's a nurse at the hospital in town."

He lumbered to his feet, and a smile lifted his heavy jowls when he saw Libby. "There's the gal who fixed up my grandson's broken arm. How are you, Mrs. Walker?"

Yay! This was good timing indeed! I thrust my hands in my pockets, watching her and Wilfred exchange pleasantries.

"I'm doing fine. How is James? Don't get me wrong, but I'm glad I haven't seen him this summer." She stepped over to join us, smiling at Wilfred.

"That rascal! He's always getting scraped and bumped but nothing that needs your attention, thank goodness." He turned to me, and his smile faded, all business again. "I'll be out a few more times as I said." He handed me a business card and then nodded before stepping away. "Have a good day, ladies!"

When he was out of earshot, Libby plucked at the sleeve of my jacket. "What was all that about?"

My jaw clenched. "More of Devon's tricks. He filed a complaint with the municipal offices about my septic system.

Wilfred had to test the lake water. He's coming back a few more times for good measure." I led the way back to the other side of the house. "What a pain. I know it's fine. Steve's guy fixed the problem."

"Ha! Wilfred is Devon's cousin. We probably should do our own tests to be on the safe side. His grandson James is a total brat, and I wouldn't put anything past Wilfred Smith either. I can get you some sample kits for the water. You should tell your plumber, Mike, about this."

She looked over at me and brightened. "So what's the big thing you wanted to show me?"

I grabbed her arm and pulled her along, walking faster to the verandah. "Aunt Maeve! She sent me a text! Apparently it takes a lot of energy to materialize, so she's sending text messages to help me! Isn't that great?"

Libby scoffed, "As I recall, she hated talking on the telephone but now that she's dead, she's sending texts? Are you sure? Maybe it's a prank from Devon or something. He might be trying to drive you insane to get this property."

"No. It's *her*! Devon couldn't know the things she wrote about anyway. I never mentioned a word about this to anyone but you." I held the door open and gestured for her to go in ahead of me.

When she reached the kitchen, her head popped back. "Wow! Amazing what a fresh coat of paint will do!"

I grabbed the phone and pulled up the message, thrusting it before her face. "See? Read that, Miss Skeptic."

As she read, her eyes got bigger and her jaw fell open. "Wow! This ties in with everything else! But how are you going to guard your mouth, let alone your thoughts? I'd have a hard time doing that and I'm more laid back than you."

"I know. But I have to try...at least until I get better at all this. Look what I did to MJ." I didn't add that my thoughts might also have led to Steve and I burying the hatchet. "Let me show you the Grimoire." I dashed into the living room where I'd left it.

When I returned, she was pouring cups of coffee for us.

"Look, I'll get the coffee. You sit and tell me what you think. Can you make out the writing?" I handed her the book, only noticing at the last moment that it was now locked again. What? I hadn't done that.

Her eyes met mine. "Do you have the key? Why'd you lock it when you're the only one here?"

"I didn't! Honest. I read it last night before I went up to bed. I left it unlocked." I looked around at the kitchen. Had my aunt done that? But why would she? "I'll get the key. I left it on the mantel above the fireplace, I think."

As I searched for it, Libby commented, "Maybe you're not supposed to show it to anyone? Why else would the thing now be locked when you left it open?"

I looked everywhere in the living room for the key, even thrusting my fingers down between the cushion and frame of the sofa. But nada. When I wandered back to join her in the kitchen, I shook my head. "Maybe. It's kind of like the feeling I got when you asked me to take you to the well. Don't take it personally but it doesn't 'feel' right. Not yet."

"Not yet? Okay, sometime in the future, then."

"That's it? Sometime in the future?" She stared at me blankly and I chuckled. "Yup. You really *are* a lot more laid back than me. If I were in your shoes, I'd be climbing the walls from curiosity!"

"Don't get me wrong! I'm curious as hell!" She shrugged. "But if it's not meant to be, it can wait, you know?"

I shook my head slowly. How two people as close as we were could be so different...

Her fingers threaded through her hair before becoming bunched fists. "God knows I could use some help dealing with Jack. The school called me yesterday. He's been skipping classes. I don't like the kids he's been hanging out with since he went back. They're older and kind of skeevy, a bad influence on him."

As I peered at her, I felt my forehead tighten. "That's funny. Mary-Jane said the same thing about her daughter, Zoe. Although she said the kids she was hanging out with were the rich ones who live on the outskirts of town."

She snorted. "Those two! They're birds of a feather. And yeah, it's the same crew that Jack's taken up with. I swear he'll be the death of me. Kevin is threatening to lay a beating on Jack if he doesn't smarten up. But that's not his place. He's his older brother, not the little devil's father." She took the coffee I handed her. "Thanks. Maybe you could 'wish' that he cleans his act up?"

I shook my head. "Nope. It might have consequences which turn out even worse. I've got to be careful." Snickering, I added, "Not *wishing* for anything but just making an innocent comment... It would be nice if your household ran smoothly. How's that for a vanilla thought?"

She crossed her fingers and grinned. "Now tell me about this party you're planning? What made you decide to do that? You've still got lots to do around here, Shannon, before the end of October." She looked down at the floor and scuffed her toe on the linoleum. "I'll help you lift this and get it out of here, once I'm finished with this coffee."

"Thanks." My stomach rumbled, reminding me that I hadn't eaten anything since a fruit yogurt that morning. As I set about making a couple of sandwiches, I answered her other question. "I don't know why I thought about throwing a party. I guess being back here and remembering all the times we got together as a gang, it just popped into my head. And seeing Stan Jones...well, it wouldn't hurt for you to hang with him a bit, even if it's just a silly, flirty thing." I grinned at her. "You don't have to be *so* laid back all the time, y'know."

"Says the woman who would have canceled getting together if it meant she'd get it on with Steve Murphy. Not that I blame you." She cupped the mug with two hands, musing as she gazed at it. "There are times that I miss it. Of course, not a day goes by that I don't miss Hank, but that..." She snorted. "It's been so long that if I ever have sex again, it would be like I was a virgin...*again*."

"Should I mention that to Stan? I'm pretty sure that would be a plus." I winked at her and brought the plate of sandwiches to the table, dodging the balled-up napkin she threw at me.

"Don't you dare! I swear I would strangle you if I didn't love you. Count yourself lucky, Shannon." She shook her head and then her voice became softer. "Seriously, the thought of being with a guy scares me. I've only ever been with Hank."

"I think it's kind of like riding a bike, Libby. There's muscle memory if nothing else." I couldn't help chuckling at that. Muscle memory. Sometimes I cracked myself up.

"It's not *that*, Shannon!" Her cheeks became pinker, and she looked away before she spoke, "Have you ever looked at porn these days?" When my head dropped forward staring at her, she quickly added, "Not that I go out of my way to watch it but I found Jack's phone."

She looked away before continuing. "When I picked it up, the screen came to life and...well...apparently it's a big thing now to not only do the bikini wax but to go completely bare. Is that what's expected these days?"

For a few moments I could only stare at her. Was I really having this conversation?

"I guess. It's not something I really thought about before. Maybe I'm lucky that my son hid his skin flicks better than yours? Totally bare, huh? I'm not sure how much of a fan I'd be about that. Wouldn't it be itchy, you know, when...?"

Her eyes flashed wider. "See! That's what I mean! Things have certainly changed from when we were in our prime!"

My chin rose. "Speak for yourself, Libby! I'm still in my prime! Okay, maybe a few days past my best-before date, but still prime for serving."

I smiled as my finger toyed with the lonely hair that had sprouted on my chin last year. As many times as I'd plucked the damned thing, it was like the proverbial Phoenix, rising again. "I'd be okay with getting *this* blasted hair removed for good! Forget about everything else."

"I hear you." She turned her head, rubbing a spot on her jawline. "I've got one too. The bane of being in our forties. Can you imagine what it's going to be like when we hit sixty?"

Laughing, I plucked at that pesky hair. "I'm going to get

this witchy wishing magic down pat, and I'll take care of all that for both of us!" I got up and took the empty dish over to the sink. "Now let's forget ripping our old-lady hairs out and settle for ripping up that floor."

TWENTY TWO

When Libby left and I flopped down on the sofa, I texted my daughter since I hadn't heard from her for a couple of days.

> How is school going? I've been busy with the renovations here. The kitchen is coming along great!

I set the phone aside and gazed out at the lake. The setting sun cast ribbons of pink and orange across the surface, which was smooth as glass. It was peaceful just sitting there enjoying some rest after working hard all afternoon. But it was worth it! The floorboards under the linoleum we'd torn up were hardwood that just needed a sanding and a coat of polyurethane to make them like new.

The phone dinged with a text, and I picked the phone up once more.

> I am swamped with papers and labs! High school never prepared me for the mountain of work in college. But I've made some friends and I'm managing to stay sane. Dad called me. He's visiting this weekend and we're spending the day together on Saturday.

I could feel my blood pressure rise as I read the message. On the one hand, it was good that Ass-hat was making an effort to see Jess, but on the other hand, I had to wonder why *now* after he'd been a virtual stranger for months.

And then it hit me. The curse I'd put on him and his sleazy girlfriend! I'd bet a million dollars his reaching out to the kids was connected to what I wished on him. Him and his hussy were having problems. I'd bet my life on it.

> Your father is coming to visit you? Not his girlfriend's daughter? Will he be alone? I hope this visit is just with you and him.

I rolled my eyes. I was fishing, but at this point I didn't care. He'd better not be setting Jess up and then leaving her high and dry like he'd done when he'd left me. It was soooooo hard to control my thoughts from piling more curses on his selfish little head. But there was no way I wanted to compound the trouble that might ensue.

> It's just him. I got the feeling when I talked to him that things aren't going as well as he'd planned with his lady friend. But I'll know better after this weekend. I'll let you know. In the meantime, I'm looking forward to the break at Thanksgiving and seeing you. Don't work too hard, Mom. Love you!

With a sigh, I signed off:

> Love you, too! Talk to you later.

I sent a text to my son, but it was just about touching base, finding out about how he was making out at school. When my stomach rumbled, I got up to fix some dinner for myself.

***

As I worked in the kitchen, I ruminated on the things which Aunt Maeve had written in her text to me. I glanced at the calendar on my phone to check what phase the moon was in. A new moon. There wouldn't be too much to see if I went outside later, but now was as good a time to start "noticing" things as any other.

With my dinner of a frozen pot pie heating in the oven, I sat down at the table. The Grimoire was closed, but the latch on the lock clicked open when I picked it up. No key even necessary this time—big surprise! I grabbed a pen and turned to a fresh blank sheet near the end of the book, writing my entry, starting with today's date.

On an impulse I doodled a small crescent-shaped moon and labeled it "New." But what to write after this? I kept drawing, creating a sketch of the well and the clearing in the forest. It was now my book, so really I could write anything I wanted. My hand seemed to have a mind of its own, filling the border of the page with flowers and vines. I would have to pick up some colored pens to flesh out my sketches.

I took a deep breath and started writing:

> *This will be my first night of going outside to sit moon gazing.*

I snickered, thinking of an old rerun of the *Addams Family*. Didn't Gomez and Morticia do that? Moon bathe?

Giving my head a shake, I tried to get my brain back to what I was doing. Aunt Maeve had advised that I take note of my mood and even physical feelings in this journey with magic. Even though I wasn't entirely sure of what I was doing, I made another entry in the book.

> *As I sit here, I'm concerned for both my children, but more especially my daughter as she is more sensitive than Thomas. But I have to trust that they will both be okay. I'm tired from all the physical work I accomplished today but also feeling deep satisfaction. The kitchen is going to be beautiful, but not only that, I had fun working alongside one of my best friends, Libby.*

I paused, rereading what I'd written. Basically everything boiled down to family and friends. That was the important lesson to be gleaned from what I'd written. Another thought popped into my head. The power of three. Aunt Maeve had said to notice and use it. Well, there were now only three people in my family. My two children and myself. My two best friends and myself were also a triumvirate. She had said there was power in the triumvirate.

My cell phone dinged with a text message, and I scooped it up, hoping for something else from my aunt. But my jaw clenched tight, seeing Devon's name. I should delete and block him from ever contacting me! But I couldn't resist seeing what that sleazeball had to say.

> I'm extending an olive branch to you, Shannon. I don't want there to be anger between us. We both know that you've bitten off more than you can chew with that house. I am willing to reinstate my original offer for your property, even though I suspect the county Health Department will condemn it.

I deliberated for all of sixty seconds before I sent back my reply.

> And I suspect that the water test your cousin did today is fine. Your latest trick isn't panning out. But just in case, I will be doing my own water test, with witnesses. Go find someone else to harass, Devon. It's not working with me.

There! I smiled. I'd gotten my message across, and I hadn't cursed him or lost my temper at all. There was hope for me in learning to control my thoughts as well as my mouth, contrary to what Libby said.

When the phone dinged again, I was tempted to turn it off. I had no wish to spoil my evening parrying with messages to Devon. But a glance at the screen shattered all the self-control I'd prided myself on.

I read the screen. "Alex Johnston."

Oh damn.

What did Ass-hat want?

TWENTY THREE

I gripped the cell phone so hard, my knuckles were ivory.

> I hope you are doing well, Shannon. That isn't a useless platitude but rather a heartfelt wish for you to be okay. Honest.The kids tell me you are working hard to fix up your aunt's old place. I'm sorry that you felt the need to leave Pittsburgh and all of our friends there.
>
> I would like us to be civil with each other, if not friends. We owe that much to our children. I was going to spend a week with Thomas over Thanksgiving but I understand you would like to have the two of them there with you. To show you that I'm sorry that I hurt you (and them!) I'll bring Thomas and Jess to your home to spend the weekend. I'll pick them up at the airport in Albany.

My mouth fell open and I reread his message. What the hell was he up to? There had to be real problems in his new home for him to make this offer! The thought of seeing him again made my blood boil! How dare he deceive me after so many years of marriage and then think a trite text message would smooth things over. Was I supposed to be grateful that he would ensure that the kids spent Thanksgiving with me?

I closed my eyes and counted to ten, willing the blood which pounded in my ears to slow down. I needed to calm down or I'd completely lose it. I was at eight when the oven timer went off to let me know my dinner was done. I set the phone aside and got up.

There was no rule that said I had to answer his text this very minute! If I chose to answer him next month, then that was what I'd do! To hell with him.

After dishing out a plate and settling myself at the table, I propped up the Grimoire before me. I'd have another look where my aunt had left off to see if there was anything else to guide me in this magical stuff. But try as I might to concentrate, the text from Ass-hat kept creeping into my head.

What was he up to? I would never be friends with him again, but could I manage to be civil if we were ever in the same room? It was bound to happen. With both kids going to graduate college in a few years, maybe get married and have their own children, it was inevitable that we'd be thrust into the same events.

I finished about half of my dinner before getting up and tossing it in the garbage. Between Devon's text followed immediately by Ass-hat's, I was lucky to manage eating anything at all. After I'd tidied up the kitchen, I grabbed my jacket and went outside.

My gaze turned up to the sky as I walked down to the lake. Above me, the dark sky was a kaleidoscope of thousands of tiny stars, but, of course, the moon was nowhere to be seen. When I reached the shoreline, I sank down onto the grass, looking at the sky.

A new moon. The beginning of a new lunar cycle. It was time to move on from the hurt and grievances to embrace new possibilities. Owning this house, creating a life for myself on my terms were things new to me. Finding a magical wishing well and learning how to use the new power I'd been granted was also new, if not completely crazy.

A breeze whispered through the trees at the edge of the lawn, the only sound in the utter silence of the night. As I sat there feeling the earth under me, seeing the water of the lake still as glass, and the showcase of stars above, a feeling of peace settled deep into my core. Along with that peace was a confidence in my own strength and power. I couldn't help thinking that I was at exactly the perfect place at the perfect time. I'd never thought much about destiny, but now the word seemed to encompass where I was in that moment.

I don't know how long I sat there just being at one with the earth and sky. It was only when the dampness grew chilly that I rose to go back inside. When I turned to face the living room, my eyes opened wider. My aunt stood watching me, framed in the large picture window. Even though I couldn't see the details of her face, I knew she was pleased to see me out there. And the funny thing was, so was I.

Whatever fulfillment was in the new moon was now flowing through me. As invisible as the sun's rays were making the grass and trees grow, the strength of the earth and sky infused my soul. Her words in the text message became clear as I stood there gazing at her apparition. This was the essence of white magic. I could practically hear her telling me that.

Things would work out with the house, with my family, and with my friends. When I went inside and locked up for the night, that same sense of peace and harmony made my footsteps lighter as I headed off to bed.

For the first time in many months, my sleep was totally sound and dreamless.

TWENTY FOUR

Two days later

I had just finished putting a second coat of paint on the kitchen cabinets when I heard the crunch of tires slicing through the gravel in my driveway. My heart leapt into my throat before I scrambled across the room to look out the window. Was it Steve, delivering the lumber and a whole lot more? Frankly, I was surprised and a little disappointed that he hadn't been there the day before.

But the guy getting out the passenger door of the small blue car was definitely not Steve. A lock of rust-colored hair had fallen over a broad forehead, and his close-set brown eyes below looked a bit familiar. The leather jacket he wore strained against a stomach that had consumed more beer than salad, but even so, he walked quickly, crossing the drive and then bouncing up the few steps of the verandah.

When I opened the door, it hit me. Roy! There was no mistaking the lopsided set of his mouth. For a moment, words failed me. Would he take a strip off me for letting Mary-Jane run into town from my place?

But then he smiled. "Shannon? Good Lord, it's been years and you still look the same."

I noticed that he held a set of car keys, twirling the ring over his finger. He gave a wave of thanks to the car that dropped him off and it left. He was here to pick up her car, of course. I gave him a quick hug. "Roy. How are you? Actually, how is Mary-Jane?"

"She's doing great! I just dropped her off at home and caught a ride out to get her car. Even though I don't think she should push her recovery, she insisted I get it home." He shook his head. "She gave Zoe and me quite a scare. Zoe is taking a few days off school to look after her while I look after the restaurant."

I could hardly believe that this was the same guy who had teased Mary-Jane to the point that she'd escaped to my house, bitching about him. "It sounds like Mary-Jane is getting round-the-clock care. I need to pop by to see her." Okay, I'll admit it; I've been putting off visiting because it was my fault she was laid up in the first place.

"She'd like that, for sure." He looked off to the side for a moment, shaking his head. "She's spending all her days on the couch, but she's no couch potato, that's for sure."

"Oh?" I was pretty sure I knew what he meant.

"Oh yeah! Even though she's stretched out on the couch, she keeps trying to do exercises! She does sit-ups like you wouldn't believe, and is bitching that she can't go out for a run!" His eyes widened. "She'd never gone running in her life, and now she's like an addict in withdrawal! And she'll only eat the tiniest portions of food that's not a vegetable. She used to be *addicted* to Oreos and milk and now says the thought of them turns her stomach." His voice was filled with wonder.

My mouth became dry as dust as he spoke. This was because of me! Because of my spell!

He continued talking. "When I left, she was doing arm curls with a couple of soup cans. I have to stop at the gym and see if I can buy her some proper weights." He turned, about to go back down the steps, but then he paused. "It's funny. When she hurt herself, it made us realize how important Mary-Jane is in our lives. I don't know what I'd do without her."

I nodded. "I'm glad that things worked out for her, with the accident and all. It had to be a real shock for you and Zoe." It might have been pushing it but I had to know. "She told you what her doctor said about her health, right? That's what prompted all this."

He nodded. "Yeah. When her knee's better, I'm going to support her any way I can." He rubbed his hand over his beach-ball belly. "I might even join the gym with her. We could both stand to lose a few pounds." He turned and called over his shoulder, "I'll tell her you'll be in to see her. Why don't you give her a call and set something up? She'd love to hear from you. See you later, Shannon."

"Take care, Roy." I let out a long sigh, watching him get into Mary-Jane's car and back out of the driveway. That was another bullet that I'd dodged with this magic thing. Maybe the reason this had kind of a happy ending was because my intentions in wishing Mary-Jane's success were totally pure?

Even though she'd hurt herself, her family had been jolted into a new appreciation of her. That part was good!

When I went inside, I sat down to record this experience with Mary-Jane in the Grimoire. I'd wished for good for my friend and after the detour of her hurting herself, it had worked out.

The path of this magic was anything but linear. You send a wish out there, and it reverberates with unforeseen consequences. With practice, as I gained experience, maybe the unexpected, negative side-effect could be controlled if not eliminated entirely.

I was so engrossed in the journal, and trying to make sense of what had happened, that I didn't even hear the truck pull into my driveway until the bang of the vehicle's door shutting caught my attention. A glance out the window showed Steve rounding the vehicle and lowering the tailgate.

My hand flew to remove the painting bandanna from my head and let my hair down. I stopped at the mirror in the hallway to check that there weren't blobs of paint on my face or that I didn't look like a raccoon with smudged mascara under my eyes. All the while, my insides were doing flip-flops, remembering our last kiss and flirty exchange.

I called to him as I walked over to his truck, "Hey, stranger! I was wondering if you'd make it out this week. I just finished my painting so your timing is pretty good."

"Hey, Shannon! Believe me, I wanted to pop out here yesterday but I couldn't get away. My employee had a dental appointment in the afternoon, and there was no one to mind the store." He smiled and pulled me into a bear hug. "But I'm here now." He kissed my neck, sending a fresh set of shivers up my spine. "I couldn't stop thinking about you."

My fingers threaded through his hair, letting my head fall to the side, abandoning myself to his caresses. "It was a long few days for me as well." I snuggled in closer so our bodies pressed together even more. "We can unload the truck later, if you'd like." From the physical state of both of us, neither one of us wanted to wait a minute longer.

"Oh, yeah. A woman after my own heart." His arm still held me close as we walked across the yard to the verandah. Laughing, he added softly, "This brings back memories of my teenage years. It felt like I was a constant walking hormone back then." He kissed my ear and whispered, "You have no idea how many times I've dreamed about this with you."

It felt like every cell in my body was vibrating with pent-up energy. This was a sensation that felt brand new to me, all over again. To be with a guy as nice as Steve was, not to mention drop-dead gorgeous. "Oh, I think I've got a pretty good idea about those dreams. Had more than a few myself, y'know."

He pulled the door open and held it for me, meeting my gaze with blatant longing that made my knees weak. As I stepped by him, a car horn sounded. My stomach dropped through the floor. If it was that guy showing up to take another water sample, I was going to drown him!

When I spun around, my forehead furrowed trying to recognize the dark-blue car that was driving up to my house.

When the car door opened and a lanky teenager stepped out, Steve murmured, "That's Kevin Walker, Libby's kid. What's he doing here?"

Great. If it's not one thing, it's another...Argh! "I think he's here to cut my grass."

Kevin waved. "Hi, Shannon! Hey, Steve. Sorry I didn't call,

but I just finished cutting Mrs. Phelps's yard. It's such a nice day, and I had an hour to spare so I thought I'd pop over."

Forcing a smile, I walked down the steps over to where he was now getting his lawn mower from the trunk of the car. "Hi, Kevin. That's awesome." It was hard to keep my voice even after the rush of lust that had coursed through my body. "Thanks!"

Steve came up behind me and stood with his hands in the back pockets of his jeans. "Hey, Kevin. I was just dropping off some firewood and supplies to Shannon." He looked over at me and smirked. "This is quite a busy little spot today."

My eyebrows rose and I blew out a long breath. "Yeah. Do you need my help with that lumber?" Turning to Kevin, I smiled. "This is really nice of you, Kevin. I'll pay you, of course. Do you have everything you need to do the yard?"

He set the lawn mower on the ground. "I brought the weed whacker to finish the trimming. I think I've got this covered." He started pushing the mower to the grass bordering the driveway.

"Great!"

Steve pinched my waist, making me jump to the side. His voice was just above a whisper as he leaned closer. "You're getting your lawn trimmed and even getting your weeds whacked! Aren't you the lucky gal!"

I glared at him before letting out a laugh. "Shut up! It's bad timing, but he means well." As we walked to the back of his truck, I looked up at him and winked. "Maybe it won't take him long to get the grass cut. How long can you stay?"

He started stacking a bunch of firelogs in his arms. "I have to be home by four. My kid's out of school then, and I like to spend an hour or so with him before his mother picks him up. Why don't you come for dinner at six? We could pick up where we left off."

"Sure, or you could come here. I haven't cooked a decent meal since I moved in. I've been so busy being a home handywoman that I'd like to fuss with making something special." The funny thing was that I really didn't want to leave, even though Steve's house was perfectly fine. "Plus, you said you would check my chimney so we could snuggle next to the fireplace."

I started grabbing firewood and grinned at him. "I guess you're really going to have to check my chimney, huh?"

When the lawnmower became a noisy drone, he raised his voice, "Just as soon as I stack this lumber, Ms. Burke. I think there's a ladder kicking around here. We'll get your fire going before the night is over."

My cheeks flushed, and after a quick glance to see that Kevin wasn't paying attention, I leaned into Steve. My lips brushed against the fold of his ear when I answered, "That fire will be an inferno if I have anything to say about it."

He pulled back, and his eyes met mine in a slow, smoldering look. "I'll hold you to that, Shannon."

***

It was pushing six that evening when I finished showering and getting dressed. I'd chosen a pale-pink wrap dress that was comfortable yet showed a little cleavage and thigh. With my dark hair falling over my shoulders and with my tanned complexion, it was really flattering, if I did say so myself.

The roast beef was done and resting on the counter as I put the Yorkshire pudding in the oven on a high heat setting. Everything was pretty well ready, the table set with candles and some colored maple leaves as a centerpiece. When I heard the tap on the door, I yelled for Steve to come in.

When I turned from the stove, my mouth fell open. It wasn't Steve standing in the doorway of the kitchen: it was Devon.

"Something smells pretty good." He did an obvious once-over with his gaze taking me in—from my heels right up to my face—while a small smile played on his lips. "Wow! You look lovely, Shannon."

My eyes narrowed. "What are you doing here? I've said everything I had to say to you in my text message. You aren't getting this place no matter what tricks you try." I tossed the oven mitts on the counter and took a step closer to him, leading with my upturned chin.

He held his hands up, palms facing me. "I came to apologize, Shannon. I actually didn't set that thing up with Eric—the problems with your septic. He made a mistake and I trusted him. I'm sorry." He looked down for a moment, lowering his hands. "As far as your water test; I checked with the office who did it. You're good. No septic issues leaching into the lake. I wanted to deliver that news personally. Along with my apology. I'd like to be friends, Shannon."

I stared at him silently for a few beats. He actually looked sincere, although I still didn't trust him. "Okay. You've said your piece so you can leave now. I'm expecting company any minute now." Knowing how much Steve disliked him, the last thing I needed to start a romantic dinner was Devon still there in my kitchen. He might be trying to make amends, but his timing was terrible.

"Yeah. Sorry. I'll get going. I left a bottle of wine in the hallway. I hope you and your company enjoy it." He started to turn but then stopped when Steve burst into the house.

"What are you doing here, Booker? Haven't you done enough damage trying to trick Shannon into selling?" Steve kept walking over to Devon until he was only inches from his face. The two of them were almost the same height, glaring at each other.

"He's just leaving, Steve. He came to apologize and tell me the water test came back okay." But it was clear that my words fell on deaf ears when Devon spoke.

Devon crossed his arms, his eyes flitting between the two of us. "So, it sure didn't take you long to make your move on Shannon, Steve. Of course it wouldn't. Even if she wasn't gorgeous, she's a woman. God knows you've slept with every single female in town and even some of the married ones." Devon let out a snide chuckle. "The only one who resisted your bedside manner was your *wife.*"

Steve's hands shot out, bunching the lapels of Devon's leather jacket. "Shut your trap, Booker!" He yanked back, almost causing Devon to lose his footing when he was pulled through the doorway.

"Get your hands off me, Murphy!" Devon's arms arced up and broke Steve's grip. "Don't worry, I'm leaving." He looked over at me. "I'd be careful having anything to do with this jerk, Shannon. I seriously think you can do better than this phony."

Steve made a rush at him, but Devon was quick as a cat dodging out the door. "If anyone's a phony, it's *you*, Booker! Get the hell out of here!"

My eyes were wide as dinner plates watching the two of them. When Steve turned and walked back into the kitchen, his face was flushed and a vein pulsed in his temple. He straightened the collar of his shirt and flexed his head to the side, before meeting my gaze.

"That guy! Nothing is below him. I swear. The nerve of him showing up here after what he did to you." He slipped his jacket off and tossed it on the back of a chair before stepping closer. "Sorry about the rough stuff but he had it coming, Shannon."

When his hands rose to rest on my shoulders, I flinched. Devon's words about Steve being the town stud kept pinging in my head. I looked up at him. "What the hell was he talking about with you being with every woman around here? I knew you dated a lot after your wife left, but 'married' women?"

Married women had hit a nerve. On the one hand, it really shouldn't matter as I wasn't interested in any kind of serious relationship at that point, but tomcatting with married women made my blood boil. That was too close to what I'd just been through with Ass-hat. I caught the eye roll before he answered.

"I *told* you about that. After Amy left me to be with Suzanne, it shook my confidence. I mean, as stupid as it sounds, I couldn't help but wonder if I had driven her to becoming a lesbian. I reacted badly. Yeah, I became a tomcat on the prowl, but honestly, no married women. What set Devon off was that I dated a woman he was hot after."

I nodded as I searched his face for evidence that he was lying. At this point, I could only go by what my friends had said about Steve and also about Devon. Libby and Mary-Jane both disliked Devon. But aside from the two of them stating the obvious that Steve was hot as hell, they hadn't said much about him bedding every woman in town. Was it as simple as what Steve had said?

"So who was this woman that Devon had a thing for? Were they an item, or was it just that he was interested in asking her out? What happened?" The oven timer dinged, and I shifted out of his grip to take the Yorkshire out.

Steve opened the cabinet next to the stove and got a couple of glasses out. "Before I get into all this, I need a drink, Shannon. Can we just sit and talk for a while, so I can explain it?"

I took the Jack Daniels from another cabinet and poured two healthy doses. "Sure. Just don't complain when the Yorkshire puddings fall flat as pancakes." I led the way into the living room and took a seat on the sofa, waiting.

He plopped the half-empty bottle of whiskey on the coffee table before taking a seat next to me. "Her name was Cynthia Granger. She works at the town records office, so Devon knew her from his business dealings."

"So how did *you* know her? Is she still around?" I made a mental note to ask Libby and MJ about this Cynthia Granger.

He took a long swallow of his drink before he took my hand, looking into my eyes. "I met her at the Timber Wolf. It's a bar downtown that's best known as a hookup joint. Like I said, I was dating a LOT! *She* came onto *me* and that's how it started."

He was silent for a few beats before he smiled. "Devon didn't stand a snowball's chance in hell with her. She's a loner and definitely didn't want to get tied down to a guy with a kid. We had a blast for a few weeks, but she ended it before it got too serious. That's it. But Devon blamed me when she refused to go out with him."

"It sounds like he really liked her. Why wouldn't she go out with him, I wonder? He's successful and pretty good looking. I get it that she doesn't want to get serious, but why date you, and not him?" There had to be more to this than what he was saying. They were both not only good looking, but they were each successful.

He shook his head and shot me a foul look. "Maybe she doesn't like manipulators and crooks? I don't know. You'd have to ask her. I never discussed Devon with her, despite what he thinks. He just can't understand that not all people fall for his BS."

"So she's still living in Wesley? Do you ever see her?" I hated sounding like I was jealous, but it came out like that anyway. Damn! How did a simple romantic dinner get so complicated? The sexual sparks that had zipped between Steve and me had sure sizzled out.

"No! Well, I see her when she comes into the store and sometimes on the street but that's it. We're friends, but the 'friends with benefits' thing is long over." His finger trailed over my cheeks as his gaze met mine. "Like I said the other night when you were at my place, finding a woman to share a laugh and conversation with is more important to me than sleeping around. Plus, I've got Byron to think about."

The fact that he'd said this to me already, even before Devon's accusations, hit home. Devon was trying to make trouble once again. But he'd succeeded in slowing things down between Steve and me. I smiled at him. "Let's have another drink while I put the finishing touches on dinner. C'mon." I stood up and reached for his hand. "You can whip the potatoes while I make gravy. I'm getting hungry."

He rose, and his grip on my hand tightened, turning me to face him. There was a sheepish smile on his lips before he spoke, "I never got a chance to tell you how nice you look, Shannon."

I leaned in and gave him a quick kiss. "You just did. And thanks. You look pretty great yourself, even without the macho display of throwing Devon out on his ass."

He rolled his eyes and sighed. "I didn't plan that, believe me." He followed me into the kitchen, continuing, "I don't like that he feels he can just pop out here. I mean, you're here alone for the most part."

I looked back at him. "I can handle Devon. Don't worry about me. I don't expect him to try a trick like that again, but if he does, I'll be ready. I'm not exactly helpless, Steve." To say nothing about this newfound magic I'd stumbled into or the fact that my aunt was still hanging around watching over me.

"I know, but I can't help but worry. I'm not far away, and you can always count on me, if he does bother you again."

"I think he was being genuine when he apologized." I shrugged. "But you know what? Don't know and don't care. Let's talk about something else." I passed him the potato masher and pushed the pot closer to him. "What do you do for fun when you don't have Byron with you? Do you like to hike or go out on the lake fishing?"

He chuckled. "Fishing is more my dad's thing. I don't have the patience. He's taken Byron out a few times. I like to hike though, especially at this time of year when the fall colors are on display. How about you?"

As I stirred the broth for the gravy, I glanced over at him. Had he ever come across the Witching Well during one of his hikes? "I like to go for long walks in the forest too. We should go together some time. You must know every trail around here."

"Yup! I've trekked these woods countless times, in all seasons. I know these parts like the back of my hand. I've seen lots of animals, even a few bears."

"How about bobcats? I almost hit one when I first drove here and I saw one the other day. Actually the same one, I think. I always thought they were really shy around people."

He stopped still and looked over at me. "A bobcat?"

When I nodded, a dark look came over his face for a moment. "What's wrong?"

He gave his head a small shake. "Uh, nothing. I've just never seen one in these parts, I guess." He made a small shrug. "I think you should be careful around them; they can be pretty dangerous."

It wasn't the wildlife I was interested in. "Aside from

animals, what's the strangest thing you've come across out in the woods?" Without waiting for his reply, I added, "Something I find kind of weird is when you stumble across a grassy glade right in the densest part of the forest. I mean, it's kind of like a fairy ring or something where no saplings have taken root. That always surprises me when I find that."

"Around here? I've never come across anything like that. I'm usually battling the underbrush when I wander off the beaten path. As for weird things, nothing but abandoned deer stands, but that's not all that strange." He finished with the potatoes and took a long sip of his drink.

So even though he knew these woods like the back of his hand, he'd never come across the well. And Libby had no knowledge of it either. It was just Aunt Maeve and myself. It was kind of like we'd been chosen or something.

"Your Aunt Maeve…"

My head jerked up and I peered at Steve. It was almost as if he'd read my mind, thinking about my aunt.

"She was a nice woman, but a lot of people thought she was…*eccentric*. I mean, she never married, and she lived out here on her own, running this small resort. It's probably a lot more common for a woman to choose that lifestyle these days, but back then, she was a maverick."

"She did have some good friends though, even if she was kind of a loner." As soon as the words were out of my mouth—*loner*—I thought of the woman who Steve had dated and who Devon had been so hung up over. Cynthia. He'd said she was a loner too.

His eyebrows rose and he added quickly, "For sure she had friends! I remember Mabel Dwyer and Ruth Viner used to be here visiting sometimes in the summer. And there were a couple of men as well, although I don't know their names. I don't know if they were even from around here."

"Yeah, she went out on dates a few times over the course of the summer. They'd go out to dinner, as I recall. They never spent the night, at least not while I was here. It's funny, I kind of forgot about Mabel and Ruth until you mentioned them.

They can't still be alive?" I took down serving dishes and started filling them with vegetables and meat.

Steve made a move to help but I waved him off. He leaned against the counter, still cupping the glass of whiskey. "No, both Ruth and Mabel are long gone. They died before your aunt."

He paused for a few beats before adding, "It turned out good for you that she left you this property. Your ex still lives in Pittsburgh, right?"

It was my turn to do the eye roll. "Yeah, with his girlfriend. They'd been dating for a year before he left. Her daughter and mine go to the same college, if you can believe that." I handed him the platter of meat and then picked up the other dishes to take to the dining room.

"I can't believe he would ever leave you. What a jerk. But his mistake is my gain. If not for him, I'm not sure we would have ever seen each other again." He held my chair as I took my seat. He came around the table to his place setting, doing a fist pump. "I can hardly believe that I'm having dinner with Shannon Burke! Considering how much of a crush I had on you, this is a dream come true."

When he took a seat across from me, I smiled at him. "I never thought I'd be dating again, Steve. I feel kind of out of it, if you know what I mean. But it's more fun than scary."

He laughed, "It *should* be fun! I can't imagine you being nervous or scared around any guy. You were always so much fun to be with. I used to hate Ron Adams and Sean Webb. They were always flirting with you, and you never even noticed me."

Oh my God. It had been years since I'd thought of those two guys. They'd both joined our crowd the summer I turned sixteen. Their families had moved to Wesley that year. Ron had been a blond, blue-eyed hunk, while Sean had been shorter with a face that was so perfect he was almost pretty. "Whatever happened to them?"

"Sean moved away after high school, and Ron is married with three kids. He's the principal at the Catholic school."

Steve helped himself to a generous helping of beef and the Yorkshire pudding. "If this tastes as good as it looks, then I'll think I died and went to heaven."

"No guarantees on that since we got waylaid making dinner." I poured some wine that I'd left decanting on the table. "It's hard to believe so many years have passed since those summers. We didn't have a care in the world back then."

"Wrong! I was always worried you'd start dating those guys and I'd be totally cut off from seeing you. Looking back, I was kind of a stalker when it came to you. I guess it could have seemed creepy if not for the fact I was tagging along with my big brother."

"I'm not sure you ever got past stalking, Steve. I mean *twice* I came back from a hike in the woods and there you were, waiting for me here." I grinned to let him know I was kidding. "Should I be worried?"

"Yes. That's the scary part of dating me. Fun, but still a little frightening. You never know when I'll bust in and start a fight with someone or be roaming around your yard checking your septic system. You pays your money and you takes your chances." He smiled and took a long sip of the wine I'd poured.

"I'm not paying you anything. It's enough that I'm feeding you. You're pushing your luck here, fella." I chewed slowly, my eyes twinkling at him as I waited for his comeback.

"No, I'd say you owe *me*, Shannon. Don't get me wrong. Dinner's wonderful, but you promised me an evening of snuggling by the fire. It won't take me long to get that stoked up and burning." His eyes were hooded as he looked over at me, while a smile curled the edges of his lips.

"Stoked and burning? You ARE talking about the fireplace, right? You sound pretty confident that it'll catch right away." I couldn't resist adding, "But you've got a ton of practice, I suppose."

"That's the word on the street, even if that information is ancient history." He wiped his mouth and then set the napkin aside. "Seriously, if all we do this evening, is sit and chat or play gin rummy, I'm good. I'm stoked to be here with you."

I had to think about that for a few moments. Devon had soured the excitement, but it was still nice to be together. And the fact that Steve wasn't pushing for anything more scored points as well. I stood up. "If you get that fire going, I'll bring in dessert. It's just ice cream, so nothing special. We'll have a few drinks and play it by ear. Although playing gin rummy using my ear is going to be a challenge."

Steve rose and stepped over to me. "I don't know what to make of you sometimes, Shannon." He folded me into his arms and kissed the top of my head. "This is nice, being here."

He picked up some of the dishes and carried them into the kitchen. I watched him, smiling as I took in the broad shoulders and cute butt, accentuated with every step. He was totally hot and available. The ball was in my court as to how far to take this.

I felt a faint chill roll across my shoulder before whispered words brushed my ear. *"Arousal and attraction are gifts carrying power. You honor the Divine Mother when you accept your true nature."*

My mouth fell open. My gaze shot to the side and then all around the room hoping for a glimmer of my aunt's presence. Even though I couldn't see her, I knew it was she who had whispered in my ear. My heart pounded fast as her words resounded through my body.

Aunt Maeve was here with me, witnessing this seductive interplay with Steve! She was encouraging me to have *sex* with him? Not that I needed much encouragement on that front. But it was more than just the fun of being intimate. I thought of the erotic sketches which Alice had drawn on the pages of the Grimoire. It was not only the phases of the moon that could amplify power in a white witch, but sex could too?

I smiled as I gazed around the room. Okay. If that was another step in my discovery of my path, then who was I to deny it? I was all about honoring Mother Nature. It didn't hurt that Steve was not only a nice guy but hot as hell.

TWENTY FIVE

My hands trembled slightly as I carried the tray with small bowls of ice cream and coffee laced with Baileys liqueur into the living room. Steve turned and then rose from where he squatted, poking the embers in the fireplace. He'd doused the lights so that only the flickering of candles and the flames in the hearth shone.

I could feel my tummy begin to tingle in that *sooo* delightful way as I set the tray on the coffee table. Even with the blatant flirting earlier, things had suddenly become very real. The ambience was pure seduction, and the guy only inches away, gazing at me with bedroom eyes, made my pulse race. I felt like I had fallen into the rabbit hole, like *Alice in Wonderland*. It had been years and years since I'd felt this level of excitement.

Steve sat down on the sofa and then patted the spot next to him. "Just sit with me for a little while and enjoy the fire. No pressure, Shannon, but I wanted to create a magical atmosphere with the candles, dimming the lights."

When I sat next to him, he reached for my hand, lifting it to his lips. "This is nice, right?" The look in his eyes was now questioning rather than overlaid with confidence. It reminded me of the way he looked when he was a teenager. Who am I kidding? He's six years younger than me; back in the day he was barely thirteen when I spent my last summer here.

I leaned in and kissed him gently on the lips. "Yes. It's perfect." Instead of pulling back, I snuggled closer, running my fingers through his hair as I kissed him harder. I felt his breath, warm on my face, his lips and tongue tasting like wine and mint; I didn't even see him pop one in his mouth. My own breath skittered as our kiss deepened and we sunk back into the cushions of the sofa.

His fingers caressed my cheeks and then lowered, softly touching my neck and then gripping my shoulder. When his mouth left mine, he trailed kisses down to the curve of my neck and shoulder. All the while, my heart pounded fast against my ribs as I gave myself over to the pleasure of his touch.

"Oh, Shannon, your skin is like silk." His voice was husky as he nuzzled my neck, his hands lowering to slip inside the loose gap of the dress's neckline. My breath caught in my throat while my body became molten.

I felt a vibration on my thigh which was immediately followed by a chirping sound. Shit! It was his cell phone. He paused for just a moment and our eyes met. When I arched up to kiss him again, yearning for this to continue, he sighed.

"I have to take this. That's Amy's ringtone. It might be about my son." He pulled back and sat up, already reaching in his pocket for the phone.

Every cell in my body that had been tingling at his touch deflated. My breath was uneven, but I forced myself to take a deep breath to calm myself. I watched Steve's face tighten after he answered. From where I sat, I could hear a woman's high-pitched voice talking fast into the phone.

"I'll be there as soon as I can." He ended the call and stood up. "It's Byron. He fell down a flight of steps and lost consciousness. That was Amy. She's at the hospital with him. I've got to go." He shoved his phone back into his pocket and looked at me. "Do you want to come with me?"

"I don't think I should. I don't have a place there and would just be in the way." I hurried to my feet, walking after him through the room. "God, I hope he's okay. Was he still unconscious when he got to the hospital?"

Steve strode down the hall to the front door. "I don't know." He stopped before going outside, peering at me with worry etched in the lines of his forehead. "I'll call you later, as soon as I know more. Sorry about ruining your night with this, Shannon."

My eyebrows arched to my hairline. "Don't be sorry! Just go! But drive careful, okay?" He turned, and his feet practically flew across the verandah and down the stairs. I clutched the edge of the door as I stood watching him get in his truck and then speed out of my driveway.

Even though I'd never met his son, my eyes filled with tears. I could totally *get* Steve's fright and worry, hearing that his kid had gotten hurt. It was a parent's worst nightmare. When I closed the door, I leaned my back against it.

"Please. By whatever power that's in me to pray for Byron, let the boy be okay. Give strength to Steve and the mother of this child." The words became a mantra in my head as I stood there silently.

After a long time, I pushed away from the door and went into the kitchen to grab my cell phone. When I went back to the living room, the ice cream was a melted soup, and the fire had been reduced to orange embers. I added another couple of logs to it and then flopped down onto the sofa.

When I'd wished for success for Mary-Jane, it had ended with mixed results—a bad sprain, yet her family was being nicer. Now I'd just wished for Byron to be healed. It just *had* to work.

I picked up my phone and sent a text message to my son and daughter, letting them know I loved them and missed them.

I settled in, sipping the coffee I'd made earlier. It might be a long night, but I needed to hear from Steve that his kid was okay.

TWENTY SIX

It had been close to midnight when Steve sent a text to me about his son. Byron was in an induced coma to alleviate some of the swelling in his brain from the fall down the stairs.

Now, sitting at the kitchen table the next morning, he called again to let me know that his son was still unconscious. My eyes closed as I listened to his voice hitch, barely keeping the tears at bay. I couldn't imagine the long night of suffering that he'd had to endure waiting at his son's bedside.

"Is there anything I can do to help you?" I got up, pacing back and forth across the kitchen. This was terrible news, and all I wanted to do was help in any way I could.

"No. But thanks. The doctors said that they'll keep him like this for another twenty-four hours and then check the swelling. It's a waiting game, I'm afraid."

"What about food? Do you need me to bring something to you? How's your ex and her partner holding up? Just tell me what you guys need." I bit my lower lip, trying to keep myself from crying. But as he'd just said, there wasn't anything anyone could do but wait.

"We're good. Say a prayer if you want to do anything. I'm going home to take a shower, and then I'm coming back here. I'll talk to you later today." With that, he hung up.

I rinsed my coffee mug and then grabbed my jacket. There was one thing that I could do to help out Byron and Steve. I'd visit the Witching Well and implore that being who lived in it to help me. The first time I'd seen it, I'd made an offering of the Jack Daniels in my thermos. Should I try another offering? I put my cell phone in my pocket and looked around the room.

"Aunt Maeve? I need some guidance here! I've got to do *something* to help Byron get better. You were pretty quick letting me know about getting it on with Steve so how about some advice with this? You've got to help me!"

When my cell phone buzzed, I grabbed it from my pocket. I could feel my eyes widen at the same moment my jaw slowly fell open when I saw the text message for an unknown caller.

> Use the four elements—earth, air, fire and water. Go to the well and take a white candle and a flask of lake water. Use your bare hands to scoop a handful of soil from my garden. Make sure it's the garden! When you make your offering, your very breath as you say the following incantation will provide the necessary air.

> Divine Mother, I beseech you to hear my plea to heal this boy, Byron Murphy. Accept my pure offering of water, earth and fire. On the blood of your servants Alice Hunter and Maeve Enid Burke and on my own blood, I implore you to heal this boy.

> When you return, record this in the Grimoire. Take note of everything in your life in the week following this, paying particular attention to patterns of three. Expect a setback of some kind in your dreams and goals as the universe will extract a price when energy is realigned.

> Now GO!

Oh my God! For a moment all I could do was stand there blinking at the message she'd created on my cell phone. But then I flew into action, grabbing a white candle from the living room, a thermos for the lake water and a plastic baggie for the soil. When I stepped outside, the wind just about took my breath away. The sky was pregnant with dark clouds threatening a downpour at any minute. I tugged the hood of my jacket up over my hair and raced down to the lake. It seemed like even the weather—strange and foreboding—echoed the task I was about to do.

I knelt at the lakeshore and filled the thermos with water, practically freezing my fingers as I held the container. After capping it, I headed for the side garden that Aunt Maeve had always maintained. The fact that she had specifically said to use that soil wasn't lost on me. There had to be some kind of special power in that spot that she'd cultivated for her garden.

The soil was reasonably soft so it didn't take long to scoop up a handful and slip it into the bag. I jogged most of the way down the road and into the forest where the well was. The rain started about halfway there, so by the time I reached the clearing, my jacket and knapsack were drenched. I took a deep breath, peering at the well as I walked over to it. This *had* to work.

I slipped the backpack off and took out the bag of soil. I couldn't remember the exact words or if these offerings had to follow some kind of order. A quick glance at the phone and I repeated the incantation, whispering softly. Starting with the earth, I then emptied the thermos of water down the well. It took me about a dozen tries to get the candle going, shielding it from the rain with my upper body.

"Divine Mother, I beseech you to hear my plea to heal Byron Murphy. Accept my pure offering of water, earth, and fire. On the blood of your servants Alice Hunter and my aunt Maeve Burke and even on my own blood, I beg you to heal this boy."

I waited for what seemed like an eternity, staring down the well as the rain pelted my shoulders. Would she answer? I desperately needed some kind of confirmation that this would work.

The power of the triumvirate flashed in my mind, startling me. Yes! I repeated the incantation two more times, and even before I finished, the voice in the well boomed out.

"Your offering has been accepted. The child will be healed before the day is done."

I let out a long breath, clutching the slippery stones of the well. "Thank you, Divine Mother, or whatever power that will help, thank you!" Tears filled my eyes, mixing with the rain dripping off my chin.

The walk back to my place passed like I was in a daze. I hardly felt the cold wind and rain whipping the hood of my jacket back or the chill in my soaking-wet sneakers. When I stepped through the door into the warmth of my house, a wave of exhaustion rolled through me. My legs were heavy, throbbing with a deep ache like I'd run a marathon as I stripped the wet coat off. A shiver gripped my shoulders and spread through my core.

For a few minutes I just stood there trembling. If anyone had told me six months ago that I'd be living in my aunt's home in the Catskills and that I'd be dabbling in witchcraft, I would have asked them for some of the drugs they were taking. But I'd just made a sacrifice at a mysterious well and spoken an incantation! And I'd done it to help the son of a man I'd come damn close to sleeping with the night before. Crazy as it all sounded, I'd never felt more alive...and *important.*

Important? I shook my head as I headed for the stairs to go up and take a long, hot bath. *Yeah, important.* I had a place in the universe, and had been called, or maybe *chosen* was a better word, to become something greater than just being Alex Johnston's wife and the mother of our two children. This was a lifeline connection to powers that I'd never known existed.

While the tub filled with hot water, I peeled the wet jeans and socks off. I stood watching my reflection in the full-length mirror mounted on the back of the bathroom door. My fingers were white, numb with cold, as I tugged my shirt up and off. My gaze lowered from my eyes, the color of a clear blue sky, to my lips which held a purplish tint.

I slipped my bra off, freeing my breasts. Instead of cringing that the perkiness of youth had been literally sucked from them from nursing two children, I smiled, cupping the underside in my palms. These were the full breasts of a woman who had nurtured life. My fingers slid over the slight roundness of my belly, admiring the space that had once been swollen with my babies. It would never be flat as it had once been but that didn't make my stomach any less beautiful. Hips that had become cushiony were like a fine wine that had aged well.

When my panties fell to the floor, I actually let out a throaty laugh, remembering the conversation with Libby about being "bare down there." Ha! I was perfect in every way! For the first time, EVER, I saw the beauty and perfection of my body.

The Divine Mother.

I smiled, thinking of that phrase that Aunt Maeve had used. For me it meant Mother Nature, but it might have meant something different to her.

When the scent of lavender filled the room, I stepped into the tub filled with hot, sudsy water. It was only when I sank down into the heat that I really felt the chill which had seeped into my bones. I turned off the tap and sank back, closing my eyes. Life was good, and I wouldn't trade places to be the wife and woman I'd once been. For the first time, I could honestly feel peace in my heart. What Ass-hat had done had created the framework to put me exactly where I should be.

In my Aunt Maeve's home in the mysterious Catskill Mountains, carrying on her legacy of witchcraft. I'd been chosen. It was up to me to tend to the property and use the power of the Witching Well.

Little did I know that this would be the last time I'd feel so alive and at peace.

TWENTY SEVEN

It was three days after visiting the well in the cold autumn rain. Lying on my sofa, I felt like a steamroller had run over my body, backed up, and run over me a few more times for good measure. Every muscle ached, while my nose was a constant running faucet.

Libby sat on the chair across from me while I was propped up with a ton of pillows under my aunt's crocheted afghan. She'd gotten the fireplace going, and the heat was starting to break through the constant chills racking through me.

She held a mug of tea in both hands, looking over the rim at me. "If you aren't better by tomorrow, I'm dragging your ass into the clinic. You've got the flu, Shannon. That isn't something you want to fool around with."

I grabbed a tissue from the box on the coffee table and dabbed at my nose. "I'm fine. Why would I go to the clinic when I have my own private nurse making me soup and filling me full of aspirin?" Even though I tried to sound upbeat, I couldn't remember the last time I'd felt this horrible and for such a length of time.

"I'll stay with you until six, but then I have to leave to go to work. I start my stint of nights today. Steve said he'll drop some dinner off later. After that he wants to visit Byron at Amy's place. I wonder if your spell, or whatever it was you did, was the thing that helped his son recover?"

I pushed myself higher on the sofa and threw the covers back. The soup combined with the fire now had drops of sweat rolling down my temple. "Byron got better the same day I went to the well. Trust me. It worked. And that's how I got this stupid flu. Aunt Maeve said I'd have a setback. So this is probably it."

When I was settled once more, I looked over at her. "So Mary-Jane's actually up and walking? That's kind of fast, isn't it?"

Libby rolled her eyes. "Too fast. But there's no stopping her. I had a hell of a time convincing her to stay away from here. She wanted to make her famous chicken soup and bring it out. But Roy was on my side. He didn't want her to risk getting what you've got." She laughed, "He took out a family membership at the gym, and I think it's wearing him out. She made them go *twice* the first day, and then they were there almost all afternoon on the second day."

I bobbed my eyebrows at her. "Part of my wish was for her to feel almost orgasmic pleasure in exercise. Five will get you ten that the gym's not the only workout they're getting. Roy should be so lucky to get a supercharge in his sex life."

"That's funny, but it's not an image that I want to dwell on, if you don't mind. I probably won't be able to hide the smirk when I see them next." Libby stood up, "I'm getting another, do you want a refill?"

I shook my head. "I'm tea'd out. Help yourself though."

At the knock on the front door, my forehead tightened. "That can't be Steve, already. And Mary-Jane is forbidden to visit."

Libby shrugged. "I'll see who it is. You stay put." She walked out of the room, and I could hear her open the front door.

I cocked my head to the side, trying to hear who it could be. It was a male voice, but I couldn't make out what he was saying. Footsteps followed and I grabbed the afghan, once more covering myself up to my chin.

185

Devon stepped into the room, carrying a bouquet of sunflowers. I could only stare bug-eyed at him, showing up out of the blue like that. Especially after the dustup with Steve a few days ago.

"Hi, Shannon. I heard you were under the weather, so I wanted to bring you something to cheer you up. How are you feeling?"

Libby stood at his side, shooting daggers with her eyes. Her voice was clipped when she held out her hands. "I'll take the flowers and put them in a vase."

I noticed she didn't extend an invitation to Devon to have a cup of tea. He handed her the bouquet and thanked her before taking the chair that she'd vacated.

"I've got the flu so you shouldn't stay. I'm probably contagious. But thanks for the flowers, Devon." My smile fell and I added, "And before you ask, I'm still not selling this place to you." I watched him sigh and then edge forward in his chair.

"That's not why I'm here, Shannon. I know you don't believe me, but I *would* like to be friends. Is there anything you need? I can pick up meds or take-out food. Just say the word." His head tipped to the side as he gazed at me. "You really don't look well, Shannon."

"Thanks. I don't *feel* well."

When a picture of the fight between Steve and Devon flashed in my mind, my eyes narrowed. "Steve told me about the thing with Cynthia. I also know he went through a period of serial dating after his marriage fell apart. So if you're here to throw some more shade on Steve, don't bother."

He stood up. "You heard his side of it. Someday when you're feeling better, I'd like to sit down and tell you my side. Maybe we could have dinner together."

Libby walked in just at that minute, and she shot a look over at me, hearing his offer. "Right now, Shannon needs her rest if she's ever going to shake this bug." She set the flowers on the coffee table, mouthing the word "No!" while her back was to him.

Devon nodded. "Okay, I'm leaving. I promised my dad I'd take him to his doctor appointment anyway, so I should get going." He tapped my foot as he passed by. "I hope you feel better soon, Shannon. See you later, Libby. I'll see myself out."

When the door closed behind him, Libby gritted her teeth. "I should pitch that bunch of flowers! There's probably poison oak or ragweed buried in it, coming from that guy!"

"No, I don't think so. I actually think he's trying to be nice." For the next ten minutes I relayed the fight Steve and he had a few nights ago when he'd showed up out of the blue. When I finished, I asked, "So what's the story with this Cynthia? Steve described her as kind of a loner. He said she broke it off with him before it got serious."

Libby flopped down in the chair again. "A lot of people don't like Cynthia. You know who she is though, right?" When I shook my head, she continued, "Your aunt's friend Ruth... Cynthia is her granddaughter."

"Wouldn't that make her too young for Steve or Devon? I don't understand." Ruth had been Aunt Maeve's friend even though she was a good ten years older than Maeve. I started to try to do the math figuring out how old Cynthia would be but gave up when Libby spoke.

"I'd guess she's in her mid-thirties. So Devon and Steve dating her isn't odd. But *she* is. Don't get me wrong, I like Cynthia. But a lot of people in town, well, more like the *women* in town, don't like her. She's a free spirit, if you know what I mean."

"In other words, she sleeps around, right? With married guys?" That had to be it for the women in the town to not like her. Having been on the receiving end of that stick, I was inclined to agree with them. Women who went after married men were skanks in my books.

"No. Not that I've heard. She can have her pick of any single guy as I understand it. I met her at the clinic when she came in one time. She's smart and knows what she wants. And being married is definitely not something she's interested in." Libby shrugged. "As far as I'm concerned, if that works for her, it's nobody's business but hers."

"Yeah." And then another thought hit me. "How did Devon find out I'm sick, I wonder. I know he didn't hear it from you."

"Probably he heard it from Roy. It's a small town. Everyone knows everyone's business, Shannon." The smile disappeared from her face. "I don't like the way Devon just shows up here. That's the second time in less than a week. I'd speak to him about that if I were you, Shannon."

I nodded. "Yeah. Even though I think he sincerely wants to be friends, I don't like that either. He's pretty persistent. If I were here alone, it might be harder to get him to leave."

"Exactly."

The aspirin and warmth in the room combined to make me sleepy again. I stifled a yawn before Libby offered, "I'm going to tidy up in the kitchen and let you catch some sleep. That's the best thing for you right now."

I sank down on the sofa, snuggled under the afghan, and closed my eyes.

***

It wasn't until I heard voices in the room next to me that I woke up. A glance at the window showed that the sun was low on the horizon. I must have been out for hours.

Steve stepped into the room. "How's the patient today?" He eased in next to my feet at the far end of the sofa. He reached for my hand and gave it a squeeze.

"I'm doing okay. How's Byron?" I sat up higher, making more room for Steve. Before he had a chance to answer, Libby spoke from where she stood in the doorway.

"I have to go to work now, Shannon. I'll pop over tomorrow again to see how you're doing."

"Thanks, Libby. With any luck I'll be up and around and better company. See you later." I turned back to Steve, waiting for the update on his son. Although I knew that Byron was okay, thanks to my visit to the well, I wanted to know how quickly his recovery was coming along. Just how good *is* magical healing?

Steve's face lit up when he spoke, "He's pretty well back to normal, although he's trying to milk this for another day to get out of going to school. You'd never know that he had a concussion so bad they put him in a coma."

Yay, magic! From a coma to heading back to school? That's pretty damn good as far as I was concerned. I smiled before a giant sneeze erupted.

He handed me the box of tissues and grinned. "I just wish you were feeling better. I feel guilty leaving you alone here. Would you like me to stop around when I finish visiting Byron to check on you?"

After blowing my nose, I quipped, "This isn't the bedside manner I was hoping for, Steve. Thanks, but I'll be fine. What did you bring me for dinner?"

"Wonton soup, rice, and curried chicken. And bear claws to have with your morning coffee." He rose and went over to the fireplace to stoke it up and add another log. When he turned to face me, there was a scowl darkening his face, "Libby told me that Devon stopped in for a visit. Do you want me to have a word with him?"

I know he was just showing care and concern, but his "take over" approach made me bristle inwardly. I shook my head but bit back the reply that threatened to leap from my tongue. This was too similar to what had led to our first argument, when I'd had problems with the septic. I didn't want another spat, so I just said, "I'm going to speak to him about that, don't worry. I'll handle it, but thanks."

He put his hands up in front of him. When he spoke it was clear that he was also thinking of the argument we'd had over Devon. "Just offering. You do what you need to do." He came over and placed his hand on my forehead. "You feel pretty warm. Should I get you more aspirin?"

I took his hand from my face and held it, looking up at him. "Yes, please. And a bit of soup if you don't mind." When my cell phone buzzed with a text message, he picked it up from the coffee table and handed it to me.

My chest tightened, seeing Jess's picture on the small screen. I'd been so sick that it had been days since I'd talked to her. "It's my daughter."

"I'll leave you to it while I get your soup and drugs." With that he left the room.

My forehead tightened as I read what she'd written.

> Hey, Mom! I saw Dad on the weekend. We had a nice day, (just the two of us!) Which is understandable when I tell you what's going on. He and Linda aren't together now. He's even looking for his own apartment. He kept apologizing for what he'd done, upsetting my life and Thomas's life. He said if he could do it over, he never would have left. He asked about you, Mom. I kind of felt sorry for him, TBH.

I sat still as a statue, blinking slowly as I reread her message. What the hell? Ass-hat and the skank were *through*? Oh my God! I didn't need to be a rocket scientist to know that this was because of the witching wish (curse?) I'd put on both of them. While I was glad he'd finally apologized to Jessica, my gut shrieked a warning at the last line of her text, especially since he'd sent me a text earlier in the week, which I still hadn't bothered to answer.

When Steve came back, carrying a tray with the soup, water, and my pills, I was still holding the cell phone in my hand. The look on my face must have alerted him because he set the tray down on the coffee table quickly.

"What's wrong? Your daughter's okay, isn't she?" He eased down next to me on the sofa, peering at me.

I was still in a state of shock but managed to answer, "Yes, she's fine. It's the ex." I gazed at him silently. There was no way I was going to get into the part I'd played in all of this, because of finding that well. The one person I could talk to about it had already left to do her shift at the clinic.

"What happened to him? He's not *dead*, is he?" Steve's forehead furrowed while his eyes bored into me. He reached for the phone, but I moved it away before he could take it. This was my business and I'd handle it.

"No, he's not dead. He met with Jess on Saturday. He broke up with the woman he left me for. He told Jess he regrets leaving me." God! Of all the times to hear all of this! I was weak as a kitten and still feeling like shit. But I'd have to come back with some kind of response to my daughter.

Steve sat back, watching me closely. "So...how do *you* feel about that? Would you take him back if he asked you to?"

"No! I would never even consider it! He betrayed my trust in him!" I jabbed a finger at Steve. "He not only had an affair, it went on for two years! How many other times did he step out before her? When I begged him for us to go to counseling, he said his mind was made up!"

My breathing was harder now. "On top of that, during the divorce proceedings, he fought me tooth and nail over every dime! Alex *killed* any sense of trust I could possibly have in him. You can't have a relationship if trust is gone. He did that, not me! It's tough luck for him that his plans didn't work out the way he wanted."

Even as the words left my mouth, I felt my chest tighten. That wasn't entirely true. I'd played a big part in upsetting his new life. I felt a twinge of guilt, but I'll admit—not all that much. If that makes me a bad person, I can live with it.

After a few beats of silence, Steve commented, "Don't get me wrong, but from what you said about your marriage, you were the junior partner, Shannon. He made the money and the bulk of the decisions while you kept the house running smoothly. Now that his relationship ended, he probably feels you'll cave and take him back."

I snorted. "Yeah, I wouldn't put it past him." I took a deep breath thinking about what Steve had said. "You know, even if there was a way of getting past the trust issue, I don't ever want a life with him again." I shook my head no back and forth a bunch of times. "I saw a nasty, selfish side of him I can never unsee." I looked around the room. "As difficult as it is with fixing this place up, I like my life."

"Still, over twenty years of marriage. That's a long time to just toss aside." When I glared at him, he held his hands up like a traffic cop. "Just kind of playing devil's advocate here, Shannon." His head tipped to the side." So what are you going to say to your daughter? That's the tricky part, I guess."

"Yeah. If only I could fix this." My big regret was laying that curse of impotence on him. To compound matters, I'd also wished for them to fight like cats and dogs. I'd cursed both of them but had created a landmine for myself.

"What do you mean, *fix it*? But if you mean fix it for your daughter, I get that. This is hard on kids, even if they're pretty-well grown." Steve reached for the tray and then set it on my lap.

Watching him, I let out a long sigh. Of course he didn't know the whole story. And if he did, would he believe it? I picked at the crackers, crumbling them as I thought of what I'd write when I answered Jess.

Steve rubbed my leg. "I hate to leave you like this, Shannon, but I'd better go if I want to see my son before he goes to bed. But I'll stop around after the visit to see how you're doing .I think you need some company or at least someone to spoil you a bit."

I smiled at him. "Thanks. I'll probably be fine, but I'm glad to hear how Byron's doing. One of these days, I want to meet him."

Steve stood up and leaned over to kiss my forehead. "You'll meet him soon, I promise. Is there anything else I can get you before I leave?"

I squeezed his hand. "You've done lots, thanks! I'll see you later." I watched him cross the floor and then disappear down the hallway. When the door snicked closed, I set the tray back on the coffee table. I had to get a reply off to Jessica.

TWENTY EIGHT

I t took me a few different tries to compose a careful response to my daughter.

> Hi, Jess! I'm glad you had a nice day with your father. It's unfortunate that things didn't pan out for him and Linda. But that's life. Things don't always work out the way we hope they will.
>
> I'm getting over a nasty bout of the flu but my friends here have been great in nursing me back to health. I'm getting antsy about getting back to fixing this place up for Thanksgiving with you guys. I'm also thinking of throwing a Halloween party to get to know more people in town. You know Halloween has always been my favorite holiday. Christmas is too commercial and Thanksgiving is exhausting.
>
> I bet there'll be some pretty crazy parties on campus at Halloween. I wish I was there to help you with a costume like I've always done but I'm sure you'll come up with a good one on your own. Have fun but drink

responsibly, okay?

I clicked send and closed my eyes, letting out a silent prayer that I'd avoided any landmines. The fact that Jess actually felt sorry for Ass-hat after his life had unraveled was more a testament to her forgiving nature than anything else. That last sentence in her text about him regretting leaving us rankled in my gut. That was the bullet that I'd wanted to dodge. Was he trying to set the stage for us to reunite? And the nerve of him to even hint about that with the kids.

It was never going to happen.

It was time to send a reply to his text from last week. I had to nip any of this BS in the bud before it became a weed choking me.

> Alex, I heard about your visit with Jessica on Saturday. I'm glad that you are finally connecting with her again. I would like things to be civil between us for the sake of the kids but that is as far as I'm willing to go. I can send Thomas money to come here for Thanksgiving so don't bother driving him. Of course, I'll do the same for Jessica.

There. I hit send and set the phone aside. I don't know whether it was anger or worry that propelled me to my feet, but I'd somehow gotten a second wind. I took the tray back to the kitchen to reheat the soup and food that Steve had brought.

When it was ready, I piled the Grimoire and a pen on the tray as well. Aunt Maeve had advised that I write my experience in casting that spell for Byron's health but I'd become ill before I'd had a chance. Well, now was as good a time as ever.

After stoking the fire with another log, I settled in to eat and continue the journal entry. I'd gotten about halfway through dinner when, of course, my cell phone dinged with a text message. When I picked it up and saw Alex's name, the muscles in the back of my neck tightened. "Shit! Now what?"

> I'm sorry to hear that you are sick with the flu, Shannon. That's rough. It was great being with Jess and speaking with Thomas earlier today. I absolutely insist on driving the kids to your place for Thanksgiving! It's the very least I can do after all that's happened. As I told Jess, I really regret everything this past year. I realize what a colossal mess I've made in everyone's life, especially yours. I hope to talk with you at Thanksgiving. I really miss you, Shannon.

> Love, Alex

My fingers splayed out, dropping the cell phone like it was a hot ember. SHIT! I just knew it! That twist in my gut had been absolutely right about what he was up to. He was wheedling to get back with me and using the kids to do it! The fact that he knew I was sick with the flu proved that he'd just gotten off the phone with Jess. And letting me know that he'd also talked to Thomas was the coup de-grâce.

"Love, Alex" As if he even knew what the word meant! I *had* to respond. There was no way I could leave this hanging.

Double shit! I was getting sucked in again, having to deal with his crap. But immediately after that thought, my shoulders fell. A big part, if not the *all of it* was because of *me*! I'd helped to create this mess with that damned curse I'd laid on him.

> I'm sorry that things didn't go well for you with Linda. But things will never be good between us, if that's what you want to talk to me about. I just want to put that out there before you raise any false hope in the kids' minds. Don't do that to them, Alex. They've been through enough this past year. Everyone has to move on. I certainly have.

I turned the phone off after I'd hit send. This was BS. I wasn't going to spend the night going back and forth with Alex or even with Jess. But when I turned to pick up the tray to continue eating, I discovered my appetite had vanished. Picking the tray up, I headed to the kitchen and plugged the kettle in. I needed a drink to settle my nerves, but considering I was sick, maybe a hot toddy would help with both things.

A bourbon, ginger, lemon, and hot water would ease my throat as well as my frayed nerves from the exchange with Ass-hat. As I waited for the water to boil, I looked around the room. "Aunt Maeve? I understand why you never married. Although I don't regret having two wonderful kids, my life is much simpler without a spouse. Especially a lying sack of shit like Ass-hat."

"Careful. Thoughts have power but words are supercharged."

I jumped back, hearing the voice in the kitchen. It was her! Her voice and even the air seemed to shimmer a bit beside me. Shit! Had I done it again? If this was the way it was going to be all the time, guarding my thoughts and words, did I really *want* this power? I'd already made a mess of things with Ass-hat and his skeevy girlfriend, complicating my own life in the process.

But what had I said that I needed to be reminded to be careful? "Life is simpler without a spouse?" Was that it? Was I sealing my fate that I'd never fall in love or marry again? At this point, it didn't seem like that bad an option.

"You never married, yet you had men in your life, Aunt Maeve. It doesn't seem so bad, y'know?" But if I'd expected an answer, none was forthcoming. I turned to add hot water to the mug I'd doctored with spices and bourbon. I was sick of being sick, and if this concoction helped to sweat the remaining flu from my body, then hell yeah!

For the next hour, I sipped my drink and wrote in the Grimoire. I wasn't even aware that I'd fallen asleep until Steve stood next to me, gently shaking my shoulder.

"Shannon? Let me help you up the stairs and get you settled in bed."

I sat up slowly and took his hand to help me to my feet. "Thanks. How's your son?"

"He's great! I think he's even going to school tomorrow. We had a nice time playing video games." He put his arm around my waist, leading me to the stairs.

"I'm happy he's better. Can you do me one favor? I'd like to take a long bath before I go to bed." I looked up at him. "Stay the night with me. It's not the romantic night we'd planned, but I'd like you next to me when I fall asleep."

He kissed the top of my head and helped me up the stairs. Whether we ever became more than friends was totally up in the air, but for just one night, I really didn't feel like being alone.

TWENTY NINE

The next morning when I awoke, I saw Steve tiptoeing across the room to the doorway. Considering he was built like Jason Momoa, tall with brawny muscles, him stepping like a ballerina made me smile.

"Good morning."

He spun around at my voice, barely hiding the surprise in his eyes. "Sorry. Did I wake you?" He came back over and placed his hand on my forehead. "You don't feel like you have a fever. I was going to make you a coffee and bring it up."

As I lay there, I realized that my throat didn't hurt anymore, and the muscle aches had disappeared. It was only when I started to get up with legs that felt like cooked spaghetti noodles that it became clear my strength was still sapped. "Coffee would be great, but I need to start moving around again. I'll come down."

He took my hand, helping me rise. "It was nice just laying next to you, Shannon, even if you do snore like a chainsaw." Pulling me close, he planted a kiss on my forehead.

I pinched his waist and murmured, "I don't snore. But yeah, I'm glad you stayed. I suppose you need to dash off to get ready for work."

He looked back at me as I followed him down the stairs. "I could stay if you need me to. If that's the case, I'll need to make a call to cover manning the store. You tell me what you want."

"No, that's okay. I think Libby's coming out later. I'm actually feeling much better today. I'm tired of lying around. I need to get outside and get some fresh air." I followed him into the kitchen and flopped down onto the nearest chair. Shit. Even that short walk from my bedroom to the kitchen had tired me.

Steve set about making a pot of coffee and then he opened the fridge. "I'm going to make you a decent breakfast before I leave. You look like you've lost weight since you've been laid up."

I grinned. "So it's not all bad, right? You know what they say, 'You can never be too rich or too thin.'" But my stomach rumbled in disagreement.

"You don't need to lose any weight, Shannon. If anything, you could stand to put on a few pounds." He took the carton of eggs and a package of bacon from the fridge.

"Speaking of weight loss, I wonder how Mary-Jane is doing? Maybe I'll ask her out for a visit. I'll make sure that she gets a ride, though, or she might be tempted to jog here." I got up to get my phone from the living room.

Before I even had a chance to ring Mary-Jane about coming out, it buzzed with a text message. From the ringtone, I knew it was my son.

> Hey, Mom! I hope you're feeling better today! I heard you were sick with the flu. I was just wondering about that resort you inherited. If Dad drives me to your place for Thanksgiving, maybe he can stay in one of your cabins? It would be more convenient than getting a hotel room (if that one-horse town even has a hotel!). It would be great for all of us to have dinner together, like a family again.

"Shit!" It was all I could do to not fling the phone across the room.

Steve raced into the room, stopping short when he saw me standing there with the phone in my hand. "What's wrong? Are you okay?"

My teeth ground so tight, they clicked. "I'm okay. It's my ex pulling his stunts! Now he has my son advocating for him, trying to set up a Hallmark Thanksgiving for the family. Thomas even suggested that his father stay at one of the cabins over that weekend! Can you believe that?"

"Let him stay in a cabin. Just don't turn the heat on or leave bedding. He'll soon leave." Steve grinned and placed his hands on my shoulders. "I'm kidding. You do what you want. Just because your ex is moving heaven and hell to make something happen, you don't have to do anything you don't want."

"He's using the kids to make this happen. Jessica felt sorry for him when she saw him. And now Thomas is adding his two cents. I asked Alex not to get their hopes up, and, of course, he's doing the opposite." It wasn't just that Ass-hat would make me the bad guy eventually when I nixed this, but he would be putting the kids through the emotional wringer again.

Steve put his arm around me, walking us both back to the kitchen. "I was afraid that this wasn't the last of him wheedling to get back with you, Shannon. It sounds like you need to talk to both your kids. They need to know that their father created this and you can't be expected to fix it."

"I think you're right about talking to the kids as opposed to sending text messages. I've got to set them straight about their father and me." I wandered over to pour coffee for us while Steve continued with frying eggs. The smell of bacon filled the kitchen, reminding me that it had been days since I'd managed to get anything besides soup and liquids in me.

When he set the plate in front of me, I smiled at him. "Thanks for everything you've done. This is wonderful." When he fixed another plate and sat across from me, I wondered about my kids visiting me at Thanksgiving. What would they think if they knew I was dating? Even though I hadn't been the one who walked out, ending the marriage, it would still be an enormous shock for them to see me with anyone other than their father, especially since we'd only been divorced for six months.

"Penny for your thoughts?"

My gaze lifted from my plate, jerked back into the here and now. From the way Steve examined me with narrowed eyes, it was clear he knew that my attention wasn't on the breakfast we shared. "Uh, I was thinking of my kids. Just wondering how they're going to react to me dating. I think they'll like you—"

"Shannon, I think we need to slow this down." His head tilted to the side and he reached for my hand. "Don't get me wrong. I'm attracted like hell to you but…"

The breath froze in my chest, waiting for the other shoe to drop. We hadn't actually become a couple but he was breaking up with me? Another guy was about to walk out the door? I pulled my hand back and set it in my lap. "But what? We're not exactly rushing into anything here, Steve. What with your kid, me getting sick, and now my kids—"

"It's only been six months since the divorce, Shannon! Trust me, I've been down this road when Amy left. I dated so many women. It was a rebound mindset, I know. So why shouldn't the same thing be happening with you?" Worry lines etched across his forehead while his eyes bored through me.

And then it hit me. This was because of what I'd said out loud the night before. I'd said that life with a man complicated things. Aunt Maeve had warned me about controlling my thoughts and words. And now it was looking like Steve was walking away.

He sighed as he stood up. "Should I take your silence as agreeing with me, Shannon?" His mouth pulled to the side before he continued, "If there's a chance that you will get back with your ex, even if it's mainly for your kids, I don't want to stand in the way." His voice lowered to practically a whisper, "I also don't want to be hurt anymore, Shannon."

My chin rose as I stared at him. "That's the real reason, isn't it, Steve? You are afraid that I'm going to hurt you. I told you that I'm through with Ass-hat, but you really don't believe me, do you?"

I stood up, going toe to toe with him. "You don't know me at all, Steve. You're in love with a teenage version of me. Well, this is who I am now, Steve. I'm not perfect. I've got kids and baggage like most divorced women in their forties."

His hands rose to grip my arms. "That's what I'm talking about, Shannon! You need to sort this out with your kids and with yourself. I'm not ashamed of being afraid to be hurt. I've got things happening in my own life! Shit, my kid was in a coma this week! I don't need any more drama in my life right now."

When he tried to pull me into his arms, I pushed him away. "Stop it! Get out of my house, Steve. That's what you want to do, so go!"

He grabbed his jacket from the back of his chair and stormed across the room. When he reached the doorway, he turned around. "I don't want this, Shannon. I mean, I want us to be more than friends, but right now, I think it's best for both of us if that's all there is. You need to sort things out with your family and I need to be there for Byron."

"I'll deal with things in my life, Steve. Don't you worry about me, buddy. I'll be fine." It was hard to keep my voice from breaking. This was all way too much like what I'd endured when Ass-hat had left. Except that this time, he wasn't leaving for another woman after sneaking around with her.

Steve nodded. "Yeah, you will. But it's going to take more time for that to happen, Shannon. I hope you still consider me a friend because I would do anything for you." With that he turned and left the house, closing the door behind him.

I sank down in the chair, letting the tears flow. I knew deep down that I wasn't in love with Steve. In time, maybe that would happen, but right now, it was mainly just attraction. What really hurt was the feeling of failure...again.

Like in my marriage. Was it my fault? Could I have done more in my marriage that would have prevented the breakdown? I thought of the times that I'd been tired from keeping house, looking after the kids, and falling into bed while Ass-hat had pushed for us to have sex. I'd always considered our sex life to be normal for a couple married twenty years. It was usually three times a week but it was never enough for Ass-hat. No. He'd wanted more and found it in Linda.

When I felt the light touch on my shoulder, I jerked in my seat.

"He was never good enough for you, Shannon. I knew it the first time I met him. It's why you never came to see me after you were married. You knew I didn't care for Alex, and he never liked me either."

The sound of Aunt Maeve's voice and her words released a torrent of tears. I collapsed forward, laying my head on my arms, letting the floodgates fall open onto the wooden table. Guilt twisted my gut knowing that I should have insisted on going to see my aunt despite Ass-hat's machinations to keep me away. And it *had* been machinations! All those boring trips to Florida or going to visit his relatives in New York, had been ways to keep me from coming back to the Catskills to see my aunt.

It was a blessing that my mother had died shortly after we'd been married. At least I didn't have to feel guilty for cutting her out of my life. Ass-hat had only met her a few times and had disliked her on sight. She'd led a hard and lonely life, unlike his mother and father.

I pushed myself up and grabbed a tissue to blow my nose. Why was I blaming myself for Ass-hat's treachery? He'd sneaked around with some skank for years to ensure he'd have a relationship in place when he left. And now that it was blown to bits, (thanks to me!) he wanted his old life back. The fact that he was using the kids to accomplish that showed he was a lowlife, who cared only about his own life, not theirs.

"Maybe Steve was right to walk away, Aunt Maeve. I need to deal with this, now that the jerk I married is manipulating my kids. I'll be damned if I'm going to let them be hurt again by that asshole."

I let out a fast sigh. A feeling of peace washed through me.

I'd be okay. But I'd have to be super-careful about how I went about accomplishing that.

The fact that the magic of the well was now a part of my life really complicated things. It might have seemed like an amazing thing at first, but I was realizing that magic came at a price. I'd have to guard my thoughts and words before I made a total mess of things.

THIRTY

I had barely settled on the sofa after showering and getting dressed—the first time in three days—when there was a tap on my front door. When I heard Mary-Jane's voice calling from down the hall, I decided the reply to my son's text would have to wait. I hadn't seen her since her accident!

"Mary-Jane!" I rushed from my seat to greet her. My eyes opened wider, seeing her shed the leather jacket revealing skintight yoga pants and a long-sleeved T-shirt. Although it had only been a little over a week, I swear she'd lost ten pounds at least. More importantly, her skin practically glowed, and her eyes sparkled above a wide grin.

I gave her a big hug before saying hi to Libby standing behind her. "You look great! How's the knee?" I stepped back, still gobsmacked, checking out her tummy and hips. Maybe even more than ten pounds?

"It's a pain getting around sometimes, but all things considered, it's fine." Now it was her turn to examine me, touching my cheek. "You look pale, Shannon. How are you feeling today? I brought chicken soup that will have you better in no time."

Libby stepped forward and quipped, "You actually look like you're going to live, Shannon. It's good to see you up and about." She brought the Dutch oven with MJ's soup into the kitchen.

Oh God, it was good to see these two! Especially after the

blowup with Steve. "I feel tons better, although I'm still a bit weak. Mary-Jane, I can't get over how healthy you look! How much weight *have* you lost?"

She preened, rocking back and forth on her heels and toes. "Five pounds! I know it's not much but I'm exercising! When I put my jeans on yesterday, they felt loose, so that's progress. I feel great."

I couldn't help but laugh knowing the part I'd played in her outlook. When Libby joined us walking down the hall to the living room, we shared a smile. "How was work last night? How are you even up after working the graveyard shift?"

Libby shrugged. "It wasn't busy. I actually napped during my lunch break and then slept when I got home. I'm okay, but I'll have to leave around four to catch another hour or so." She glanced over at MJ. "This one wanted to walk out to see you, but I'm the healthcare professional here. You both need to let up on pushing yourselves."

Mary-Jane scoffed, "Are you kidding me? I haven't felt this alive in years! If I'd known my sex drive would go into fifth gear, I'd have taken a gym membership out *years* ago." Her forehead tightened before she continued, "Come to think of it, whenever I exercised in the past, it was horrible. But it sure as hell isn't now!"

I looked over at Libby, who was having a hard time keeping a straight face. I added fuel to the fire when I asked, "How is Roy coping with all this? I heard you made him join the gym too."

Libby hurried over to put a log on the fire and stoke it up. I saw her shoulders quiver as she silently laughed.

Mary-Jane remained standing, extending her arms and alternating curling them. She was obsessed with this! Her smile was sly when she answered, "Let's put it this way. He's got an appointment with the doctor to get some little blue pills. We've had to schedule more shifts at the restaurant for Zoe so that Roy and I would get more privacy."

Libby turned around and held her hands in front of her. "Enough! TMI, Mary-Jane! Just be careful that Roy doesn't have a stroke or heart attack from all your demands." She took a seat in the chair, smiling at Mary-Jane. "You know, you can take a seat for a while. You don't always have to keep moving."

Mary-Jane stuck her tongue out at Libby and began arm rotations. "It makes me feel good. Don't knock it till you try it, Libby."

Libby rolled her eyes and turned to me. "Is Steve stopping over later? I know you aren't sick but it's nice to have some help with dinner."

I let out a long sigh. "I don't think that Steve will be stopping by anymore." Libby's eyes opened wider and she leaned forward in her chair. Even Mary-Jane paused in her arm exercises. I proceeded to fill them in on the texts from my kids and Ass-hat, ending with the blowup with Steve that morning.

Mary-Jane had taken a seat next to me on the sofa. "I'm sorry that this is happening to you, Shannon. After what your ex put you through this past year, you shouldn't have to deal with this. And then there's the crap your kids have to go through *again*."

Libby tried to offer encouragement, "As awful as the scene with Steve was, I think he may have a point. In fact, he may be doing you a favor, Shannon. You need to sort this out with your kids." Her voice became softer, "And with yourself. Twenty years is a long time to toss aside. Are you sure that you could never forgive him and be together again?"

"Are you kidding me? There's no way, Libby! As I said to Steve, the trust I had in Alex is *gone*."

Mary-Jane started to say something, but I continued on, "I'm not that same doormat who was married to Alex! I'm *me* and I have to say I *like* being me! I'll do everything I can to protect my kids from getting caught up in Ass-hat's pipe dream , but that's all I can do. Thank goodness I have the time to cushion that blow. Thanksgiving isn't for another six weeks."

Mary-Jane rubbed my shoulder. "You'll handle this, Shannon. You're smart and you're a good mother. As far as Steve is concerned, he said he would do anything for you. He still cares. After this blows over, maybe then you'll get together."She shrugged. "Or not. He's not the only single guy in this town, if you decide you want to date again."

"Thanks. It's nice to hear it from you." I smiled and straightened my shoulders. "For now, I'm going to keep on with fixing this place up and trying to be supportive to my children. That's all I can do."

Libby frowned. "So are you still going ahead with this Halloween party? I know you love Halloween but will this place be ready?"

Mary-Jane's eyes lit up. "Yes! Libby told me you're planning a party. Please don't cancel, Shannon. I'll help you with the renovations and getting ready for it. You can count on me for catering!" She jumped to her feet. "I've got two weeks to lose another few pounds so I can fit into my old Cat Woman costume. Roy's costume will be snug, but I think he can squeeze into his Batman one."

I gaped at Mary-Jane and then turned to Libby. "It looks like I *have* to go through with it. Not that I mind. It'll give me added incentive to get back to work here. I'd like to get that kitchen floor sanded and varnished."

Libby smiled. "I'll get my Kevin to do the sanding. Those machines are too heavy for you. Mary-Jane and I will both help you with the other stuff. I think having a Halloween party will be good for you. You need to meet more people in this town and have some fun. What better way than with a costume party?" She was silent for a few beats. "What will I wear, I wonder?"

It felt like a load had dropped from my shoulders, seeing my friends offer to help and get so excited about this party. Libby was right. It was time to have some fun and get to know more people. I winked at Libby. "So not going as Nurse Goodbody? The fireman's going to be here, you know."

Mary-Jane shrieked and put her hands over her mouth laughing. "No way! For years, I've been bugging our Little Miss Prude to go out on a date with him. I've got the perfect costume idea for you, Libby! Elvira! You can show off the girls in a skintight dress open to your navel. Wasn't she every guy's fantasy back in the day?"

Libby's eyes almost popped out onto her cheeks. "Absolutely not going to happen! I'll think of something a bit more modest but attractive." Her eyes glinted when she turned to me. "You have to be a witch, Shannon! We can get a cauldron and some dry ice. It'll be perfect, right in character." This time she winked at me.

That exchange went over Mary-Jane's head. She looked over at me. "Will you ask Steve to the party?"

The air got sucked out of the room at her question. I felt my stomach twist into a knot. "I guess. We're friends, I suppose, so why wouldn't he want to be at the party? I'll have to get your help making up a guest list. I think twenty or thirty people could fit in here okay. If it's nice weather, we could have a small bonfire outside."

Libby's mouth tightened before she spoke, "Not Devon Booker though. Although he could probably come as he is—a snake in the grass."

Mary-Jane nodded and then continued with twisting her body at the waist, hands on her hips. "Or he could be a sneaky fox. Yeah, I'd leave Devon off the guest list, especially if Steve is coming."

Libby jumped to her feet and grabbed MJ's upper arms. "Stop! You need to get off your feet to fully heal that knee. If you don't, I swear I'm gonna slip you some valium." She frog-marched MJ over to the armchair and then forced her to sit. "I'm going to heat up that soup. You two stay put and I'll be back with lunch."

When she left, Mary-Jane popped up from the chair, resuming her waist twists. "We really need to get that woman laid, Shannon. She's been celibate way too long. She's withering into a spinster right before our eyes. The next thing you know she'll end up with thirty cats or something."

Nodding, I got up to stir the fire. "I think she's more attracted to that fireman than she lets on. She just needs a little nudge."

I glanced over at her. "You know, she told me about her

son Jack getting in with the same crowd your daughter was hanging out with. How's that going with Zoe, Mary-Jane?"

She stopped for a moment, gazing at me. "Zoe has been too busy fussing over me to hang out with those jerks. This injury really shook Roy and Zoe up"—she flashed a warm smile—"for the better. When she's not underfoot at home, she's working in the restaurant or doing schoolwork. My kid's okay, but for Libby's sake, I wish I could say the same for Jack. If he stays on this course, he's headed for trouble. He's a big reason why Libby is such a homebody."

As she spoke, I willed myself to just listen, no hoping or wishing for better things for Libby or Jack. I'd dodged a bullet with Mary-Jane, but I wasn't going to press my luck with my other friend. Libby would handle her kid, and the dating thing would come in due course. I sure as hell wasn't going to "wish" for any solutions for her.

I was saved from commenting when Libby walked in carrying lunch on a tray. She shot a dirty look at MJ before setting it down. "*Sit down* and eat. You both need the nourishment."

She set the tray on the coffee table and handed me a bowl of soup. "I had the strangest dream last night. Your aunt was in it. She kept asking me to check on you, Shannon. It was almost as if she was at the nursing station sitting next to me."

Again, the two of us locked eyes. Libby knew that my aunt was haunting my house but MJ didn't. So if Libby felt Aunt Maeve's presence near her, then something was up. But what? "That's odd. I wonder why you dreamed of Aunt Maeve."

Libby took a seat next to me. "I'm not sure. But I'm glad that we're here. Especially after hearing about your ex's latest stunts." There was a smirk on her face when she added, "Sometimes karma's a bitch, right?"

Yeah. In more ways than one.

THIRTY ONE

The next two weeks passed in a flurry of activity. True to their word, Libby and Mary-Jane spent practically every minute of their free time out at my house, helping with refinishing the kitchen floor and even giving the living room a fresh coat of paint. All of the worn carpeting had been removed and carted away, leaving us scrambling to finish the floors in the hallway and dining room. But it had all been worth it. The place looked amazing!

The afternoon of the big party, Libby's son Kevin cut the lawn for the final time of the season. As he drove away with his lawn mower poking out the trunk of his car, I noticed that he'd forgotten his gas can. I set it under the verandah, making a mental note to give it to Libby later.

Seeing Kevin reminded me of my own kids. My feet felt like blocks of concrete as I trudged up the stairs, remembering the conversation I'd had with them over a week ago. I'd even managed to set up a Zoom video call linking the three of us. It still stung recalling how they'd accused me of being unfair to their father and begging me to give him another chance.

They had bought into his sob story, hook, line, and sinker. I'd had to endure listening to how he was beside himself with remorse for breaking up our family, and ashamed that he'd taken all of us for granted. It was only after he left that he realized how much he loved ALL of us. Yada. Yada. Blah Blah.

Jessica had gone first with tears in her eyes, openly sobbing and pleading with me to give him another chance. Then came Thomas's more practical approach. He told me I was being spiteful and small minded. He'd even used my own words I'd taught him as a young child, against me. "Forgiving a wrong frees you from anger and hurt."

Yeah. Right.

I'd done the best I could in calmly stating my case. What was broken between their father and me could not be fixed. The best they could hope for was a level of kindness and civility in how their parents dealt with each other. That had gone over like a lead balloon, of course.

It put a damper on my mood when I should be excited about the party, which would start in about four hours. I had to set this Ass-hat issue aside and deal with it later. With a bit of luck, the kids would understand by Thanksgiving, so we'd see each other then.

My stomach sank even lower. If it wasn't settled, would they even visit me then...or at Christmas? Shit, I *missed* them. This was the longest I'd ever gone without seeing them.

But for now I had this party to finish preparing for. I checked the kitchen when I went inside. There were hors d'oeuvres arranged on trays to look like skeletons, witches, and hissing black cats. Orange and black streamers hung from the ceiling, crisscrossing between diaphanous spider webs. There was a large galvanized washtub filled with ice and many bottles of beers. All kinds of liquor lined the counter, along with sleeves of red plastic tumblers.

The dining room table had been pushed to the outside wall to make room for guests mingling. A grouping of pumpkins, squash, and corn stalks completed the decorations there. A quick glance at the living room showed everything was as ready as it could be, with the wood in the fireplace waiting for just one match. The witch's cauldron that Libby had recommended was set near the window, overlooking the lake. It just needed some dry ice to get it roiling.

I went up the stairs and poured a nice long bath, using my favorite scented bath bombs. I had plenty of time to enjoy a leisurely soak and could primp and pamper myself before putting my witch dress and cloak on. It was an original, scrounged from Goodwill and the dollar store, but it still managed to be flattering, showing off my figure without being overtly sexy. Considering I only knew a handful of people coming to my party, I wanted to make a decent impression.

Thank God for Libby and Mary-Jane. They handled choosing the guest list and making the invites in person. If they hadn't, I'd be lucky to have six guests. They managed to get a lot of the old gang from bygone days. People I haven't seen in almost twenty-five years.

An hour later, I stood in front of the mirror, primping and turning to admire how I looked in my costume. The slit in the side of the dress showed off the red-and-green-striped knee socks and the ankle boots. The V neckline was a little more plunging than I wanted, but a black-lace camisole peeked up, covering most of my cleavage. I pressed my finger against the fake mole on my chin, trying to secure it better. I'd given up trying to get the plastic nose affixed over my own nose. The greenish shade to my skin tone would just have to do. The only thing left was to sweep my hair into a bun and put the witch hat on.

I tidied up in the bathroom and was about to go downstairs when I noticed my aunt's bedroom door was ajar. My eyes opened wider and I hurried into the room. It had been over a week since I'd had any visit or contact with my aunt. Maybe she was letting me know she'd be at the party in spirit if nothing else. The scent of lilies hit me when I stepped into the room. My gaze scanned the area looking for that shimmering in the air that I'd always noticed when she was around. The Grimoire on the pillow next to the photo of the Witching Well caught my eye.

I'd hidden the book in my room so Mary-Jane wouldn't stumble upon it when she'd been helping me out earlier in the week. And the photo of the well had been returned to hang above my aunt's dresser.

My eyes narrowed. "Aunt Maeve? What are you up to?" I tucked the Grimoire under the pillow and set the photo on the dresser. "Is this your way of telling me you're here? I was hoping you'd make an appearance to see your house filled with people you once knew. How long has it been since this house had a party in it?"

When there was no response, not even a faint touch or cool breath on my cheek, I shrugged. "I promise I'll lock this door so that no one wanders in to touch your things, how's that?" As there were still last-minute things to do before guests arrived, I hurried out of the room, setting the lock on the door before closing it.

I took the tray of brownies that I'd prepared earlier from the fridge and turned the oven on. There was no way I could forget the brownies, not after promising Stan Jones, the hunky fireman who'd helped me find out where Ida-Red-Car lived. Gosh! That seemed like so long ago after all that had happened.

When the front door opened, I called out, "Is that you Mary-Jane? About time you got here with your catering! I think that's why a lot of people accepted the invitation."

When I turned, it wasn't Mary-Jane standing in the doorway. It was Steve. I stopped short, and my mouth fell open, gazing at him. It wasn't just that I hadn't spoken to him in two weeks since that morning—he looked amazing! He was decked out as a pirate, with a white, ruffled shirt open to the navel, displaying dark hair between two ripped and tight pectorals, while it looked like he'd been literally poured into the tight leather pants.

"Hi. Or should I say 'Ahar, matey'?" It was hard to get the words out, past a mouth that felt like it had been stuffed with cotton. It didn't help that my pulse rate had rocketed into the stratosphere. Oh God he was *hot*!

He handed me a bottle of rum and his smile seemed kind of sheepish. "I hope you're okay with me being here. I came early in case you needed some help getting set up before your guests arrive." He stepped closer, and his gaze sent a thrill right through to my core. "You look awesome, Shannon."

I gulped and turned to hide the blush, which probably was melting the green face cream. I set the rum with the other bottles. "Thanks. It's totally fine. We're friends, right? I'm happy you came."

His hands rose to rest lightly on my shoulders while his head lowered, his lips so close to my ear, I could feel the warmth of his breath. "I've missed you, Shannon. I can't believe how often I thought of you."

I spun around and eased back from his touch. "Don't start this again, Steve. Not now. I've done a lot of thinking about what you said. I think I need some more time before we can ever be more than friends. I need to be on my own for a while."

His eyebrows rose, and it took a few beats before a smile lifted his lips. "Let's have a drink, Witch. It's Halloween! For just one night, let's forget who we are. Tonight I'm a rakish rogue, and you're deliciously wicked. I stake a claim to the first dance, deal?"

The twinkle in his eye accentuated the boyish grin. It was hard to resist his charm, but I was going to give it the old college try. "Sure. Since you're here early, you might as well make yourself useful. Pour me a Jack Daniels while I pop these brownies into the oven. After that, maybe you can start a fire in the fireplace while I get my cell phone and speakers set up with music. "

I sneaked a glance at him as I opened the oven door. If he was taken back by my gentle rebuff, he sure didn't act it. The smile never left his lips as he got us two drinks. I decided to keep the conversation in neutral territory. "How's your son?"

"Great! He's with Amy tonight, making a Spiderman costume. He's totally stoked about going out trick or treating tomorrow night." He turned and handed me a tumbler of Jack. "A toast, to Halloween and your party. And to magic moments."

For a moment I peered at him. Why did he say magic? But

then I took a deep breath and smiled. It was Halloween, an innocent remark. "Yes. To all the ghouls and goblins I'm going to meet tonight."

The banging of a car door followed, and I rushed to the window. A group of people, one of whom looked really familiar even in just the light shining from the verandah, poured out of the vehicle. I leaned closer, squinting my eyes. Oh my God. It was Ida-Red-Car, decked out as Raggedy Ann, skipping up the walk with a tall, Raggedy Andy beside her.

Wow! People didn't lose a minute in getting here. I went to the door and threw it open, while Steve hurried to the living room to get the fire going.

Ida-Red-Car stood at the door grinning. "Trick or treat, Shannon!" Her hands clasped together in front of her as she rocked back and forth on her feet.

"Ida! I'm so glad you could make my party! Come in! No tricks, okay?"

She flounced by me, and when the group was inside, proceeded to introduce her husband and the other couple, a pair of zombies. George and Lesley O'Brien. "Pleased to meet you. Come in, and help yourself to beer or whatever poison that's lined up on the counter. The mix is in the cooler with the beer."

They'd hardly swept by me when I noticed another vehicle enter the driveway. Oh my God! Where were Mary-Jane and Libby? I'd hoped that they'd be here to help me with introductions and hostessing this gig.

I watched a lone figure emerge from the large vehicle. From the swagger and breadth of his shoulders, straining the white buckskin jacket, I knew it had to be Stan Jones, Libby's fireman. His boots clacked across the wooden verandah and he touched the broad rim of a white cowboy hat, dipping his chin. A black mask covered his eyes, but not that dazzling smile. "Howdy, ma'am. Lone Ranger at your service."

"Stan!" I gave him a warm hug and pulled back, grinning up at him. "You look great! If I had a contest for best costume, you'd win. Come in! Let's get you a drink." I opened the door wider, leading him into the kitchen where the others were still getting drinks and nibbling from the trays of food.

When they saw him, they gushed and chattered with him, leaving me free to get the music set up. I hurried down the hall to the living room. When there was another tap at the door, I asked Steve to get it. In no time flat I had "Monster Mash" blaring on the stereo speakers before I headed to the door to greet the latest guests. As I passed the kitchen doorway, I noticed that the group there was laughing, having a good time.

I edged past Steve's frame at the front door to see who had arrived. Oh my God. It was a beautiful woman with a mane of brunette hair, secured from her forehead by a Wonder Woman headband. She wore a cape, but it did little to hide the tops of her breasts straining against the tight costume, while tanned legs glistened above dark boots. Her ice-blue eyes left Steve's to fasten her gaze on me.

"Shannon, this is Cynthia Granger. Cynthia, this is Shannon Burke, the hostess of this crazy party."

For a moment my mouth fell open, staring at her. This was the serial dater who Devon and Steve had fought over? Small wonder, she was stunning. "Hi. It's nice to meet you! Please come in. I love your costume!"

Steve stepped back, and for a brief moment our eyes met. He gave a small shrug and followed Cynthia and I into the house.

"Wow! I haven't been in this house in eons! It's exactly the way I remember from when my grandmother and I visited your aunt. I'm so glad that you're living in it and not selling out. Your aunt would roll in her grave if you did that." Cynthia squeezed my arm as she looked around at the kitchen and hallway.

I liked her right away. "Thanks. I'd like to hear more about your visits here. But it will have to wait. I hear another car door and should go greet the new guests." Turning to Steve, I asked, "Can you look after getting Cynthia a drink and something to eat?"

I turned to go back to the door, hoping like hell it would be

Mary-Jane or Libby. This was fun but nerve racking since I only knew a couple of people here. Some backup would be greatly appreciated!

When I stepped out onto the verandah, I saw three people emerge from a SUV. They were wearing masks, so I had no idea who they were. The tallest one had a plague-doctor mask while the other two wore full rubber masks of Porky Pig and a zombie. It was odd that they walked shrouded by dark capes, totally silent as they approached.

The two shorter people stepped forward, staring at me quietly.

"Hi! Great costumes. Uh..." My forehead tightened, and for some reason my gut twisted in a knot. Why were they just standing there, not saying a word? "Who are you?" It popped out before I could stop it.

The two shorter figures lifted the masks up and off. My mouth gaped open, seeing my son and daughter standing there. But when the third figure lifted the plague mask, my mouth snapped shut.

Ass-hat.

THIRTY TWO

"Mom!" Jessica stepped forward and threw her arms around me. I stood mutely as she gushed, "We thought we'd surprise you! We know how much you love Halloween!"

When she stepped back, Thomas hugged me. "You look great, Mom. It sounds like a rocking party going on."

Again, I let him hug me as I stood still as a statue, my gaze locked with their father's. Waiting.

Finally, he spoke, "Shannon, I know this is a surprise, but the kids and I wanted to spend Halloween with you. When we heard you were throwing a party, it just seemed like the perfect opportunity." His face was perfectly calm, not even a trace of nervousness at showing up here like this, out of the effing blue! My face felt like it was made from stone as I glared at him, while he looked like this was as natural as returning home from a trip to the grocery store.

Steve's voice behind me made me jump. "Shannon? Are you coming in?" When I didn't turn or answer him, his words became quicker. "Are you all right? Everything okay here?"

I glanced back at him, "Steve, this is my daughter, Jessica, and my son, Thomas. Their father, Alex, decided to bring them to my party."

"Oh. I see."

Immediately, I turned to him. "Please go back inside and make sure my guests are looked after. I want to speak to my family in private." My words were clipped as I struggled to keep the burning rage from erupting. It was clear from the surprise in Steve's eyes that he knew I was barely holding it together.

When he left, I looked at both of my kids. "I wish that you had talked to me before you decided to drive here. I thought I made my position regarding your father perfectly clear."

Jessica took a step closer, reaching for my hand. "Mom. We thought that coming to your party would be a good icebreaker for all of us. We knew you would never agree to meet with us on your own, so we decided to just show up."

When I saw headlights turn into my drive, I pulled Jessica to the side, walking down the few steps to the yard. "There are more people showing up. Let's not make a scene here, okay? We'll talk at the side of the house where we can have privacy."

Thomas piped up, "There doesn't have to be a *scene*, Mom. Let's just go inside and have fun. We can meet your friends and maybe you and Dad can talk later. You're making waaay too big a deal about this." He followed on my heels while I could hear Ass-hat walking a few feet behind us.

When we were at the side of the house at the periphery of the light shining from the verandah, I couldn't hold my temper any longer. Ignoring Thomas and Jess, I turned on Ass-hat. "This is all your doing. Your little fling with Linda ended, so you decided to try to piece your family back together."

"Wait a minute, Shannon! That's not fair. The thing with Linda ended, yes. But I'm *glad* it did! It was like there was a spell on me when I left you for her. I love you. I realized how much I really loved you when you weren't in my life. I think that's the reason why it didn't work with Linda and me."

My eyes flared wide, and I gritted my teeth to keep from screaming, *Liar*! I knew why his thing with Linda ended, and it had nothing to do with missing me! Or the kids! His dick didn't work, and that's what he was really missing.

"See, Mom? Dad made a terrible mistake. He's sorry. Why can't you just talk to him for a while about this?" There were tears in Jessica's eyes when she sidled closer to me.

Rather than the waterworks softening my position, it had the opposite effect. My blood practically boiled, seeing this added hurt in my daughter, a hurt that Ass-hat's selfishness was causing. My hand rose to swipe a tear from her cheek. "It isn't that simple, Jess. Your father betrayed my trust in him. He caused a lot of pain in my life as well as in your life and Thomas's life. There's no going back."

Thomas put his arm over his sister's shoulder. "Dad hurt us, sure! But what do you think you're doing right now, Mom? You could fix this, if only you'd get past your own stupid ego. We can be a family again, but you're turning it down without even hearing him out! This is your fault now."

"Enough!" My heart broke, hearing my son's condemnation. I was the innocent one in the marriage breakup. *He* had cheated, not me! I glared at Ass-hat. "How dare you do this to our kids! You had to involve them in your scheme to get back with me. You're a *coward*! The only person you care about is yourself! Take the kids and go. You never should have come here, let alone drag them along as some kind of shield."

Ass-hat's face grew harder, his eyes narrowed as he stepped closer. "You aren't being reasonable, Shannon. Can't you see how much pain you're causing our children? We aren't leaving until you and I have talked. Stop being such a bitch, at least for the kids' sake." His hand thrust out to grab my arm, closing on it like a vise.

"Let go of me! The only one who caused them pain is you! And you're *still* doing it!" I tried to shake his hand from my arm but his grip got even tighter.

"Get your goddamn hands off her, pal!"

My head turned at the new voice. Devon? Oh my God. I'd been so wrapped up in the argument with the kids and Ass-hat that I hadn't heard him approach. His eyes were locked with Ass-hat's as he kept striding over.

"Mind your own business! This is my wife and kids here. It's no concern of yours. Screw off!" Ass-hat had turned to the side partly facing Devon but keeping his hand grasping my arm. "Shannon! Tell him to go back to the party. We don't want some kind of scene in front of the kids."

My foot in the sharp-toed boot arced up, catching Ass-hat on the shin. "Screw you! You should have thought of that when you chose to involve them, Alex!"

"Mom! Stop this. Let's just talk," Jessica pleaded.

Devon's fist bunched in the folds of Ass-hat's cape, yanking him away from me. His teeth were gritted tight before he shoved Ass-hat, knocking him off-balance and to the ground. "The lady asked you to leave."

He looked over at the kids who stood wide-eyed, staring at the scene. "Sorry, kids but he should never ever lay a hand on your mother. It looks like the party's over for you guys." He looked over at me. "Unless you want them to stay, and I'll escort this jerk off the property."

Thomas reached over to help his father up from the ground. "We're all leaving. C'mon, Dad. I can see why you left Mom. She's a total bitch." He grabbed Jessica's arm and started frog-marching her back to the SUV. "I never want to see you again, Mom."

His words sliced my heart into pieces. All the while Jessica sobbed, begging me to stop this. I felt my world fall apart, staring as my son and daughter got in the vehicle.

Ass-hat hurled a parting shot, "You can kiss the support I send you goodbye until we resolve this, Shannon! Go on back to your boyfriend! I'll look after our children."

I shrieked at him, "Go back to Linda! Oh, wait. I guess she threw you out, so you can't." I rubbed my arm where he'd crushed it with his paw. What a disaster! A totally needless mess that he'd created. What made it unbearable was that now my kids couldn't stand the sight of me.

Devon pulled me into his arms, rubbing my back. "I'm sorry this happened, Shannon."

But as quick as he had reached to comfort me, I felt his hands scrape along my arms as he was wrenched back. I jerked back, seeing Devon laying on the grass while Steve stood over him with his fist raised.

THIRTY THREE

I was hardly aware of Ass-hat peeling out of the driveway and gravel being hurled high from his screeching tires. Steve picked Devon up by his lapels and only missed landing a knockout punch to his jaw when Devon's leg shot out, knocking him off-balance. "Get off me, Murphy!"

Oh my God! As if the nightmare with my kids and Ass-hat wasn't enough, these two grown men were trying to kill one another! For a few moments I could only stare in horror. A sharp pain streaked through my chest, jolting me. Shit! Was I having a heart attack? As quickly as the pain had struck, it was gone, leaving me feeling lightheaded and dizzy. I heard the front door bang shut before shouts filled the air.

"Stop it!" I rushed over, tugging at Steve's shirt, but strong arms gripped me, pulling me back. The next thing I knew, Stan and a couple of other guys pulled Steve and Devon apart. All the while the air was blue with Steve's curses.

I stepped in between the two sides, holding my hands up, like I was separating the red sea. "Enough! You both have to get the hell out of here! I can't deal with this! This can't be happening!"

When Ida-Red-Car came over and tried to put her arm around my shoulder, murmuring words intended to calm things, I turned on her. "Please! Get away from me! I can't cope right now! I. Just. Can't. Not now! You don't understand. My children..." Tears choked off anything else but I didn't care. I turned and brushed by the group of people standing there, racing across the yard and then into the house.

My feet practically flew up the stairs. I ran into my room and slammed the door. When I fell onto the bed, my shoulders wracked with sobs. What a failure I was! I couldn't even throw a party without it erupting into an out-and-out brawl. And even my best friends had deserted me when I'd needed them the most. But the worst thing that could ever happen had happened.

My kids despised me.

I don't know how long I lay there crying my eyes out when my bedroom door opened. I felt a hand on my shoulder, and I rolled over, expecting...hell, I don't know who I thought would be trying to comfort me, but it sure as hell wasn't who I saw.

Cynthia?

Her eyes were rimmed with sadness when she murmured, "Everyone's gone home, Shannon. I'm sorry about what happened tonight, even if I'm not really sure what *did* happen. I think you need to get some rest, so I'm going to leave now, okay?"

I nodded numbly and watched her turn and go out the door. What a complete disaster my life had become that the only one who showed a modicum of kindness was a complete stranger. That's all I had to show for myself? *What a loser I am.*

What made it even worse was the fact that *I'd* initiated the blowup with my kids. If I hadn't put that curse on Ass-hat with Linda, he'd still be with her and I'd still have a good relationship with Jessica and Thomas.

Wait.

That curse had been a justified, angry thought that any woman who'd been lied and cheated on would have! This wasn't my fault. Not really.

NO! It was that damned Witching Well of Maeve's and its so-called magic. It had caused more problems in my life than it had ever solved. And I was cursed to have found it! I couldn't live my life like this anymore! My jaw clenched tight as the pieces fell into place.

I had to destroy it! It was the only way I'd ever be free of its malignant influence in my life. If I had any chance at all of getting my children to love me again, I had to burn it down. And I knew where I could find the fuel.

Ten minutes later I strode down the pathway armed with a pack of matches and the can of gas that Kevin had forgotten at my house. Branches and the underbrush clawed at my cape as I picked my way along a dark path, lit only by the light of a crescent moon. Twice, I almost tripped on stones that littered the trail leading to the well. It was hard to find my way, but, by hell, if it took me till dawn, I would find that blasted well!

The screech of a wild animal—that bobcat probably!— came from deep in the woods but I wasn't fazed. Even if it stepped out onto the path, it wouldn't stop me. I'd had enough of that stupid, magical well. How had Aunt Maeve lived with this curse? No wonder she had never married or had children. She probably knew the stakes would be too high, burdened by that cursed well like an albatross around her neck. Well, that was her, but I knew I wouldn't bear that fate.

Finally I came to the clearing. I stood there panting, catching my breath before I would splash gas all over it to destroy the damned thing! I'd burn what I could and come back with a sledgehammer to knock the rest of it down. For now, I just wanted to burn it! With renewed resolve I walked over to it. As I unscrewed the cap from the plastic jug of fuel, I hissed curses at the creature in the well. "You damned bitch! You've ruined my life. Well, it ends tonight. I don't care if you're a witch from *Salem*, you are going to go back to hell where you belong."

I lifted the can high and tilted it.

"STOP!"

I jerked back. My heart pounded fast as I realized that the voice hadn't come from the well...but from somewhere behind me!

"Shannon! Oh my God, I'm so glad we found you!"

I turned and saw two figures emerge from the stand of trees. As they got closer, my jaw fell down to my knees. Libby? Mary-Jane?

THIRTY FOUR

Libby rushed across the grass while Mary-Jane gaped, taking in the trees surrounding the strange little glade. I shook my head from side to side, not believing my eyes. What were they doing here? Why?

Libby took the container of gas from my hand. "Shannon, take it easy, okay? You're going to set yourself and the whole forest on fire if you're not careful. It's a good thing we got to you in time."

"But how?" The nightmare of the party and my kids leaving me in disgust flashed in my mind. I tried to wrestle the container from her grip but Mary-Jane pulled me back.

"Stop, Shannon! Libby's right." She glanced over the lip of the well into its depths. "What the hell is this? Why are you trying to burn it? Hell! I don't even know what this well is all about, but I know you need to stop, Shannon. Your aunt—"

"What about my aunt? Why are you two even here?" I swayed on my feet and reached for the stone wall of the well to steady myself. A wave of dizziness flooded through me as I gulped big mouthfuls of the cool night air. Forget a heart attack! It felt like I was going to stroke out if anything.

Libby set the gas container down and reached for my hand. "What Mary-Jane tried to tell you is that your aunt appeared to both of us in a dream."

"It was more like a daydream, really. I zoned out even though I was doing a bench press. The damned weights just about—"

"Mary-Jane! Whether it was a nighttime dream or zoning out doesn't matter! The important thing is that Maeve appeared to *both* of us." Libby turned to peer at me. "She said you were in dire trouble, Shannon. Maeve told Mary-Jane and me to come to this well, that you needed us. She even lit the way through the trees so we could find you."

"What? But why?" None of this made any sense at all.

Mary-Jane snorted. "I think it's obvious. She didn't want you to incinerate yourself and half of the mountain. What I don't get is why you're out here at night. And what happened to your party?" She pulled the cloak she was wearing tighter around her body, peering at the trees around us. "This is seriously creepy. Can we leave now?"

Ignoring her, Libby spoke, "Something happened to make you want to destroy this well, Shannon. Your aunt came to Mary-Jane and me to help you. It's clear that she thought if you burned this well, it would be very, very bad for you."

Again, tears threatened to spill as I looked into her eyes. The concern on her face and the fact that my kids hated me brought me almost to my knees. "Ass-hat showed up at the party with Thomas and Jessica."

"Oh shit, shit, shit." Libby's hand rose to rest on my shoulder. "That's why you're out here. It must have been pretty bad."

Mary-Jane's gaze flitted from Libby to me. "There's something you're not telling me, guys! I get that her ex showing up wouldn't be good! Hell, it must have been awful! But why come out here to torch this old well? That's just crazy!"

She leaned in, staring into my eyes. "Why did Maeve appear to both of us? I kept asking Libby on the way out but she wouldn't tell me." Rubbing her uppers arms, she shivered. "Can we go back to your house to talk about this? It's seriously creepy out here, not to mention cold."

I shook my head, trying to make sense of it all. "No, Mary-Jane. This is where we need to be, right here, at this well while we figure this out." I looked at Libby again. "The scene with Ass-hat and the kids went really bad. I lost my temper and told them to leave. Thomas said he never wants to see me again. It's all because of this well and that curse I put on Ass-hat."

"You *can't* destroy the well, Shannon. Think about it! Maeve urged Mary-Jane and I to come out here to stop you. If we hadn't, things could have gotten way worse. As for Thomas and Jessica...they're your kids. They're angry and hurt...again! But they'll come around, in time."

Mary-Jane's hand rose like a traffic cop's. "Hang on! Did you just say she put a curse on her ex? A curse? What the hell—"

But Libby ignored her and continued, "Maybe there's something we can do to reverse that curse! Something so that he'll get back with Linda or find some other woman."

"You guys are talking crazy, here! I don't know why your aunt came to me and made me come here, but this is nuts, as in total loonytunes! I'm cold, and I'm going back." Mary-Jane started to step away, but my hand shot out to stop her.

"Wait! It needs to be all of us here! There are three of us. Three. My aunt wrote about the power of three." My gaze shot to Libby. "You saw that too!"

"Yes! If the three of us standing here beside this magic well combine a wish to reverse the spell, it might work! Your Aunt Maeve said there is a ton of power in a triumvirate. Well, there's three of us here!"

"Magic well? Did I just hear you say, 'magic well'?" Mary-Jane edged close to the well's opening and peeked down. "Seriously?" When she turned to fix her stare on Libby and me, she said, "You two are serious. You really think this is a *magic* well."

Libby nodded. "Try to keep up, Mary-Jane! Yes, a magic well! We have to try something to fix this mess, Shannon." Her eyes narrowed. "You made an offering to this thing when you stumbled onto it. If Mary-Jane and I are going to help you, maybe we have to make an offering too. But what? What can we offer that will give us the same magical power that the well gave to you?"

I blew out a huff of frustration. "This just keeps getting better and better." Mary-Jane looked up at the sky, blinking slowly. "Okay. If this will get us out of here any faster, I'm willing to try anything." She tugged her purse out, which was hidden by the cloak, and lifted the flap. "I've got credit cards, some cash, lipstick, or my little emergency sewing kit. Take your pick."

I looked at Libby. "Blood. I think we need to offer our blood to make this work." The sewing kit would have a needle. We could prick our fingers."

Libby quickly added, "Mingling our blood will strengthen the bond between us. I know this sounds like a juvenile trick, but I think it applies here."

Mary-Jane jerked back, holding her purse tight to her body. "Blood? Are you crazy? You're a nurse, for God's sake! You're not supposed to expose yourself to other people's blood and fluids...unless it's sex and you've been with them like forever!"

"Well, I don't know about you, MJ, but my dose of the clap cleared up last week. I'm good! How about you, Libby?"

She grinned. "A little Hep A won't kill you."

Mary-Jane took a step back. "Sure! Laugh all you want, but you're not getting any of my blood, you ghouls!"

Libby towered over her, walking slowly toward her. "You wouldn't sacrifice a little prick of blood to help Shannon get her kids back? C'mon, Mary-Jane. Why do you think you're doing so well in your weight loss and exercise? You have Shannon to thank for that. She blessed you with that wish. The least you can do is this one little thing."

Mary-Jane leaned to the side, her head appearing at Libby's side, staring at me, "*You* did that, Shannon? That's why I'm obsessed with exercise and sex? That's why the pounds are falling off my fat ass?"

"Yeah. I was worried when you told me what your doctor said. I wished for you to succeed."

"Oh yeah? When?" She stared at me in disbelief.

I took a deep breath. "Remember when you brought over the Chinese food? And you were talking about your doctor warning you about your weight and gall bladder problems?"

She blinked at me and nodded.

"Before we started eating, I silently wished that this time you'd really stick with your diet, and that for you, exercising would be as pleasurable as sex..." I let that hang in the air for a moment. "*Orgasmic* is the term I used."

Mary-Jane let out a gasp.

"You barely ate a bite, and the next morning you woke me up with jumping jacks. Remember?" I started to cry. "And then...and then you went out running and sprained your knee!" Oh shit! Another oddball screwup that she'd gotten hurt...because of me.

Mary-Jane handed the purse to Libby. "Here. You win. But if I get hepatitis or some disease, I'm coming after you. The sewing kit's in a little pink case." She walked over and stood next to me. "So what does this make us? Some sort of coven or something?"

I gave her a hug. "I think a coven is thirteen, but I'd say we've got a start on this. Thanks for agreeing to this, Mary-Jane."

She eased back and scowled at me. "You two have got some explaining to do when we get back to your house. I don't like being the third wheel, left out of everything. You should have told me!"

I looked over at Libby when she appeared beside us, armed with a sewing needle. "You're the nurse, so it's up to you to do the pricking."

Mary-Jane elbowed me. "Stop. I hate the sight of blood, especially when it's my own."

"All to help the big prick with his little prick!" The craziness hit me like a Mack truck, making me giggle. Soon Libby and Mary-Jane joined in.

The sharp pain that sparked in my finger cut the laughter short. "Ow!" Soon Mary-Jane let out a yelp when Libby stabbed her finger.

I held my finger up and over the well, watching as a drop of blood oozed from the pad. Libby's finger nestled against mine. We looked at Mary-Jane who rolled her eyes before joining her finger to ours.

"By the power of the earth, wind, fire, and our blood, we ask that the impotence spell on Alex Johnston be reversed. Please help my children Thomas and Jessica forgive me." I stared down into the dark depths of the well. A gust of wind lifted my hair, swirling around both Libby and Mary-Jane.

The voice which spoke from the darkness below was almost drowned by the wind rustling the trees around us. "By the power of three, so mote it be."

My mouth fell open, and I saw my own look of shock mirrored in Libby's and Mary-Jane's faces. On impulse I murmured, "So mote it be."

Without missing a beat, Libby and Mary-Jane repeated the phrase.

"So mote it be."

THIRTY FIVE

A half hour later, the three of us were back at my house, snuggled close to the fireplace, munching on food and drinking. On the way back, Libby and I filled Mary-Jane in on all the supernatural visits from my Aunt Maeve as well as the "wishes" that had created havoc in my life. At first she'd been angry as hell that we hadn't let her in on things, but now sitting there, she was excited about it all.

"So we're kind of like witches, right? If I want to get back at someone or wish them well, then I've got that power, right?" When Libby and I shot a look of horror at her, she quickly added, "Not that I'm going to do that. Not until I find out more about this. Especially after seeing the trouble it caused for you, Shannon."

There was silence for a few moments before Libby spoke, "It's funny, you know. I went into nursing because I've always had a lot of empathy for sick people. I've always had the ability to tell when something's wrong, even when a person denies it." She looked over at Mary-Jane and me. "I'm getting a strong sense that ability might have just ratcheted up to a whole new level."

Mary-Jane nodded. "I still can't get over Maeve showing up in my daydream. I swear I could practically smell that perfume she always wore. It was kind of floral but with a bit of patchouli oil mixed in. It was so vivid."

Libby's head tilted to the side when she looked at MJ. "It was more a 'feeling' that I got. That Shannon needed me. And then when you showed up at my door, telling me the same thing, I knew."

Her forehead furrowed. "But what about Roy? How'd you get away without him? He wanted to come to the party, right?"

"Yeah, he did. He had his costume on, ready to go out the door. But I told him I needed to help Shannon. And that I needed to do it alone." She took a deep breath, "He's been so good to me since my accident. It's like he has a brand-new appreciation for me." She brightened. "All he said was be careful and to let him know I'm okay."

She jumped up and grabbed her purse. "Which I promptly forgot to do. Give me a few minutes." She took her phone from her purse and then wandered out of the room.

"Don't tell him about the well! Make something up, but don't tell him!" Libby raced after her but paused at the doorway, looking at Shannon. "Want another drink? I think MJ and I are staying the night. We've got a lot to figure out with this stuff."

"Sure." When she left I stirred the fire, gazing at the flames. There *was* a lot to figure out with this magic stuff, but at least I had my friends helping me. I smiled as a heavy but warm feeling washed over me. A faint brush of air caressed my neck and whispered words filtered into my ear, *"You have gathered your triumvirate."*

"Oh my God, she's here! She's standing next to you, Shannon! Maeve!"

I turned at Libby's voice and saw the shimmer of my aunt's form next to me. She wavered in the air, and her smile was just barely visible. Her presence lasted until Libby and Mary-Jane were seated beside me at the fireplace.

When her image faded, I stared at my two friends. "We are three. Our trinity is complete."

Mary-Jane shook her head from side to side. "Nope. We are just getting started."

The END

EPILOGUE...

Two months later:

Practically the last thing I wanted to do was have dinner with Libby and her family on Christmas Eve. But she wouldn't take no for an answer, not after seeing me spend Thanksgiving alone, hoping and waiting for my kids to show up. Even though I'd tried countless times to repair the damage with Thomas and Jessica, even offering to fly out to visit each of them at their schools, they'd turned me down. They were both still angry about me refusing to even meet with Ass-hat. Needless to say, I'd shed many a tear over our estrangement.

I leaned closer to the mirror, applying some mascara to my lashes. Although I tried my best not to dwell on this painful situation, times like this...holidays like Thanksgiving and Christmas were slap shots to the gut. My lips were a tight line thinking of Ass-hat. He'd tried a few times to contact me, but there was no way I was letting him anywhere near me. He'd screwed up my relationship with my children when he'd shown up unannounced at my Halloween party.

As far as reversing the curse, there was no way of

knowing if it had worked or not. And, frankly, at this point, I was beginning to care less and less. He could suffer from impotence for the rest of his miserable life for all I cared. But Libby and MJ didn't agree. They'd really been affected by how we'd come together after Maeve's urging.

Plus, they were just being supportive, like they'd always been.

Despite the constant ache in my heart from my children's reaction, I'd carried on with the renovations, even starting on one of the cabins. Mary-Jane and Libby had helped with some of it, that is when we weren't having our weekly dinner together, exchanging notes on this magic, witchcraft thing.

I smiled thinking of our celebration the last time we'd met. Mary-Jane was ecstatic about losing twenty-five pounds! She'd gotten a new hairstyle and a ton of flattering clothes to show off her new curves. Of all of us, she was the one most excited about our newfound magical power, immersing herself in research about what we now called "the craft."

When she'd wanted to do a spell to nudge my kids into forgiving me, both Libby and I had nixed it. Mary-Jane hadn't experienced the negative that could result, and I sure as hell didn't want to make matters worse.

It was funny...since that night at the well, Libby had changed the most. There was an otherworldly quality about how she approached life now. She'd always been empathetic, but now it was like she could "see" into other people's hearts and sense their feelings. She even claimed that she could see a colored haze surrounding people that indicated not only their state of health but their mood. I sighed. That was probably why she was adamant that I join her and her family for Christmas Eve. Thanksgiving had been brutal.

My cell phone dinged with a text message and I went to the bedroom to get it. Even though it wasn't Thomas's or Jessica's ringtone, there was always the chance that it could be them, right? My heart fell, seeing Steve's face appear above the text. We'd patched things up enough that we were friends, but it was disappointing that it wasn't my kids reaching out.

> Hey! I wanted to get an early Merry Christmas out to you since tomorrow morning is going to be chaotic here. Byron and his two mothers are coming over in the morning to exchange gifts. Maybe I can stop by for a drink with you on Boxing Day? Have fun at Libby's!

I texted a quick reply.

> Happy Holidays to you too! Say hi to Byron and let me know if he likes the video game I got him. Having a drink sounds great!

I slipped the phone in my purse and trudged down the stairs. Actually having a drink right now, or maybe ten drinks, sounded better than going out to be with Libby's family. It would only remind me of the hole in my life, not seeing my own kids.

It had snowed the night before, so before I could do anything, I'd have to shovel my drive and hope that the plow hadn't left a wall of heavy snow at the road for me to clear. Even so, when I looked out the window at the gray lake under a clear blue sky, the evergreens surrounding it dusted with snow, I had to admit that it sure was pretty.

I went to the door to pull on my boots and parka. Just as I was about to open the door, my cell phone rang. My heart stopped, hearing Thomas's ringtone. In a flash I yanked it from my purse and answered it.

"Hello?"

"Hi, Mom. Is the offer for Christmas dinner still open?"

My eyes opened wider and I grinned! "Of course. I'd love for you to come here for Christmas." But my second set of ears, the mom ones, heard the undercurrent of sadness in my son's voice. "What's up?"

"It's not just me, Mom. Jess will be with me. We were supposed to visit Dad in Pittsburgh, but he canceled at the last minute. He's spending Christmas in Aspen. I'm pretty sure he's not going there by himself. I heard a woman's voice in the background when he was on the phone with me."

My eyes narrowed thinking of that bastard tossing the kids aside once more, but I kept my voice calm when I answered. "I'd love to see you and Jessica. You have no idea how much I've missed you. Are you flying in? When can I pick you up?" The anger that I felt at Ass-hat dissolved in the happiness of seeing my kids.

"We get into Albany at eleven tomorrow morning. We thought we'd stay with you for the week. Think you can put up with us that long?"

My heart raced in my chest, and tears welled in my eyes—happy tears! "I don't know. Think you can put up with me for a week? Of *course* it's okay! I am over the moon to see you guys. I have to warn you though; I mailed your gifts to your dorms last week. I wasn't sure I'd see you."

There was silence for a few beats, and I held my phone out checking my connection. Finally he spoke but his voice was strained. "I'm sorry for what I said to you, Mom, the last time I saw you. You've always been there for Jess and me."

I sighed. "That's in the past, Son. What's important is having you here. I'll be at the airport to pick you up. I can't wait!"

"Yeah, me too! I feel awful about not calling you before this."

I shook my head. "You're calling me now, and that's what counts. I'll see you tomorrow."

When I hung up the phone, I closed my eyes thanking whatever powers in the universe had intervened to make this happen. But then it hit me. The Witching Well. Mary-Jane and Libby had joined me in reversing the curse on Ass-hat. It must have worked if he was going to Aspen with some woman.

And back to his old self-centered ways.

Whatever.

I'd have to hustle if I was going to make it to the store in time to get a turkey and all the fixings. I would call Libby and Mary-Jane while I was on my way to town.

At the sound of a vehicle in the driveway, I opened the door and looked out. A truck with a plow mounted on the front pushed snow and came to a stop at the edge of my walkway. The door opened and Devon leaned out. Oh my God! I hadn't seen or heard from him since that Halloween party. I had to smile, seeing the comical red-plaid trapper hat almost eclipsing his face.

"This is my Christmas present to you, Shannon. You really should think of getting a plow guy or mount a blade on your truck. You're living in the mountains now, woman."

"Totally! Thanks! I need to do that, all right!" I could hardly believe that he'd shown up at exactly the right moment to save my ass. Again. He'd also decked Ass-hat when he'd grabbed me. And his words, "You're living in the mountains now" took me by surprise. It looked like he finally was acknowledging that I wasn't going to sell the property.

Things were working out. I felt a brush on my shoulder and smelled my aunt Maeve's perfume. For just a moment there was a glimmer of her face smiling at me before it faded. *"So mote it be"* sounded in my ear.

Yes. There'd been some negative reactions when I'd placed the curse on Ass-hat, but now things had balanced out. This magic thing wasn't half bad.

And as Mary-Jane had said that night, "We're just getting started."

AUTHOR'S NOTE

Shannon and her besties really are 'just getting started'. There's a lot more coming down the road for these three gals. Sure, they're intrigued and excited coming into magical powers. But…

Nothing in life is free, right? I mean, you have to *buy* a lottery ticket before you can win, right? Yes, these gals have some surprises coming down the line, some good and some…well, pretty bad.

This is the first book in my new series. I have three books planned. The second installment is in the process of being edited and will be available by June, 2021. I'm just finishing up the third and final episode and plan to have it published by August, 2021. Probably earlier, but I don't want to make promises I can't keep!

Here's a quick peek at the cover for Book 2 of 'Hex After 40': **'Spellbound'**

ABOUT THE AUTHOR

Michelle Dorey, writing as 'Shelley Dorey' is the author of more than a dozen spine-chilling novels featuring ghosts, haunted houses and the supernatural. She has been on the Amazon best seller list many times throughout her career.

A voracious reader of the masters like Stephen King and Dean Koontz, she decided to try her hand at writing after going on a Ghost Walk in the enigmatic city of Kingston, Ontario, Canada where she lives. Her first book, Crawley House was inspired by a true tale of a family's nightmare, living in a home owned by Queen's University.

"Expect the supernatural when the bedrock of a city is limestone. Throw in the fact it is bordered on three sides by the mighty St. Lawrence River, The Rideau River and Lake Ontario and you are in for some thrills and chills of the paranormal variety--which of course is my cup of tea."

Does she love Kingston? You bet! Her husband Jim, a transplanted native New Yorker born and raised in the Bronx, agrees. Michelle and Jim like nothing better than spoiling their two pugs with treats and long walks in their neighborhood. Funny, but the slightly neurotic dogs always refuse to go for a stroll in the cemetery nearby.

OTHER WORKS

All of Michelle Dorey and Shelley Dorey books are
exclusively available on Amazon
Women's Paranormal Fantasy By Shelley Dorey
The Mystical Veil Series
Hex After 40 Series
Celtic Knot Series

Ghosts And Hauntings By Michelle Dorey
The Hauntings Of Kingston Series
The Haunted Ones Series
The Haunted Cabin

Made in the USA
Middletown, DE
10 October 2023

40568418R00141